ADAPT OR DIE

by

CHARLES NUETZEL

The Borgo Press
An Imprint of Wildside Press

MMVII

This book is dedicated to my wife,

Brigitte Marianne Nuetzel,

with all of my love

FIRST COMPLETE EDITION

CONTENTS

About the Author 4
Introduction...5

Chapter One 7
Chapter Two...16
Chapter Three..29
Chapter Four 39
Chapter Five...53
Chapter Six..61
Chapter Seven 74
Chapter Eight 84
Chapter Nine 96
Chapter Ten..107
Chapter Eleven...122
Chapter Twelve 134
Chapter Thirteen 139
Chapter Fourteen...152
Chapter Fifteen...167
Chapter Sixteen 175
Chapter Seventeen..184
Chapter Eighteen..195

Epilogue 211

ABOUT THE AUTHOR

Charles Nuetzel was born in San Francisco in 1934, and writes:

"As long as I can remember I wanted to be a writer. It was a dream I never thought would materialize. But with the help of Forrest J Ackerman, who became my agent, I managed to finally make it into print.

"I was lucky enough not only in selling my work to publishers but also ending up packaging books for some of them, and finally becoming a 'publisher' much like those who had bought my first novels. From there it as a simple leap to editing not only a sci-fi anthology, but a line of sci-fi books for Powell Sci-Fi back in the 1960s. Throughout these active professional years I had the chance to design some covers and do graphic cover layouts for pocket books & magazines."

Much of his work in covers and graphics are a result of having had a father who was a professional commercial artist, and who did a number of covers for sci-fi magazines in the 1950s and later for pocket books—even for some of Mr. Nuetzel's books.

In retirement he has become involved in swing dancing, a long time lover of Big Band jazz. But more interestingly world travels have taken him (and his wife Brigitte) across the world, to Hawaii, Caribbean, Mexico, Kenya, Egypt, Peru, having a lifelong interest in ancient civilizations. His website is full of thousands of pictures taken during these trips.

INTRODUCTION

I've never been an over-sensitive writer; I have been fairly practical concerning publisher's requirements and/or policy needs. I used to consider writers who complained about having their stories ruined by the editor as being somewhat childishly unprofessional. But there are times when a publisher goes too far.

This book was originally published in hardcover as *Last Call for the Stars*, which was not my title for the novel. It was also butchered by the editors who cut it by one third to fit their length requirements. They deleted very important background, and even, to my horror, much scene-connecting material. It was as if the editors had taken an ax to the manuscript and aimlessly chop-chopped! What was left was a badly connected comic book of action, without any real inner guts left.

The theme of the book came out of the concept of Deep Freeze: have your dead body deep frozen to be thawed when science found the cure to what killed you (and any damage caused by the deep freezing process itself).

So I approached it this way:

What would happen is a man, whom I called General Hal Grant, went into the Frozen Death before he turned senile? It would be his last grand adventure. What would the future Earth be like? How many years would have passed since he was deep frozen? Assuming he survived Deep Freeze itself.

If a body could be cured of all illnesses that led to death, then Immortality was a very realistic promise.

And what were the implications of Immortality? Just consider one simple thing like: is it possible to stay in love

5

with another person for eternity (forgetting ideals and/or religious belief systems)?

Nothing turned out as Grant had expected!

Upon revival he and some twenty-plus other men and women, from varied time periods on Earth, were faced with the challenge of adapting to unexpected harsh realities or dying!

The title was obvious, and has been now reinstated along with over 20,000 missing words. The original manuscript had been written in the late 1960s, so some updating was required, plus new material added to more fully develop other characters. I think it is a far better book than the original novel would have been if not brutalized by editorial cuts.

I got some very good, tough advice from an internet friend, Heidi Garrett, who had read the hard cover edition and asked to see the revised version as soon as it was finished. I sent her a copy of the first full draft via e-mail, and over a three-day weekend she not only discovered typos and lines that were questionable, but pointed out redundant material, which needed fixing. All this was done via continual e-mail exchanges during that furiously busy weekend. I agree with her claim that *Adapt or Die* is a totally different story from *Last Call for the Stars*—and far better!

CHAPTER ONE

The old man hesitantly stepped out of the air car, turned, and looked at the large neon sign on top of the roof entrance to the thirty-story building with a feeling of uncertainty.

INTERNATIONAL FREEZE, INC.

...the sign said. He paused long enough to turn full circle so that he could take one last look at the large city of Los Angeles Major, a sprawling jungle of steel buildings clawing its way into the smog-filled sky like some perverse gray monster. This was his last look at the world that had given him birth, and even though he was a little late for his appointment, it was impossible not to stretch the moment out a little longer than necessary.

His senses were blurred with age. Through the thick, artificial eye lens, it was difficult to take in every detail, impress it on his mind.

This image would have to last a long time—if things worked out right.

He was an incredibly old man, even for the twenty-first century, a few months past a hundred and twenty. The lines in his face showed deep scars from a youth spent in the battlefields. When he walked, it was with a limp from a wound suffered as a result of his first battle as a young foot soldier. A hollow, pock-marked face revealed a dim purple scar at his right temple where shrapnel had hit him in another battle, one of the many forgotten little wars that had been a part of those youthful years.

Slowly he faced the entrance to International Freeze.

7

When he moved toward it, he had an air of weariness that comes only with age. Yet there was something in his eyes, the set of his squared jaw, that seemed determined, even excited. His relatives had not wanted him to go into Deep Freeze, for it cut down the years in which they would have their "Uncle Grant"—the war hero—with them.

But this was the Big Adventure that General Hal Grant could not resist, the last he would experience in the world he knew.

Deep Freeze offered a new life sometime in the far distant future. Deep Freeze would hold his aging body until science finally discovered a new kidney, a new heart, and a cure for the kind of advanced old age that was enfeebling his brain. Deep Freeze and a new life faced him. His old body would remain, but it would gain an immortality that he had never dreamed possible as a young boy. And he was following many old friends who had gone on before.

A shiver shot down his spine as he stepped into the large lobby and started toward the neatly shaped young girl who stood behind a long, plain counter.

As he stepped up to her, he could not help but wonder if this new life would offer a restored vigor and physical ability to desire young women like her. That thought annoyed him, for it had been along time since he had thought about women as a young man thinks of them—a blessing only old age rationalized. Now he wondered if this last adventure was not, in some minor part, the old search for manhood, the ego desire which made middle-aged men chase young women, in order to prove they were still virile. He rejected the idea immediately.

"Yes?" the young woman offered brightly in a smooth, friendly voice.

Grant realized that her manner was part of the training of all the personnel of Deep Freeze. Every action was calculated to offer a sense of well-being and solid security to those who were about to enter into an unknown but promising future in frozen death.

"I'm Hal Grant." His voice crackled high-pitched and strained.

"Just one moment, sir," she said, flashing that well-practiced smile once more. She turned to the panel in front of her.

Grant looked at the milling people, both young and old, who moved through the large, undecorated lobby and in and out of the two corridors on either side of the reception desk.

He returned his attention to the girl as she said, "Yes, you were supposed to be here fifteen minutes ago, sir."

"I'm sorry. The right of old age to be a little late." His eyes twinkled as they met hers.

"Never for Immortality." She picked a card out of files at her right and extended it to him. "Down the corridor to your right, you'll find a room marked 17B. They're expecting you. And good living in the future."

Hal Grant's face wrinkled into a smile at this last remark as he started off in the direction indicated by the woman's delicate hand. It was interesting that they never said "good luck"—bad for the image! Luck was for the young and living, not for those about to die. There were a lot of probable accidents that could take place in Deep Freeze, or—more importantly—afterwards. Maybe they would never find a cure for his old age illness. And even if they did, would the world be one to which he could adapt? He would need luck. But these questions did not bother him. No adventure offered a sure guarantee of success—and that was what made it an adventure to Hal Grant—the element of disaster, danger and death.

Upon finding the door marked 17B, he gave one quick glance at the long, wide corridor with its off-white, plain walls, lined with countless doors on either side. A sense of the world slowly closing in, squeezing away inch by inch, assailed Grant. A shiver of doubt held his hand from the doorknob. It wasn't too late to turn back. Not yet. He could go down the corridor and out the front door and have the twenty-first century he knew, the small apartment with all his metals on the walls, all his little trinkets that had been collected over the years. And a few more years to live. Then Deep Freeze.

His shoulders squared. The hollow chest attempted to expand as he took a deep breathe. Over the years his frame had pulled in on itself, slashing his height, shrinking the bone-structure until he was far smaller than in his youth. A hundred and twenty years could do that to a man.

No, he would not turn back!

This was an adventure he wanted to seek out, grab while he was still mentally alert enough to enjoy it. A few years of life now did not make any difference. Feeble-mindedness was not for General Hal Grant, hero of half a dozen wars. So his thoughts ran as determination once more set in.

He opened the door and closed it behind him. His heart pounded painfully as he faced the all-too-small room.

It wasn't what he had expected. This was to be his grand exit from the world of his birth. Bands should be playing. This was the old soldier's famous fade away.

He faced a tiny nook with a long bed-like bench in the middle, a cabinet with surgical equipment at the right, and pale off-white walls.

A man in a green surgeon's smock stood in front of the bench, his face contorted into a friendly greeting.

"Oh, hello, sir. This is a pleasure I never expected," he announced smoothly. "I've read so many things about the General Grant since I was a child."

"Civil War General Grant, I—"

"No. Hal Grant, and—"

"History forgets its heroes fast!" Grant observed with a slight ironic smile on his face.

"Nobody will forget you, sir!"

"Yes, they will, my boy. History slips back further and further into the past, and events, men and wars, kings and nations become footnotes. As I became the fad of this day, to overshadow even a greater Grant—a distant relative—so events of the future will overshadow my moment of...so-called glory!

"I doubt it, sir—"

With a General's wave of a hand, Grant cut the man short. "Please, let's get down to business before I change my mind."

For only a moment a smile flickered on the other's face; then he nodded. "As you wish, sir. But would you—"

10

He pulled a small pad from the smock, extended it with a pen. "For my son. Just something like: Dear Jimmy, with best wishes, General—"

Irritated, yet vaguely pleased, for this would be the last of countless autographs, Grant shakily struggled over the pad. It took longer than he had expected, and by the time he was finished, there were two other men in the small room.

"Now, sir," one of the newcomers said, "if you will undress."

After that, "Just lie back on this bed and relax. In mere moments you will be on your journey to the future and immortality."

This is a recording, Grant mused at the bright voice and overly smooth words.

The three men worked so smoothly and with such speed that Grant had no time to think about anything other than following their instructions.

"There, sir," the head doctor announced, after pressing an injector against his right arm. "The rockets are now blaring, the first stage is shooting you up into orbit, and in only a few moments you will be...."

The voice faded. The world of light closed quickly around his weakened vision, then pinpointed. The vague sense of panic returned. He didn't want to die. What little life had been left to him was suddenly more valuable than any vague possibility of immortality. His mind spun in an effort to speak, to call it off. Quick mental pictures of the last couple of weeks—the interviews with the staff of International Freeze; signing away all rights to his estate, other than personal belongings that might be taken and stored with his body; the naming of those who would receive his insurance payoffs—all the details that set right the past and arranged for the possible future, all attacking his mind like jarring physical shocks, calling him back to the present

Then all light flickered out, and he was in total ink darkness where nothing moved, where all was silent.

There was a momentary sense of coldness.

After that, nothing.

* * * * * * *

"This is the new shipment for Rocket G-857?" the supply officer inquired of the shipping clerk. The young clerk handed him a list of names.

The cold breeze of winter whipped the two men's jackets as they stood just outside the monstrously large spaceship, which loomed behind them like a gigantic night shadow on the space field.

"That's the last of them, too, sir," the shipping clerk announced.

"Well, that makes five thousand. It'll be quite a load. Send them up."

"Where's this one heading?" the shipping clerk inquired conversationally.

"Star GY17—with an alternate of D-K900."

"Good chances?"

"Same as usual. If the two alternates don't work out, it will search as many star systems as possible until it finds one or runs out of energy banks or some other disaster meets up with it."

"I still can't get used to it."

"You will, once you've been around for a time."

"But it seems so unfair."

"How so?" The supply officer frowned down at the small, younger man. He looked as if he were just out of college.

"Well, they don't have any choice."

"What does choice have to do with it? The governments have to do something. And the stars might as well be colonized. We solve two problems at once. And there is still a good chance that everything will be fine. We don't just point at a star and go to it. The scientists pick the best possible stars, with known planets, and the ships are programmed to check things out before landing. If there's no Earth-type planet on the first system, then it moves on to another programmed choice. After that, who knows? Luck will have to be with them."

"But if the second choice is—"

"Look, you worry too much. In the first place, only a small percentage will survive the trip and revival. Even the ship itself may suffer all kinds of damage during the trip or even in the landing. But they have a chance. They're written off, in any case. Those are the facts of life, boy."

"But they didn't figure on this. The contracts read quite specifically: Deep Freeze until recovery is possible, then revival."

The young man was giving the usual college gab-room arguments. For a moment the supply officer felt annoyance. Then he sighed.

"And where are you going to put them on an over-crowded planet? Even with Mars, Venus, the moon, we have no place for them. Everybody wants immortality. They want it now. International had a choice to make: rid itself of the backlog or stop doing business. Immortality for the now living, not those bodies some five hundred years old. They have their health back and a lot more than they expected. And if they come through it, a world, a whole world, and none of these overcrowded beehives we have to live in."

"It still doesn't seem fair," the young man objected.

"Forget fairness! Get on with it! I don't have all day to argue over the morality of this. The government made the laws, not me. I only load up the ships. The ships go out, and some of them will survive to reach the stars. Some will find planets on which human beings can live—what few survivors are left in hopefully still functioning ships. Immorality, man! This is better than the other choice, outright destruction of the bodies."

He looked down at the list, and one name stood out, partly because it was the only high-ranking officer and partly because he was sure he had seen it before. After a moment he placed it as being from one of the history texts he had studied in school. General Hal Grant, war hero.

Well, he thought, the old boy ships out on this one. It's a good ship, and the destination has better than a fifty-fifty chance of turning out all right. Wonder what the old boy will think if he's one of the few survivors of the long trip, when he wakes up in a robot ship on some alien planet.

Then the supply officer quickly forgot about the general, and merely glanced over the one hundred other names of men and women, born over a period of several hundred years. They were all from totally different cultures and would awake together, if lucky, in a wildly primitive, virgin world. And they would adapt to it or die one by one.

* * * * * * *

Rocket G-H7, the Interstellar City in Deep Freeze, sat on its launching pad, the night winds pressing unnoticed against the dull hull. It awaited the countdown in total ignorance. But once the launching sequence had been initiated, the robo-brain would take control and send electronic impulses surging through its wires, its cell banks, its micro chips; then, like some giant creature from an alien world, it would lift off into space, slip beyond the solar system; and then, under full power, it would build up to almost the speed of light, launching itself to the stars.

Over a thousand miles away, a human mind signaled a finger, the contact button was pressed, and the sequence instantly began. In microseconds the command reached into the ship's inner computers, activating its control centers.

The Interstellar City in Deep Freeze, Rocket G-H57, became a volcano in reverse, its monster tail roaring savagely against the launching pad. Red flames, then blue and white, fired from its rockets as the ship slipped up into the night, cut through the atmosphere, and then felt space chill and burn its opposite sides. Electronic messages raced through the circuits, checked the five thousand deep-frozen passengers, noted that twenty-three already showed signs of decay from the shock of take-off, with more than a hundred other bodies in the danger zone. Fluids raced to those scattered casket-like chambers. All but the already decaying twenty-three survived, rebuilding their body rhythms to normal. The robo-memory banks made a note to keep careful watch over those who had just been serviced. At the same time the central brain was taking over all the functions of the ship's drive and steering controls. More electronic impulses flashed through the circuits, and the ship turned, its body aimed at a distant star so faint that its light was impossible for human eyes to see even in interplanetary space.

The robo-brain relaxed its efforts, the generators took

14

on a slower beat, and the solar batteries began to store up the needed energy that would take it on this long journey. Until it hit interstellar space, its job was finished, other than to carefully watch the five thousand passengers—less twenty-three—in its huge storage chambers.

Once it reached a billion miles beyond Pluto, the interstellar drive burst suddenly into life, driving the ship forward on a surge of powerful rockets that continued to burn until their energy bank's allowance had spent itself. This might have been a day or a year in human time, for mankind's science had not fully determined the effects of close-to-light drive on the human time scale. But it was generally estimated that the Interstellar City G-H57 would reach its first destination in over a hundred years of Earth time. For its passengers it did not matter. A few hundred years for the semi-dead meant nothing.

CHAPTER TWO

The shock of awakening was totally different from what General Hal Grant had imagined it would be. All his ideas of revival from Deep Freeze had been hazy, but this was totally different from what he had heard from the few reports people supposedly made on revival. Maybe they had been faked.

Dim awareness of being came first, then vague dreams that were memories:

* * * * * * *

He was slipping up on a small rise, gun in hand, the hot sun beating down on his naked back, the summer breezes thick with the scents of apple pie and turkey roasting in the oven. He leaped up over the weed-covered mound, shouting, "Surrender or you die!"

"Junior, come on in. Dinner is ready," came his mother's voice from the house behind him, only to change suddenly to the voice of the gruff top sergeant who had pounded him through basic training. "Get up, you slobs! Momma ain't gonna fix no breakfast this morning. Up on your feet! Dress, double-time!" His bunk was kicked over, and he felt the hard cold floor of the barracks hit his face. The foul smell of men living together in tightly packed quarters choked his throat, and suddenly he realized he was in some battlefield ditch, packed in with five of his buddies, mud painting his uniform, hot rain soaking his body like some filthy slime. The far distant sound of a cannon blasted; a man's scream of agony as death clawed away life cut into the air; the crack of a rifle came from his left. Then a voice

16

screamed in terror at his feet. "I can't go on! I don't want to die. Don't want to die!" He was, Patton-like, slapping the face of the whimpering young boy, not much younger than himself. Then the face slowly changed into another, then another, repeating the scene in different places, different times, those horrible moments when young kids broke under the first hard day at war.

The scene shifted and he felt the soft arms of a dark-haired girl circle his body, drawing him down onto the clean white linens, pulling him close to supple curves of feminine flesh. Lingering caresses, hot, deep kisses sent trembling need through his own frame. His eyes feasted on her up-turned naked breasts, his lips lowered and smothered against their soft warmth. Somehow the texture of the skin, the fullness, changed. Her whole body transformed, melding into another, then another. He was being served a Mardi Gras of faceless female forms. They bandaged gaping wounds in his young soul, soothed the aching need for love and tenderness—and offset the harsh cold horror of all the killing.

A slender face formed more solidly before him, smiling teasingly with flashing blue eyes. "Captain Hal Grant, we will be married, and I will bear your children, and we will have all the happiness that was meant for two people in love." The face crumbled in an explosive burst, and he saw the young girl's body twisted under the weight of an army jeep.

A bar surrounded him. His mind was dazed in a fog of liquor; the glass in his hand was a thousand glasses, held over a thousand nights drinking away the taste of harsh bitterness at the loss of his Judy, the only woman he would have been happy with. She was dead now, like himself.

For a moment, Grant felt a strange sense of freedom, as if something long forgotten made all this important. But that moment of doubt vanished.

He was talking to a man, some fifty years younger than himself, sitting in a small living room, a fire blazing in the stone fireplace. Outside the wind howled, and through the window he could see the snow-covered hills, the trees heavy with white.

"I want to marry her, uncle," the boy told him in

17

painfully serious manner.

"You're only twenty. You have your life ahead of you."

"I don't know, Uncle Hal. I think maybe a guy finds the right person one time in his life, and if he doesn't grab it then, it's too late!"

Grant thought about that for a moment, and remembered his Judy, and the fact that there had never been a woman to replace her. "Maybe you're right, son, I don't know. Maybe you are right."

The room suddenly began to fade away.

He was being given his general's promotion, then the endless staff meetings, the endless years of running battles behind a desk, then retiring quietly, and going on long lecture tours, signing autographs. He was a popular speaker in those later years, and the memories of all those faces looking up at him with admiring eyes set like a photo in his mind.

* * * * * * *

The dark fantasy dream-visions had frozen, then simply faded. For a moment he thought of how so many faces had gazed longingly up at him.

So many were admiring young women who would have easily offered themselves up for a night of passion in the arms of the celebrity-general. But time and experience had changed his attitudes concerning intimacy. Without the central feelings of deep caring, a one-night stand was empty. Youth enjoyed fast links to passionate young bodies; maturity sought deeper, longer-lasting connections. There had been far too few of those love affairs. Too many quick one-night escapes in his youth. In the last years he'd been pretty much alone.

It took a moment for his awareness to focus on reality. Consciousness had simply lifted up out of darkness which was like some strange death. It took a long time to sort out what might be happening to him.

Suddenly he knew that all this was the memory of an isolated, dead past. Instantly this became a conviction without logic to support it.

18

Next, Grant felt terribly cold. It was a coldness of the bones, a strange, eerie, frightening cold from which he might never escape. Then he distantly remembered such a coldness before death had grabbed life away.

Next, sound touched his ears, bright, brilliant sound, far sharper than he had been aware of for years. His hearing had been dulled by age. But this sound was clear, very close. His brain responded to this realization with a shockwave of emotion. The nerve endings that had been retarded upon going into Deep Freeze were now sharp and alert as he had never remembered them as being.

So far he had not moved a muscle, and did not know if this were even possible.

But now he was totally alert, his mind sending impulses throughout a stiff body.

And memory flushed through his brain with such sharpness that it actually hurt. What had started as memory-bits had folded outwards, and his life stretched behind him like a long pathway to the present.

Nothing had gone wrong! He knew that now. Deep Freeze had given him new life, new body strength, and alertness!

Something pressed his right arm; then a sudden tingling sensation assailed Grant. It quickly spread like a narcotic through every cell and nerve.

Dim light started to form. First it was a glowing fog in jet black; then the fog expanded, brightened to become hazy forms, dim lines and shapes far above in the distance.

Grant suddenly became aware he was lying on his back in a small, tightly formed "casket," his eyes open, looking straight up at a ceiling that could have been miles away. After a moment he realized that it was only about a foot above his head.

He focused on the metal, taking in details his artificial eye lens had never been able to notice. He even wondered if his eyes had ever been quite this good in all his life. Probably so, but years had dimmed memory.

Sounds like metal sliding against metal came from his right. He tried to turn, but could not, nor would his eyes move.

19

Panic threatened. What if he would have life only in this static state? He fought the panic.

Something pressed into his left arm.

A convulsive shiver shot through his frame. For a moment Grant just lay there, waiting. Instinctively he knew that it was now possible to move, that the last injection had totally freed him from paralysis.

Where are the doctors? his mind wondered, alarmed.

He felt several shockwaves eat through him. The idea that he was alive was startling. The last memory before going out had been total terror. Now, here he was, hearing and seeing far better than ever before.

Grant attempted to look to his right and found to his pleasure that his eyes moved freely.

The first thing he saw was startling in itself. It was natural to expect to find doctors in white uniforms caring for him. Instead, he was apparently in some wall cubicle lining a long corridor. On the opposite wall was a series of seven-foot-long, three-foot-high glass-covered bunks. He could see other men lying in Deep Freeze.

For some time he stared at the small wall cubicle immediately opposite him before his shocked senses could even begin to understand what they were seeing.

A pale white skeleton was stretched out, arms in repose, jaw and mouth set in a death grin.

Grant's muscles coiled; his body shot up. His head hit the top of the cubicle, stunning him.

He lay back, eyes closed, breath laboring against the shock of awareness.

Then slowly he slipped to the floor. The metal under his naked feet seemed to be vibrating slightly. He didn't attempt to puzzle that one out. Instead, his attention centered on stack upon stack of cubicles lining both walls.

His immediate impression was that scores of people were sleeping in Deep Freeze, but after even a casual examination, it became obvious that they slept only in death. Some were skeletons, others in different degrees of decomposition.

Stunned, Grant started moving along the long corridor toward the door at its end.

His next shock came as he heard a low moan when he

ADAPT OR DIE, BY CHARLES NUETZEL

was but a short distance from the door. All the "caskets"—as he now thought of the cubicles—had revealed dead bodies. The moan was like some hideous cry from a grave.

He turned and immediately placed the sound's location: just above his head, to the right. A casket door was open.

Grant reached up, and a third major shock froze his action.

His eyes were paralyzed on his fingers, his hand. They were strong, slender, well-muscled, the veins hidden under firm, smooth flesh.

These are not my hands! his mind roared.

His gaze now ran the length of his arm and found it swelled with corded muscles, the flesh thickly massed with dark black hair. He looked down at his legs, his stomach. It was not the body that had gone into Deep Freeze. His fingers revealed firm flesh, a sharp, angular jaw. They touched his head, where it had been bald for some fifty years. Thick curly hair grew there.

"What's happened?" a deep voice interrupted his search.

Immediately Grant looked up to see a young, slender, blond-haired man staring down at him. The other looked like a college track runner. The face was lean, but healthy.

The man said, "You look like you've seen a ghost. Why aren't you dressed?" Then, more puzzled, "Where are we?"

Grant immediately took command of the situation. The puzzle of his youthful body would have to be solved later.

"Name's Grant," he said in a rich, low voice, totally unlike the squeaking crackle that had gone into Deep Freeze. "Went into Deep Freeze at age 120."

"Just a kid, then! But then I knew that, your DF date was recorded in the history books of my time." The other offered a wide, generous grim. "So it worked!"

"I guess so. But as to where we are or what happened to all of these others, I don't know." His right arm had swung in a circle to indicate the frozen dead.

The other man slipped down to the floor next to

Grant and extended his right hand. "Name's Flip Kord. Went in 2185. What year is it now?"

Grant hesitated at the shock of learning he had been in Deep Freeze for so long a time, then once more turned the puzzle aside. There would be time later to find explanations.

Flip Kord asked, "Have any idea where we are?" Grant considered that question. Immediately his mind ran over all information gained to this point, including the vibrating floors.

"Machinery under us. This is some kind of storage vault. Something went wrong with these in here." He turned to the door, indicating it with a nod. "There might be some answers. I was just revived a few moments before you."

Without waiting, Grant quickly moved to the door, started to open it, then stopped when Flip Kord gave out a yell of surprise which bordered on terror.

"My body! It's not my body!" he screamed.

Grant turned. "I am—was one hundred and twenty when I went into Deep Freeze."

"Like I said, a kid! Okay, middle age," Flip grunted, recovering. "I would have been two hundred on my next birthday."

"You're not over twenty now. Twenty-five at most," Grant observed.

"You're about the same."

A sudden scream sounded from beyond the slowly opening door in front of them.

Flip Kord fairly pushed against Grant's back in his eagerness to get on the other side, for it was obviously a feminine voice sounding beyond the panel.

"Hold on, son," Grant offered, carefully pulling the door completely open.

They found themselves in a corridor similar to that in which they had awakened. This one contained women.

A tall, red-headed woman stood halfway down the corridor, her back to them. As she faced them, her hair flowed, moving, the red shifting to a silvery tint, the shadows speckled in flickering stars. Then it shifted again, to reveal more of a reddish glow, with bright golden streaks. It was an illusive shifting of shadows and light. Like the men, she was naked. Her back was facing them.

They stood there as if paralyzed, helplessly captured by the visual perfection of her form. She was a stunning woman.

Grant fought back the natural surge of animal desire that teased along his spine. He had forgotten such intense feelings.

The woman raised her hands slowly, holding them out, as if examining every detail, unaware of the two men behind her.

A whimpering gasp came from her, then elevated to a soft moan. A scream pierced the corridor's quiet.

At first, Grant was captured by sensations her image inspired. He stood there, unable to move. Stunned. His eyes just continued to flow over the lush curves of her body.

Flip murmured in a raw, husky voice, "She's a goddess!"

She screamed again, swung around and instantly glared at them.

The surge of raw desire that played along his spine was frozen by that scream.

Suddenly her attitude changed upon seeing the two men.

Her eyes focused with some effort. Then widened. Her face relaxed. The look of open terror flushed to a more sensually charged invitation—as if some inner switch had flicked on.

A slow smile suddenly tilted her full lips.

She stepped forward, and the look on her face was totally wanton. Her eyes moved from one man to the other, warm, seductive desire blatantly naked in their depths.

"Well, hello, boys. Imagine finding you here—wherever here is." She smiled in warm greeting. "My, my, aren't you the handsome pair!"

The tone of her voice, the look on that wide, attractive face, warned Grant.

He instantly knew what was required and moved.

Without so much as a word, he briskly stepped forward and slapped her. The sound was more startling than the action, reverberating in the corridor like a snapping tree truck.

A deathly silence followed. The woman started to say something, then noticed Grant's grim expression and apparently changed her mind.

"What's that for?' She sounded childlike now, a little frightened.

"This isn't the time to play coy," Grant announced sternly, turning to include Flip Kord, just in case the other was getting ideas.

The seductive expression on the woman's face had been replaced by fear, then by anger. "Who are you? What right do you have to hit me, Mardi Shores! Grand Queen of the Tri-Dee FeelGood. What right? How dare you!" She stood before him in rigid defiance and regal anger, lifting to her full height, brazenly seductive, challenging and demanding.

"Calm down." Grant felt a momentary confusion, brought on by her righteous anger and his own painful awareness of her naked body. "I'm sorry about hitting you, but I thought you were out of your head."

"Out of my head? Mardi Shores? Actress. International star. Well-known from Venus to Pluto as the Spaceman's Darling. And—"

"We don't have time for long conversations," Grant brutally informed her, once more in control of the situation. He quickly introduced Flip Kord and himself, giving dates when they had gone into Deep Freeze and their ages at that time.

She remained expressionless as he quickly brought her up to date on their mutual situation. Now her attitude was totally serious, as if for the first time she realized their true situation.

"I went in 2231, and I won't tell you when I was born. I only admit to being over a hundred and fifty. But," her blue eyes twinkled as if revealing a most guarded secret, "considering the situation, I don't mind admitting I wasn't quite a young woman when I died. Quite a shock, isn't it, coming out young like this!"

"Admitted. Now, let's do a little exploring." Grant's eyes were already beginning to take in the rows upon rows of caskets.

Mardi Shores said to Flip Kord, "You missed some living, friend. A few more years and you would have really orbited! In my time, we orbited like Jupiter! By profession...well, I was into the making of some really major ErotoAdvents."

"You said ErotoAdvents?" Flip inquired.

"Yes, you know. Sensual Erotic Advents. They were something special. Originally they were called Reality Experiences. Common folk, everyday streeters called them Feelies. Ancient Tech Talk was Virtu-Reality Jaunts, or Experience Events. ErotoAdvents became the commercial term, the tag for the industry.

"We heard that some experimentation and research was going on, but didn't believe it would procure real results so quickly. If—"

"Oh, yes, the ErotoAdvents were hot stuff, and big business. I was a Nova—a Star!"

Grant cut them short. "There don't seem to be any more survivors here. Out that door, the two of you."

He was already moving down the corridor. Casually he checked with his eyes as many of the caskets as possible, but found only decaying bodies and skeletons.

He heard the other two silently follow him. Reaching the door, he opened it and found himself in another corridor. This one had no survivors.

Flip Kord asked, "What do you make of this?"

Grant ignored the question and continued on to the door at the far end of the corridor.

Mardi Shores breathed, "It's like we are the only three humans in the world."

Suddenly the idea of being trapped with Mardi Shores as the only woman alive did not instantly appeal to him. She was unstable, a seductress. Real trouble in the wrong circumstances. At least that was his first take on the lady.

He opened the door and was startled to find himself in a circular room, about fifty feet in diameter, with six doors spaced evenly around the walls. The walls themselves were lined with speakers, switches, monitor screens, and what looked like supply lockers.

"Where do those other doors lead?" Flip wondered.

Grant guessed they would be filled with the remains of deep-frozen dead. He repressed a shudder.

Suddenly one of the other doors opened, and five men and two women stepped out one after another, dazed expressions on their youthful faces.

"What is this?" a barrel-chested, muscular man demanded, looking at Grant, then at Mardi, with blunt, obvious interest. The others merely stared.

Grant said, "We just arrived through that door." He was about to introduce himself when, one after another, the other four doors opened. From two to seven people entered the circular room from each door.

Immediately, confusion filled the air. Only a few people seemed embarrassed, all too aware of the fact that nobody was dressed. The general drift of the questions and comments were reflections of Grant's own confusion about where they were and who was in charge.

The barrel-chested man who had first spoken to Grant stepped closer and said, "I'm Lard Talor. We have to get this organized."

Grant nodded. There was a sense of mass hysteria working in the room.

"Quiet, everyone," Lard Talor shouted, turning to face the men and women. "Quiet!"

Suddenly all faces turned to Lard as if happy to have someone to attract their attention.

Lard stood facing the sudden silence, started to say something, hesitated. A low grunt sounded from his thick lips.

Somebody shouted from behind the first layer of people. "Well, what's going on?" Several voices echoed his question.

Grant turned their attention his way. "I don't think anybody here truly knows what has happened. But let me ask one question. You found others in Deep Freeze—dead bodies?"

There was a moment of mass agreement.

"Then we're the only survivors?" It was more a

statement than a question, and nobody answered. Grant wondered at his use of the word "survivors."

One voice threw it at him. "Survivors of what?"

"Deep Freeze," Grant offered quickly, without considering his answer. "I take it we were all older than we now appear. Seems that International took good care of us—to that extent. I suggest we attempt an organized search of this room. Those cabinets look promising." He pointed to the rows of cabinets lining the walls. Grant knew that he now had the full attention of the twenty-plus people. If he was to keep command, it would be necessary to surround himself with a select group of "lieutenants."

"First, I'm Hal Grant. This man who spoke is Lard Talor. Lard, pick out five men to carry on a search." Then he added, before anybody could object, "For a moment or so, let's start introducing ourselves to those next to us. State your name and the year you were placed into Deep Freeze."

Lard quickly took command of organizing the search. The six men went to the cabinets. One reached out, grabbed a handle and opened the sliding panel.

Immediately all the panels slid open. A startled murmur of surprise ran through the room. As they recovered from this, a metallic voice boomed from the very air.

"Greetings from International Deep Freeze."

All turned to the wall lined with vidscreens.

A pause followed, then the voice said, "You are now at the end of a long journey. First, you are to step to one of the clothing outlets, which are indicated by the flashing red lights on the panels around you, and you will be fitted with brief-ons. Keep close to the walls while dressing, and then wait until given instructions. Seat arrangements will be made in the meantime."

Immediately following the voice came the soft strains of music.

The twenty-plus survivors immediately started doing as instructed.

As Grant stepped up to one of the multitude of flashing red lights, under which was a slot about a foot long and an eighth of an inch high, he found himself responding to the announcement with a deep sense of relief.

Everything would be explained. No doubt this was a form of conditioning before setting them out into a strangely advanced culture they could know little or nothing about. He had to fight the sense of uncertainty ebbing through him. Was it excitement or raw, naked fear that teased though this amazingly sensitive and alive "new" body?

CHAPTER THREE

They had all been fitted with one-piece garments that fell over their heads, with side slits for the arms. It was a simple but functional covering colored a dull blue. Once the last piece of clothing had been handed out through the slots under the red lights, the robotic voice began speaking once more, while the ceiling slid away and an arrangement of connected, heavily padded, comfortable-looking lounge chairs slowly lowered to the floor on long supporting rods.

"There are twenty-four of you," the wall speakers announced, "and no doubt there are a lot of questions in your minds as to where you are and what has happened since you went into Deep Freeze." The chairs were now in place, a neat double row, twelve to a line. "Now you will seat yourselves."

Grant moved with the others and found a chair at the left side of the first row. The seats were facing a bank of vidscreens. The seat immediately formed itself around the contours of his body.

"Now you will find a little compartment to the right of your seats. Open it and drink from the small container," the voice instructed.

There were a few moments of shuffling around while the twenty-four people eagerly followed the order, for they were hungry.

Grant found a small lid-covered container filled with a yellowish liquid. This soupy substance had a pleasant, heavy-bodied flavor that seemed to attack all his taste buds. Once it had been swallowed, he felt a sudden sense of well-being, as if he had eaten a huge banquet of large roasts, butter-covered vegetables and gravy-smothered potatoes. Then, slowly, a restful feeling surged through his nerves. Immediately he realized there had been some kind of nerve sedative in the liquid.

When all attention was again centered on the wall in front of them, the voice continued.

"First, and most importantly, Deep Freeze and International has been able not only to restore life to dying bodies, healing all causes of death and results of Deep Freeze itself, but advanced science has been able to rebuild these bodies, making them youthful, young and vigorous!" This was stated with a great amount of enthusiasm.

"Your bodies will not show any signs of age until reaching three hundred Earth-years, if unattended. But Deep Freeze will not allow this. Instead, you will restore your bodies to youthfulness every fifty years. You have immortality for as long as you wish, barring accidents and acts of God!" Again the voice had swelled as if attempting to drive home these wonderful facts.

Grant felt just an edge of uneasiness. This was the hard sell before some startling shock, the old promotional sales pitch.

"International has given you far more than you might have expected." Again a short pause accented this announcement.

"Now, if you will notice the major screen in front of you, we will present to you the events that have taken place on Earth since Deep Freeze came into existence. For those of you who were used to Advents technology, we wish to point out that the ship is, at this very moment, fixing some minor malfunctions that have momentarily crippled this method of presenting our program. Therefore, we are using these more primitive methods of vidscreen projection."

The huge ten-by-ten-foot screen came into full-color three-dimensional life. For a moment it was hard for Grant to convince himself that a real live man was not standing in front of a neutral background of green.

The man smiled and said in a rich announcer's voice: "My friends, you do not know how happy I am to have been chosen to speak before you. By now you are fully revived, young, healthy, as you have never been in all your lives. You

30

have all been taught a mutual language which is so impressed into your brains that it has probably not been obvious to you that you have never used this exact form of English. International has forgotten nothing!

"And it gives me great pleasure to fill you in on some details concerning human progress since our great organization became the most popular method of persevering lives in the twenty-first century. Since then, science has discovered the means of expanding life beyond three hundred years. Deep Freeze has kept the dead and dying ready for these advancements. But with Deep Freeze, natural birth rates and expanded life came problems. Some of you no doubt remember a few of these problems. First, the crowding out of all vacant land. Cities spread across territories that in the past had been whole states. Nations became mass cities. Countries became little more than endless plasti-metal buildings. Then, high into the skies and deep into the ground, the human race expanded in its search for more room. Up into space, converting all the planets that could be converted into worlds on which man could live."

As he had spoken, the neutral screen behind him had sprung into life, showing the scenes his words described. First the smaller cities like Los Angeles Major that Grant had known; then larger ones, which rose high into the skies. After that a shot from space showing an endless line of buildings that spread out in every direction, leaving no vacant land. Finally the colony worlds of Mars and the moon, detailing the advances made there. These colonies were far more crowded than the world he had known on Earth.

A shudder rushed down Grant's spine as he took all this in. Was this the world in which he had been reborn?

The man continued as diagrams, photos, visual images of the inner workings of the cities on Earth, both upward into the sky and deep into the ground, illustrated his statements. The overall impression was a universal mass of people, living in cubicles hardly big enough to move around in.

"These apartments will fold in on themselves. Make a statement, and you will get the arrangement you desire. Wake up in bed, say what you want for breakfast, stand, and

like magic the room converts itself! Now you have a breakfast table and chairs. Food is served by robo-automatic serv-
ers from the walls themselves." The picture behind him illustrated his point.

"Now everybody wants Deep Freeze. Almost everybody can, in time, afford it if they save long enough. The
world of the twenty-seventh century is a beehive where
space is the most valuable thing in the solar system, and
Deep Freeze is expensive for those who desire it.

"International had pressures on it to do away with its
backlog. It had to either do this or stop doing business. International was the backbone of the solar system's economy. If
it went under, the governments would go under too."

The man looked dramatically serious for a long moment as the lighting on his face created dark shadows. "They
wanted us to destroy all the bodies which had been in Deep
Freeze for over five hundred years—which were being held
in Deep Freeze simply because there was no living space in
our world for them!" He hesitated for a heartbeat.

"They wanted your immortality taken from you!"

His face now quickly brightened. "But International
would never do such a thing! We have made contractual
promises that must be kept, no matter what the cost! And
you have profited by it far more than you could ever have
imagined!"

There was a murmur of agreement from those around
Grant. He felt deep within himself that he was getting the
best of the bargain, far more than he had expected.

The man continued, "Now, what could International
do? There was the problem. We went to the government, and
a magnificent solution was worked out." The picture zoomed
for a close-up of his face, which stared intensely at them.
"'Why force upon these people, who have trusted their immortality and lives to us, an overcrowded world?' they said."

There was a moment to let this statement sink in, and
Grant reacted with a shockwave of mental questioning.

"Give them a whole world of their own, a world in
which they can carve out a society and civilization to their
own liking. It was perfect. Space drives had developed that
could carry passengers to the stars. But those who left con-

32

sciously alive would not live to see the end of the journey. Man had always wanted to expand across the universe. And until now we've been defeated by the length of time involved to span the light years between the stars. No faster-than-light drive was possible. But you are among the few chosen who have succeeded in doing the impossible. With you, we have leaped across the galaxy to new worlds!"

The image cut to show the man full-figure. He stepped back, indicating a huge, gigantic monster of a spaceship behind him that started at the base with a fat body and swept up to a needle point.

"Here is an Interstellar City ship: a rocket that is able to span the distance between two stars, a city that can support life once it has set down upon a planet. This city, like the one in which you are now watching this presentation, is not only a Deep Freeze laboratory, like the one you revived in, but also a supply center, a mechanical robo-brain, which has stored in its banks all the combined knowledge of man. It is programmed to keep all of you alive, to give you immortality for as long as you wish. Everything you will need in your efforts to establish a colony is here."

The ship on the screen suddenly burst into life. Its rockets lifted it up on a pillar of white flame.

"And now, the story of your flight."

The picture went dead for a moment. Then the wall speaker said in its metallic robotic voice: "It has been well over three hundred years since you left Earth. We have traveled to one star system which proved unsuitable for human survival. As programmed, we proceeded to an alternate system."

The screen had burst into life, showing a full view of space, a pinpoint of light that was a distant star centered in jet black on the screen. Suddenly it zoomed closer, becoming a hot, fiery disk.

"This is your sun, one which is just slightly smaller than Sol. The planet upon which we have landed is about the distance of Venus from its sun, the first planet of the system of twelve. Six of the planets are made up of solid matter and could be adapted in time to human needs."

Grant was amazed that his emotions were quite calm.

He reacted to these startling statements much the same as if the speaker were telling an interesting sci-fi story concerning other people. He was completely detached, mentally and emotionally. He turned from the screen to look at the others in the room. All faces were devoid of emotion, all eyes focused on the screen.

The drink, Grant concluded, was doped. Probably better, under the circumstances.

A new scene formed on the screen when he looked back. It was a close-up full view of a large green planet, heavily cloud-covered, with just the suggestion of dark areas below which might be continents.

"This is your new world, open for exploration, perfect for human life!"

The scene panned to show three satellites, one after the other, pockmarked and bright in the sunlight.

"The largest moon is about a thousand miles across. The closest is one hundred miles; the furthest is two hundred miles across."

The scene shifted back to the world, which hung in space like an emerald. "This world is twice the size of Earth and has eight major continents. The largest one is just north of the equator, selected as a landing site because of its mild climate."

The screen now seemed to be zooming, or diving, into the planet's atmosphere. In moments a coastline revealed itself. "This is your new world, your new land, your new nation! Here, along the beautiful shore, near the flower-lined banks of this large river, you will build a new colony, prosper and live out immortality as it would never be possible on Earth."

Now the landscape view presented itself. There were rolling hills of bluish green grass, a forest of tall, huge trees, and off in the distance could be seen what looked like a herd of deer-like animals.

"All information on this world and the solar system in which you are now located is recorded in the ship's memory banks. Before landing on this planet, we recorded all necessary astronomical details. We have picked out the most mild and hospitable location for your new colony."

The screen went blank, and the voice continued for a moment longer. "At the floor just below the screen is a panel which will now open to reveal a circular staircase leading into the main sections of the ship. Here you will find living quarters, supplies, weapons, a fully stocked library and all items which might be needed for survival on this new world. Now it is up to you. Good living."

The speakers went silent.

The only sound in the room was the sliding of a metal panel, and the shallow breathing of twenty-four stunned men and women.

Grant felt the impact of what had been done to them. The raw rage ebbed up, then mellowed.

His brain felt as if it were floating in a drunken daze. For just a moment it was overwhelming, then faded. The rage was gone now. Grant had to admire how cleverly International had arranged this PR production.

They'd been nicely drugged.

Of course, he realized. International had fixed things just real nice!

Hundreds of dead bodies were in the ship. Maybe thousands. All had made agreements with International. Thousands of unfulfilled contracts and promises.

There were now twenty-four survivors.

Drugging us was smart business!

How many of them would survive the emotional shock of the truth?

Drugged we have a chance to adapt to the realities, he noted with casual acceptance. Drugged we might get past this horror now facing us.

How many of those who survived would live to attempt the building of a colony?

Drugged we're able to consider alternatives and even absorb International's con job! We've been totally and brutally abandoned. As far as Earth was concerned, we were cheaply written off.

Suddenly Grant's attention was brought sharply alert as the sound of a long, high-pitched scream slashed through the air.

Grant leaped to his feet. Several other men had followed his example, but it was Lard Talor who went into action first. He flew at the woman some three seats in front of him. Grabbing her, his hands shook her form like a helpless squirrel.

The scream rose higher.

Lard abruptly and brutally struck her. It was then that Grant recognized the woman: Mardi Shores.

A low grunt of anger came from him as the woman suddenly froze, wide-eyed.

Several other women had come to their feet, shocked by the brutality of the scene.

Grant could see all the signs. These people needed only a small push.

"Lard!" He used his most military commanding voice. "Bring her here. The rest of you settle down."

Like robots, the twenty-one men and women seated themselves.

Grant took a stance in front of the seats—reluctantly. He knew what must be done. The expression on his face was hard, commanding. It was a practiced stance, one taken countless times. He became the professional officer about to send men and women into battle.

"Set her here!" Grant pointed to the chair which he had used. His mind raced, attempted to decide on the best method to stop mass hysteria. But he did not hesitate before saying, "We'll have no more of this!" He motioned Lard to his side. "Mr. Talor will take further action against another outburst. Is that understood?"

A glance at Lard proved he judged the man right. The set expression on that brute angular face assured Grant, as much as it must have impressed the others.

"Now is not the time for hysterics!"

Grant turned to the others. "First: We are here, and there is nothing we can do to change that. International pulled one on us, but that is past history. We have been supplied with a lot more than we expected. And as the man said, we are probably better off than on the beehive Earth. So be thankful for youth, immortality, a world to conquer, and a challenge that will make our immortality worth having!" He hesitated only long enough to let that sink in. "The first thing to do is get to know one another, but in an organized manner. We want each person's specialty. We must make a complete search of the ship. Nobody goes out of the ship until given orders."

He turned to Lard. "Mr. Talor, you and Mr. Kord will report to me."

Facing the others, he said, "Is there a medical doctor here?"

Nobody reacted. "Any kind of doctor?"

A woman stood. She was blonde, trim, her features evenly cut. "I'm a psychologist."

"Fine. Step up and introduce yourself."

"Dr. Lena Hitten. I went into DF in 2199. I have worked in hospitals and—"

"Please step up, Dr. Hitten. You will be in charge of interviewing the others. We'll want information on their backgrounds." Grant fired his statements like bullets, not giving anyone time to dispute his authority. He silently thanked Lena Hitten for having picked up on his businesslike attitude.

Lena stepped forward. As she approached, he could see that she was a striking woman with a cute upswept nose, dimpled mouth, and large blue eyes.

"Dr. Hitten will take over," Grant announced. He motioned to Lard and Flip Kord, who stepped close. Backing away to the open floor, he said to the other two, "We have to hold them at arm's distance, keep them too busy to have time to question our authority. It's the only way, isn't it?"

Flip quickly nodded. Lard hesitated long enough for Grant to anticipate future trouble from him. Lard wanted to be top man.

"Okay, I see the wisdom of your suggestion," Lard admitted reluctantly.

"First, we have to organize a quick search. Flip, pick out two other men, one woman.

In the background, he heard Lena Hitten's rich voice. "And if we can do this first, I'll know how to advise Mr. Grant on how best to set things up. Now, beginning with the first row on the left, please stand, introduce yourself, give your name, the time you went into DF, any information as to your background. But at this point keep it short. Later, I'm sure, we will have forms to fill out which will detail this information. Now, you, sir?"

Already Flip had picked out two men and one woman. All three appeared to be eager to help. Grant was pleased; he had judged Flip correctly.

"Now," Grant announced as they stepped forward, "follow me.

Without another word, he started down the circular staircase which led into the rooms below.

As he reached the third step, light burst into being in the room below, and he saw a circular area, a little over ten feet in diameter, off which ran twelve corridors.

CHAPTER FOUR

Grant sat back in the chair of the large room he was using as an office. The first issue before him was a general look-see of the immediate situation outside the ship.

Lard Talor had already pushed to form such an expedition. Flip had instantly backed that idea. Almost everybody was anxious to see what their new world had to offer.

That was their first priority, Grant realized with a surge of very personal excitement. Yet he wanted to factor in all the details before rushing off impulsively. Long experience as a Staff Officer had taught him the wisdom of getting the facts first before leaping in to attack the enemy defenses.

No need to fall down unknown pits. A child didn't stop to reason, but reacted without balancing cause with effect. A mature mind knew as many facts as possible before taking action.

Even when events were moving quickly.

His attention once again focused on the document in front of him. Lena had prepared this list for his consideration.

A lot of issues, items were covered here, he realized. Some can be set aside for now.

In a general sense, International Deep Freeze had left them in pretty good shape. For the immediate future the ship was able to satisfy their needs for food and shelter. Even though it wasn't in tiptop condition, the ship was a vast center of information, tools and weapons. It contained unknown wonders which would help to make survival possible in most alien environments. They needed to discover how much damage the ship had suffered in its long voyage here. It might be self-repairing, as the promo program has suggested, but there certainly were limits. Even as nothing but a shelter, it was quite a desirable structure. A bit of Earth here on a strange world. Still, under no circumstances could they stay put forever, confined in the huge monstrous shell.

Exploration of the world itself would be a driving force to spread their numbers across the planet. Expansion of their population would be a natural reality—given time.

They were twenty-four people from different cultures and diverse historic periods.

He focused on practical issues concerning the ship, which contained all the crucial medical and even Deep Freeze technology necessary to handle just about all health concerns. Without that, the immortality now promised might be lost. There was the library, which not only contained the history and wisdom of Mankind, but a storehouse of hard information on every level.

Her list was well thought out and vast in its wide landscape. Lena Hitten was going to be a very important person in the colony.

Nervously he looked at the clock on the wall. Where is she? He was anxious to really explore some of these issues with her.

So many problems to resolve. Like what kind of morality or religious ethics would be adapted by the community at large?

Again, Grant pushed such social problems aside, realizing that most would simply resolve themselves. They were background to the harder realities facing them.

They needed solutions that would work for twenty-four different people. Without a central authority to rule with a somewhat firm hand, things could become very difficult. On a small tribal scale, such as they faced, somebody had to play Big Man—be that male or female.

And how powerful, restrictive and demanding should that leadership be? Exclusive or inclusive?

International had done an amazing job on many levels, but all these issues facing them right now were not resolvable with a mere sweep of drugs or a skilled con job.

Another item caught his attention: What dangers will the planet itself offer? Answering that would demand very

40

careful exploration of their immediate surroundings as quickly as possible.

The ship offered a lot of solutions, but by far not all. And the damage done during their flight was an unknown factor to be checked. Even a short exploration had revealed much of the ship's inner workings were totally beyond their human skills to run or fix. Everything behind the scenes was running on full automatic. They may never know more than they now knew concerning the ship.

His eyes once more looked over the list of items Lena Hitten had given him.

The weapons list concerned Grant most. Laser guns were totally new, but there was a Sergeant Whets who could handle almost all of the weapons in their supply. Lard and Whets had hit it off right from the beginning. Grant had already decided he did not trust Lard. Yet the man was a necessity to his immediate plans. Strong muscles were needed now. Such people were easily controlled by an iron hand.

The office door slid open. Lena Hitten stepped in. The brief-on moved freely around her attractive figure as she stepped forward and settled down on the edge of the desk, smiling tiredly. Without even the normal social conversational formalities, she was all business.

"Well, that does it," she announced. "It breaks down to about four major groups. Like it or not, I guess we fall back on ancient tribal patterns. Horribly sexist, but for now, it's the simple solution until we find who is best for what. The ladies mainly centered at home, researching, and men supplying food, hunting, building and exploring. Including Lard, Bel, and Flip, that makes something like eight vocally willing and best able to form an exploration team—that includes Whets, of course. Mardi Shores shows signs of emotional strain. We have her temporarily under very mild sedation."

She frowned worriedly. "I think Mardi will be okay. But it's going to be difficult for some to adjust. Normal, under the circumstances." She tapped a stack of papers on the compact metal desk. "You read these?"

"Not yet." Grant thoughtfully studied the woman.

"Well, there are eleven women and thirteen men. Out

of the women, there are three who are having a bit of trouble, but will be okay. Of the men—well, I'd say we can expect the normal personality conflicts and power quibbles. As for Lard, watch out for him. He's brilliant, but there's something disturbing about him."

"You sound concerned."

"Well, I'd say he might profit from a total mental re-vamp!" Lena forced a laugh, as if attempting to make light of that statement.

"Oh? What's that?"

"Therapy. Deep therapy. And I'm not even certain that'll work with Lard."

"Some men don't like therapy," Grant pointed out. "They find it threatening. Great men aren't afraid to face their inner demons. They aren't worried about using new tools to ferret out the dark monsters."

He shrugged as she offered, "Yes. Of course. But you're being a bit judgmental."

"Oh?" He chuckled. "I thought you'd agree."

"Looking for my approval?" she teased, with a warm, generous smile.

"Is that possible?" he countered just as a lightly.

"Anything's possible." She flushed, then became serious again.

"But this point about men like Lard. It threatens their sense of personal power and authority. The more hostile they are toward authority, the more their blocks go up. They feel they're giving up their control and power to the therapist. Some people just can't be helped. Some people aren't fixable. We're just imperfect bio-systems. Lard might be very dangerous."

They were grimly silent for several minutes.

She puzzled over Grant, eyes studying his features as if trying to read the quality of the man. "You are a natural leader. I believe you are the best one to lead here and now. Especially because you aren't interested in power over others as an end—only as a means to avoid tragedy." She hesitated, touched her lower lip with a long fingertip. "Why'd you take command as you did? I got the idea you were tired of command."

"Maybe tired of it, but I guess everybody is tired of something." Grant sighed, more wearily than he had realized. "We must all do what we are best suited for."

Grant stood looking at the small metal-walled room. In time, somebody would probably turn artist, or photographer. Then he would have to hang something up to cover the walls' bareness.

"I want to thank you for your help, Dr. Hitten."

"I think you can call me Lena," she offered softly, with something subtle deep in her blue eyes.

She was a strikingly attractive woman.

Grant realized that any man would find her more than desirable as a mate. The thought flashed across his mind, then was politely tucked away. Right now wasn't the time or place for such considerations.

Grant had given no real thought to the more long-range problems like marriage and families. To say nothing about the normal interpersonal relations, the sexual issues involved in such a close-knit society.

The immediate problem of organizing the colony before any real panic or disagreement could set in had been his first driving purpose. The last thirty-two hours, a full day for this planet, had been hectic. Exploration of the ship had come first.

The ship had several floors. The first one under the Deep Freeze compartment was the living quarters, with sleeping rooms for five hundred people. This really had staggered Grant, for it revealed that International had not expected more than five hundred to survive, if that many. The next floor was split up into lounge rooms, a theater—which could also be used as meeting place—a kitchen, dining rooms, and a play room in which there was a robotic outlet for any combination of desired supplies. One of the men Flip had picked, named Bel Lon, had gone into Deep Freeze just short of the twenty-seventh centennial and knew how to handle the robotic controls. What surprised Grant was the fact that International shipped people so recently deep-frozen, since their little lecture had indicated that only those who were in for over five hundred years would be shipped off to the stars. Nonetheless it was a break, since they needed someone who knew how to use the machines in the ship; maybe that was why International had sent men like Bel Lon.

Later, they came to stairs leading down into an armory. Below this was a major surprise, a garage for ground and air cars, which had been generously supplied to them by International. One of the women had already taken charge of this department.

After they had finished with the exploration, they ate their first meal together in the "mess hall," where Grant had brought the others up to date on their discoveries, and then assigned to Lena the job of interviewing, in detail, each member of the colony. Later, he took a long catnap, after which he continued forming plans for the colony and an exploration of the surrounding planet itself.

His eyes once again focused on Lena's form, and a strong sense of longing filled him. Yes, she was very lovely.

Not now, he told himself. We have other, more important matters to deal with.

They hadn't even set foot on this planet, yet. He had the full responsibility of leadership, something he would have rather avoided. Such responsibilities had been lifted from his shoulders many years before, after he'd returned to civilian life. But that had been centuries ago. That thought lingered for only a moment, to be briskly shoved away.

"You've been a great help, Lena," he said in an unexpectedly husky voice.

"You needed help, and I could see what you were trying to do. You've done a beautiful job. But the real trouble will come in time."

Grant waved that away. "Enough. Have the others been instructed to meet at 1800 hours?"

"Yes."

"Whom did you pick for first exploration of the planet?"

"Lard, to pamper his ego," Lena said without hesitation.

"Who else?"

"Possible choice, Art Rent. Huge man, looks the type to have on your side in a good fight, or if you're in a jam."

"Thanks!" Grant smiled. He moved to the door,

which opened automatically at his approach.

"I think," he announced, waiting for Lena, "it's about time to see about getting out of this tin can!"

* * * * * * *

They were in the lower section of the ship, a cold place of huge wheels and metal doors. This was the inner airlock.

Grant held the small laser gun in his right hand, mainly because it gave him a sense of security. He tensely ordered Bel Lon to swing the inner airlock door open.

The man had proven a real blessing, taking charge of communications. He was quickly becoming their TechManager. A pretty complete visual exploration had been made of the territory surrounding their landing sight. There was no indication they would meet with danger.

But Grant felt a sense of eerie strangeness. In the ship they were, in proxy, on Earth, with Earth-built materials. In his time things had degraded to unmanned probes and flybys to view alien worlds—and those were within the solar system.

There was a hissing sound as the air rushed out of the airlock. The huge door slowly swung open.

Lard, Bel and Art Rent followed Grant into the outer airlock, where the alien air now surrounded them.

"Open the outer door," Grant instructed, his fingers once more tensing on the laser.

He looked momentarily at the other three men. They were all grim. Only Bel showed signs of excitement. His eyes gleamed as the outer door began to slide away.

The air, Grant noticed, tasted only slightly different, probably fresher. It had the scent of perfumed flowers, of strange pleasant-smelling grass.

The four men stood there in the small airlock, looking out on the rolling plain with its dark bluish grass, which ended at the foot of a thick forest of gigantically tall trees.

Grant stepped forward. As self-appointed leader, he had logical rights to be first on the planet.

For an instant he stood there on the edge of the airlock, taking in the beautiful sight: the low grassy plains, the cliff-like expanse of the forest, the distant murmuring of the placid river. Then, leaping lightly down onto the grass-covered ground, he turned and motioned to the others. They moved next to him.

Leading the way around the huge ship, Grant found that all his senses were startlingly alert. He moved like a soldier on the battlefield. The others followed silently.

The ship was larger than he had expected, and it was fifteen minutes before they were on its opposite side. Here they discovered the beautiful flower-lined river that was supposed to flow into a huge ocean some twenty miles downstream. Here they changed course and went to the river bank. The waters were placid, some thousand yards across.

Bel's voice rang out clearly on the clean air. "What a site for a city!"

"Cities are far in the future," Lard observed matter-of-factly. "We simply won't see any—"

Grant's chuckle cut the man off. "You don't expect immortality?"

They looked at one another, suddenly aware for the first time exactly what immortality could mean to them. They would see this beautiful land slowly change into a roaring city, inhabited by their children's children down through the endless centuries.

Grant felt a deep pang of regret. It would be a shame to ruin this natural beauty. The grassy plains would slowly retreat, as would the forest, and finally a town, a small city, then a huge complex of metal, cement and stone would grow into being, perverting this paradise of nature. It would spread like a degenerate forest fire, eating away all the beauty the Creator had blessed on this strange land, seducing the virgin world, until it became a whorish prostitute, stripped of its innocence, its former glory.

Grant pulled his thoughts from that prospect and faced the direct, immediate reality confronting them. Cities would come. Now they must survive.

"This way." He started off to the left along the river bank, in a direction that would make a complete circle of the ship and bring them within the outer fringes of the looming forest.

As they moved toward the cliff of magnificent trees, ripples took shape on the river, and finally a more turbulent action on its surface, where huge stones and fallen trees distorted its calm. It wasn't until they were within a hundred yards of the forest that they made an unnatural discovery.

It was Art Rent who suddenly cried out in alarmed surprise. "Look there!" He pointed a little to their left, just a short distance from the river bank.

They turned as if pulled by one invisible string.

Slowly Grant strode toward the grisly remains Art Rent had indicated. As they closed the distance, it took the form of one of the deer-like animals, half-eaten by some terrible creature that had torn huge chunks from its tender body. Dark, almost purple blood was splattered over a ten-foot radius. The large-eyed animal now lay there on the ground, a twisted mass of flesh and pale bones.

Bel Lon made a sick grunting sound as they stood over the mutilated body. "Look at those!"

Grant was already studying what Bel Lon pointed out. What appeared to be huge claw marks were gouged deep into the tender flesh. Some creature had held the body helpless in a three-pronged grip while feasting upon its victim.

Lard expressed Grant's own feelings as he said, "I wouldn't want to meet up with what killed this."

Grant nodded. "We have to expect some struggle from the planet. There are probably creatures here that would swallow us up in one bite. What killed this must have been huge."

Art Rent suggested in an awed voice, "I'd say it was some giant bird."

A shudder shot through Grant.

"We have," Lard observed, "lasers."

With a nod, Grant commanded that they take a small piece of the flesh back with them to analyze. After that they continued around the dead animal and started for the forest.

The huge trees looked like something from a book about prehistoric Earth. The bark was heavy and deeply rutted. When Grant examined it more carefully, he discovered that it was extremely hard.

47

"Here," Art Rent offered, gently urging Grant back. He aimed his laser at the tree and pressed the small button set in the gun's grip.

A thin white beam burned through the air, then hissed against the bark. Dark black smoke whipped around the laser beam where it touched the wood.

Art Rent nodded like a man who had experienced the expected. "That charge would have reduced a man to ashes."

Lard, who was standing to Grant's right, fingered his chin. "It'll make good walls for strong buildings when the time comes for building a village."

"If we can cut it," Grant pointed out.

"We'll cut it," Whets assured them. "Just find the right tool."

They examined some of the surrounding foliage growing at the base of the trees. Bel Lon gathered samples to take back with them.

By the time they started their return to the ship, which towered high above the plain like some monster structure, the sun was already beginning to move down toward the eastern horizon, a huge fiery ball twice the size of Sol. Two of the three moons were in evidence in the north.

Lard began talking to Grant in a serious, businesslike manner. "I've been wanting to have a chance to speak to you, Mr. Grant. I think we should attempt to form a legal government and start to decide on laws that can be enforced. I've given our situation a lot of thought, and there are problems which aren't immediately evident. We all come from different cultures, so to speak, over quite a span of time. Each culture has its own idea of how to live. Just take teenagers and adults: they don't understand each other. Each generation builds its own patterns of living. We have to form one which will suit the majority and—most importantly—serve the purpose of our own future. What do you think of this?"

"I can't argue with that," Grant answered, honestly impressed by the other man's depth of thinking. Lard had seemed more the basic type, the kind who acted first, then thought. Yet Lena had pointed out that the man was highly intelligent.

48

"Such a society," Lard continued, his voice excited and high-pitched, as if he were warming up to his subject, "will need an iron hand, but one which will look out for its future. We need to...how can I put it? Having children is important. Expanding our population is of prime importance. You go along with this?"

"It is important. I've given some thought to the matter," Grant said carefully.

"I mean, that it should be...well, forced, if necessary."

"Now, wait. You can't force people to match up and—"

"You can force anybody to do anything you damned well please. And if it's for their own good—"

"The end justifies the means?" Grant offered, restraining an angrier retort.

"Well, if you want to put it that way—"

"I don't. But that's the way you put it. I fought all my life against that very principle. I don't believe it's the method to use here."

"Yet you have, in your way, done just that."

"Well, I'm not agreeable to that line of reasoning."

"Well, if it's all the same, I'd like to at least present my ideas and see how you take them." When Grant remained silent, Lard continued. "I see it this way: These people are children, in a way. Children on a new world, and they are frightened. We have to give them a harsh parental hand, forcing them, if necessary at the point of arms, to do what is best for them.

"I believe that if we can get them busy pairing off, if we can keep them active in having children, and then worry about building a colony-village—"

"Children first?"

"Why not? The ship is large enough to take care of several generations. We can make it our first obligation to explore the planet. I've looked over the stuff the ship recorded on the planet, and there's little information other than details of weather patterns and photos of the surface. We don't know what kind of animals the planet supports. We don't even know if there is some kind of intelligent race of beings here who will have to be forced into submission.

And—"

"If there are intelligent beings on this planet, I believe it would be best to learn to live with them," Grant announced firmly. "Peacefully."

"Are you kidding? Man must be the Supreme Being. We would use such creatures as slaves to do our building and—like we drove the American Indians across the continent, onto reservations and—"

"Are you foolish enough to believe that an alien race could be subjected to our rule? By twenty-odd human beings?" Grant asked, horrified by the man's suggestion. It was not only foolish, it was downright stupid.

"Why, of course. We have advanced science. You are experienced in military matters. With lasers, with scientific gadgets, we would appear as Gods!" Lard grinned as if having boxed Grant into some kind of tight web.

"In the first place, such a conversation is moot. There is no evidence of intelligent native life," Grant declared angrily. "And if we do find such, we will have to act accordingly. Chances are that such a discovery would be highly dangerous for our own survival. Chances are that with all our scientific advances we would be overwhelmed before we knew it. We have to learn to live on this planet, in peace with its natural animal life. We have to adapt to the planet, not adapt the planet to ourselves, at least for several hundreds of years. Generations away."

Grant felt annoyance with the conversation and had made no effort to hide his feelings.

Lard started to say something, then was silent for some time. Finally he spoke, but in a guarded voice. "At least you agree about the immediate need for enlarging our population?"

"I can't disagree with the basic idea. We have to reproduce, build up our numbers, and begin the next generation. There is little doubt about that. We have far more to lose in death than we ever did before. The only thing that can kill us is having our brains demolished. We have immortality at our fingertips. We can live for as long as we please. Maybe we should take a lesson from that fact, that idea, the implications it offers up. With all the time in the world at our

50

hands we should be able to take our own sweet time. What's the hurry?"

Lard laughed harshly. "You know that's not the basic nature of man...or woman. I think most of us would like to enjoy our new bodies, enjoy each other's bodies in a natural way man and woman were supposed to enjoy! And man must search, and he must have knowledge. He has never sat on his hands and calmly waited for events to take place. The nature of the beast is to lust with a hungry passion, and to expand, explore, discover. But most of all, to rule the world in which he lives. You should know that better than most people."

Grant nodded, grimly. "Yes, men can be beasts in war, in passion, and in power grabs. That's what laws and a police force is all about—controlling these less promising—"

"It is what made us kings of Earth! Aggressive mastery of the planet. And it will, in the end, make us masters of this new world we are now trapped on."

Grant shrugged. "Maybe you're right...sadly right."

"Then you agree that the most pressing need is to force a mating off of the men and women? And a society that basically needs women as care keepers and men as the rulers?"

Grant was about to say that he did not agree about forcing such a pairing off, since it would come naturally in time, but at that moment a shout of warning ripped from Bel Lon's throat, followed by Art Rent's curse of anger and fear.

Grant looked up as he heard a high-pitched hissing from above. Lard was but a foot away from him, and it was only a matter of chance that Grant was attacked by the strange, alien creature.

He got only a flashing mental picture of what was attacking him, but that was enough. Grant was convinced he was about to die. A winged creature enveloped him. It was large, covered with brilliant feathers of red, yellow, and green. A long beak, three feet in length and at least one foot high and two wide, hung over him like some gigantic canyon. Hot, sickening breath billowed out at his face, all but causing vomit to burst from his mouth. Then he felt horrible talons grab at his arms.

As his body was swept from the ground, Grant realized the dream of immortality had all been a waste of time. He was going to be killed outright. Death was coming on a far distant planet, hundreds of years in the future, in a young, healthy body. It was a mockery.

He heard shouts from those below.

Then, just as he was attempting to raise his right hand, which still clutched the laser, the bird's beak struck out at his head. The world spun; blackness pulled in around him. Grant fought to keep consciousness. The wind was fairly whipping around his body, hot and tropic. The sharp talons that held his shoulders were sending red pain through every nerve. It was hard to see through the surrounding haze. He desperately blinked while trying to focus his eyes.

For a dizzy moment he was looking down at the ground below and saw all three men with raised lasers, aiming. Lard's first shot struck the bird.

A scream of pain sounded from above. He smelled cooked flesh. The bird buckled, seemed to drop; then those gigantic wings flapped wildly, and the bird soared higher into the sky.

Again he felt the bird buckle as another laser charge burned its body. But once more it lifted into the sky, and for a moment Grant had one last look at the receding land below, the grassy plain, the ship to his right, the river and forest, and the three men standing with arms held hopelessly at their sides, watching as the bird drew him higher and higher into the sky

Blackness soothed around him. Then he was fighting to keep consciousness. It seemed only a moment, but when he got another view of the ground below, there was no sign the other men. In the distance he could see the top of the spaceship that had brought him all the way from Earth to this nameless world.

Painfully, struggling to control the gripping agony in his shoulders, Grant managed to do the only thing he could with the laser—he tucked it into his belt. All this time he was fighting to keep consciousness, but this last effort drained all strength. Blackness throbbed into being like a misty fog, enveloping all consciousness.

52

CHAPTER FIVE

Lena Hitten was watching through the vidscanners as the four men returned to the ship. She saw the huge bird swoop down, grab one of them, and then fly away. It all happened so fast that she could hardly believe it had taken place. The first reaction was hope that it would not be Hal Grant. The colony needed Grant more than the others knew. She felt deep emotion sweep through her at the thought of losing Grant, but quickly wiped it away.

Then the three other explorers started back to the ship. She waited breathlessly with the rest of the men and women in the main lounge, a huge room with comfortable sofas and chairs colored in flashing reds, greens, and yellows, giving the only spark to the otherwise functional off-white of the walls. Nobody had said a word.

As the men filed into the room one at a time, a sense of personal loss choked Lena's throat.

Lard immediately took a stance in front of the group, in the middle of the room. His face was white, drawn, his lips compressed. Then his voice boomed out like an explosion in the small room.

"We've lost a great man. I tried to save him. My laser hit the bird twice. But for a trick of Fate it would have been me, rather than our leader, Hal Grant." He paused long enough to give everybody a chance to absorb that fact. Then he took another tack.

"Whets, I want you to collect the lasers—except for yours and mine."

Before anybody could say anything, Whets began gathering the dozen weapons handed out earlier that day. For lack of a leader to speak up against Lard, the man was able to finish his job before anybody could object.

Suddenly one man in the back of the room stood and blurted out, "What's the idea?"

Lard jerked his head toward him. His eyes were as cold as ice. "About what?"

"Everybody should have use of the weapons!" the fellow announced, his voice more carefully guarded, though still defiant.

Lena recognized the man as Vern Cart. She tried to remember what particular emotional problem his interview paper had revealed, but couldn't.

Lard nodded to Whets. "Bring this man here!"

"Hey, what's the meaning of this?" Vern Cart objected, now showing signs of quick fear as the huge man grabbed his shoulder and roughly shoved him toward Lard.

"I'll have no questioning of my orders. I have only one thing in mind: keeping this colony in total control of itself! Nobody will have weapons unless issued them by Central Command. Grant totally agreed that weapons could be dangerous in the hands of hotheads. And it was our opinion that nobody should question any order given for the betterment of the others." He faced the man and demanded, "Give Mr. Whets your name! If there are any outbursts from the others, I'll take more direct action. Is that understood?"

One large man started to say something, then seemed to think better of it as his eyes glanced from the laser in Lard's belt to the hard, unbending expression on the man's set face.

Lard let a silence fall across the room. "General Grant and I had a conversation out there, and both of us agreed on several points. First, he said that if anything happened to him, I should help to carry on what he began. If Dr. Hitten and Mr. Whets will come with me, I wish to have a conference."

Lard Talor led the way into one of the private living quarters. Once the door was closed, he faced them coldly.

"I don't think that was wise," Lena blurted out before the other could begin talking.

"You question my actions?" Lard asked her with a hard glare.

54

"I'm simply pointing out that if there's no trust, there's nothing. We're a close family, like it or not."

"And all families have a father. I believe there should be a strong father image here. And a father will punish his children for not doing exactly as he says. He knows what is good for them. Do you understand me, Miss Hitten?"

"Dr. Hitten!" Lena announced. "And I was married several times in the past."

She realized that this last statement had been childish, but something burst up inside her to fight back. She had seen too much of what made Lard tick from his interview paper, and didn't like the idea of the man taking over leadership. She was frankly frightened that if the man wasn't checked, a cruel dictatorship would come into effect, with Lard's every wish becoming a command.

"Miss Hitten, on Larton...yes, that's what we'll call this planet. Larton!" His eyes gleamed brightly as he looked from Lena to Whets. "On Larton, as I was saying, we are all reborn children, with a second chance. We must forget the past and our past ideas of morality, of social order. There are no married men and women on this planet. Everybody is without a past. Everybody will have to learn to conduct himself in a new manner, following a new code of ethics. I don't think that most of the people here are able to decide honestly what is best for them, for what is best will not necessarily be pleasant. Most humans like to ride along, take the easy road, the road of least resistance. They don't like to think, because thinking is hard. They would rather play games. They would rather live a life of ease.

"I remember that national sports became such an ideal, such a preoccupation, that during the World Series everybody stopped living. All the nation watched the Series. And you know what? The nation was almost attacked during that time, because it was considered the best moment for such an attack, since all attention was on the Series! People weren't interested in scientific exploration, advancement—no, they elevated their little dull lives with entertainment, and when pressure was put on them they would take the road of least resistance.

"Now, on Larton, this cannot be. We must carve a

world out of the wilderness. We must create a new society, with new goals, new ideals, even a new moral ethic! I am willing to think and work out the problems. I am willing to direct these dear children down the path of glory and success. I know what is best in this world, because I realize the Truth!" His eyes were bright, his breath now coming in heavy gasps as he finished.

Lena was tempted to say something about his little speech, but realized that it would be too revealing to Lard. He would not like a woman exposing his weaknesses to him. He could be dangerous if he knew she saw right through his mind, as if it were made of glass.

Lard abruptly changed his attitude. "First, we have to keep control of our people—iron control! That is what Grant would have desired, am I not right, Miss Hitten?"

Lena could find no logical reason he would accept at that moment to argue the point. One part of her mind screamed to argue, to call him a weak little bully who didn't have the brains to cope with human relations, but another part calmed the raging anger with a rationalization that soothed away fear. He was a bright man, and his tests had revealed a sharp, active, though twisted mind. He was power mad. A dangerous man.

"Whets, I want you to be second in command. You know the use of the lasers better than anybody. I have a lot of decisions to make. Dr. Hitten, you will please give me all the results of the interviews. I want to know how everybody thinks. I want to know something about their historical background, what kind of society they came from." He hesitated, thoughtful for a long moment; then a slow grin played on his lips. "Have Mardi Shores bring them to me as soon as possible!"

Lena tried to remind herself that Lard Talor, regardless of all else, had proven to be a brilliant man. But she was frightened. She tried to convince herself that maybe he would do what was best for the colony. Yet doubt plagued her.

She moved like a zombie as she did as instructed. The next ten minutes were a blur to her; she remembered little. But when she was alone in Grant's empty office, sudden

56

emotion took control. Her shoulders abruptly began to shake. Tears streamed down her cheeks. It seemed so cruel, after all those ugly years in Deep Freeze, to be brought back to life with a youthful body and given immortality, only to have life swallowed totally away.

This also illustrated a drastic reality that immortality had its limits. If the body was destroyed or the brain demolished, death would befall the person, just like in the past.

It was some time before she could once again control the sobbing panic of emotions. She felt helplessly caught in a terrible trap—and there was no escape. Then Lena began thinking and realized how she must edit some of the files she'd given Grant before offering them to Lard. The next hours devoured her full attention in doing just that. Then she went out to find Mardi Shores.

* * * * * * *

Lard sat in his office, considering Mardi Shores. She had just handed over the material Miss Hitten sent. This latter fact was of little interest to him right now. Instead, Lard's full attention centered on the woman.

Visually, she was every man's image of a Goddess Sex Pot.

Her immediate hysteria that first day had concerned him. How stable was she? A tease, flirt, or harlot? Would she fit in, or be a problem? Considering his plans for the colonists and the women, she might prove a real plus. Mardi was the prime choice for a man like himself.

"I wanted to talk to you," he announced, rather all business. "About some personal things."

"Yes?" She responded in the same tone.

"About your hysteria. Is that all over? I mean, how do you feel about all this, now that you've had some time to think matters over. Have you adjusted?"

The questions were fired at the woman so rapidly that it took her a moment to merely shrug them off.

"I'm fine. It was overwhelming. If that's what you mean."

"What I mean is, we can't have unstable people running around loose."

She derailed that with, "Well, never you mind, hon. I'm just fine, now."

"Good. I'm glad." He couldn't help staring at her body. She wore her tight-fitting brief-on in a very inviting, seductive manner. The material hugged her voluptuous curves.

She seemed to preen and just sat there letting him enjoy his thoughts.

The silence lingered somewhat awkwardly for Lard. It was difficult to read the expression on her face, but she seemed pleased with herself. That annoyed him somewhat, but not enough to cool the building flush of desire.

"What did you want with me?" she inquired, in a voice that subtly suggested she was reading his mind. The woman was quite comfortable and suddenly in total control. "I was cataloging the seed samples we'd gathered when Lena told me to report to you."

Trying to regain control, Lard shrugged and said, "I wanted to see if you were doing well."

"You don't seem like a man who...well, makes a move without good reason. You want something from me."

"Yes, I suppose so. I have plans." He spread his hands wide. "They involve all of us. And especially you and me, perhaps. Are you interested in them?"

She drew closer, somehow. It was more a shifting of her body in the chair. Those eyes searched his. Inquiring. What? "Well?"

Desperately he fumbled with his hands, then muttered, "I feel we need a public policy. Something that...will get the men and women...together. You know..." He paused, awkwardly, struggling to find the right words. "The colony needs to become family oriented, and fast! Well, bluntly put, I think we all have to find suitable partners and get on with it. If you get the meaning."

"Not really." Yet her eyes met his with the amused sense of an all-knowing witch.

"Having many children. Starting families."

Her amused laughter stopped him. "I assume you don't mean...horror of horrors, match and mate?"

"What?" He was surprised by her blunt mockery. This was neither a harlot nor a dumb, timid female.

"Well, what exactly are you planning?" That was direct, serious. She leaned back, listening intently. Waiting.

Without a thought, he blurted, "Okay, I figured we should have couples matched up and pushed for early birthing—"

"That's blunt."

"Well, we're all adults here," he stated. "I'm sorry if I offended you."

"Me? Are you kidding, hon? Like you said, we're all very much adults." A flaring edge of raw sensuality burned in her eyes as they met his. "I'm for adult play all ya want. Sounds like real fun for all!"

"I want to make this a directive, a stated policy. The central principal. I figure they should all be given a short period to find a suitable partner, and if they don't, we'll match them up. What do you think? Think that's fair?"

"Call it what you will," she merely shrugged it off as so much nonsense. "It boils down to match and mate. Some will like it; others will be offended. Most will enjoy the excuse it gives them. Explore our brand new bods. Love it, Lard. A Free Love society! A nova idea. And keep 'em happy enjoying their new bods. Less time to bitch about other things. Nice thinking."

He was truly impressed by her swift insight. "Something like that, I suppose."

She leaned forward, eyes now glistening, teasing him with sultry promise. "I hope your motive is more than baby making."

"What do you think?" Now he really began enjoying himself.

She was now the predator female. "Well, I kinda think you're a big strong, powerful male gorilla! Thumpin' away in the jungle heat! Right? A wild beast who needs a real cooperative female—say, like me—to soothe away his more basic bestial passions. Right? Is that close enough for ya?"

"And you'd like that." He chuckled, delighted by this brazen side of the woman.

Mardi Shores was not only approachable, but sharply blunt about what she wanted: the leader of the pack.

Ah, what power, delicious power, he thought.

"You're quite a woman, I see," he managed in a suddenly husky voice. "And I thought you nothing more than a hysterical—"

"Bitch?" she laughed. "I'm any woman you want me to be, hon!"

"Well, you were a bit edgy! I suppose in shock."

"That was then; now I'm just shocking!" she mocked him with a wink. "Right? I think your ideas are Target One! Make your decree! I'm for it! And you and me...?"

"Yes?"

"We could be wild fun together, don't you think, hon?" It was a throwaway, almost casual retort. But those eyes met his with a warm and promising glance.

Fine, then," Lard announced, pleased with himself. "Why not go get your things and come over to my quarters this evening." He chuckled at her warm smile. "That is, if you weren't just all bluff, hon!"

"I don't bluff," she assured him, standing.

"Then go. I'll see you later." He waved her away, and watched as the woman obediently left.

I think, he realized, Mardi Shores just might prove quite an enjoyable woman.

He decided this evening might be soon enough to make his first bold proclamation concerning Birthing and Breeders. Women had to learn immediately, if not sooner, that their place was subordinate to the men, as breeders of the new human race on Larton!

CHAPTER SIX

It was still dark, but Grant was conscious. At first he did not remember where he was, and for a moment after memory did return, it was difficult to keep from believing he was still in Deep Freeze, that it had all been a strange dream while coming back to consciousness.

Then he suddenly became aware of weak movement next to him. A sick shudder ripped through his body. A feather touched his face.

Grant automatically recoiled, fighting quick nausea.

Slowly, shapes that were nothing more than darker shadows against the black night took form.

Grant reached for where the laser should have been in his belt and felt panic. It had been lost, after all his efforts to keep possession of it.

The first thing to amaze him was the fact that he still lived at all. From what the four of them had seen of the torn remains of the deer-like creature, it would have surely indicated that it had been killed by a bird like the one that had taken him. He should by now be inside the bird's stomach, half digested.

First, he had to deal with survival. Prime focus: Escape the bird. Second: Find a route back to the ship. Assuming that was even possible. He had no idea where he was, nor where the ship might be.

One thing at a time, Grant told himself. One thing at a time!

Obviously the bird was either sleeping or unconscious from the wound it had received. Grant guessed unconscious, but worked on the principle that it was merely sleeping.

61

His shoulders were burning with sharp pain, and when he moved, the pain burst like knives ripping at him. Still, many times on the battlefield he had sustained ugly wounds while struggling back to his own lines. Those almost-lost memories flashed back like a series of pictures flipped rapidly past his eyes. An almost contented groan of recognition choked in his chest.

A moan sounded. Grant realized it had come from his own lips.

He struggled to move away from the giant bird. As he did so, he pressed into a hard-packed wall. His body froze. His eyes were now getting more used to the darkness, and as he looked up, he saw the dim outlines of the largest moon through a few holes in the interlocking branches high above.

Immediately he guessed where the bird had taken him: a nest high in the branches of a tree.

How high up were they? What kind of climb down did he face? Could he manage with his wounded shoulders? He would have to.

Grant hesitated only a moment before he started to investigate the nest. It was small, considering the size of the bird, giving little room for movement around the giant creature. The nest came to his shoulders. He looked out over the edge and saw only leafy foliage. Rising on his tiptoes, he was able to look over the edge. Again only leafy foliage was in evidence. To his right was an open space, obviously the route the bird used to reach its nest.

Grant moved around the edge of the nest, always keeping away from the bird. When he had gone as far as possible, he could just make out the huge branch on which the nest was perched.

It was obvious that the only way he would reach the branch and escape the nest was by climbing over the bird. If it awoke, all his efforts would be for nothing.

Setting his nerves against the pain in his shoulders, Grant started to edge toward the bird, then gently reached out and touched its legs where they were curled up against the nest. The bird moved slightly, then was quiet. There was nothing to do but make a leap for it.

Without hesitation Grant moved, lightly climbing

onto the leg, then boosting himself out over the edge of the nest. For a terrible moment he swayed, off balance. Behind him he heard the bird thrashing in the nest. Then Grant regained his equilibrium and leaped recklessly toward the tree trunk, flattening himself against it, while helplessly waiting to see if the bird was able to attack him. After some moments of thrashing around in the nest, the creature fell silent.

Grant made a quick survey of the immediate surroundings to find some means of descending down the tree. The branches were thick, heavy with foliage, from three to five feet apart, slowly circling around and down the huge trunk. Under normal circumstances it would have been hard physical work. In his present condition it seemed all but impossible.

Slowly he started lowering himself to the next branch. It was a painful exercise, and once he had attained his goal he was forced to rest, catch his breath, and regain some of his lost strength. From then on, moving from branch to branch was torture. He was forced to stop for long periods of time, and once he was certain that his consciousness slipped. But he continued on, demanding from muscles, nerves, and mind what was necessary to fight for life, for survival.

The western sky was beginning to brighten, reflecting through the thick growth of the upper branches in deep reds, by the time he finally managed to see solid ground below. How long he had been working his way down from the bird's nest was hard to estimate. He guessed well over five hours. By then he was exhausted beyond any ability to continue.

The sky was bright by the time consciousness returned. Grant felt dizzy and feverish; his shoulders throbbed and his muscles ached. At first he couldn't remember where he was. Once his mind cleared, he slowly started moving down from branch to branch. It was some twenty feet to the ground. When he finally reached the last branch, his body was soaking with hot sweat. He rested for a moment, then jumped five feet to the soft forest matting covering its floor.

His body hit with a jar, collapsing every muscle. Panting, with the world dizzily spinning round head, Grant lay there, unable to move.

* * * * * * *

Lena silently ate her breakfast of what appeared to be fried eggs and toast, though it had come out of the ship's meal-hamper, as she thought of it.

The evening before, Lard had addressed the group. After a few words about how horrible Mr. Grant's death had been, and what a personal blow it was to all of them, he immediately got down to business, stating much of what he had told Lean and Whets. Then he began outlining his plans for the colony.

All women must consider themselves mothers, and prove to be mothers immediately. The most important necessity of their colony, even above starting to build a town, was breeding children. In time they would build a city out there on the banks of the river, but not until the distant future. All men would help enforce his demands. They would all rotate in making exploration expeditions in the surrounding territory. Women would be placed in a secondary role, first as mothers and wives. All other duties would center on the home.

Lard had not asked for comment, and he received none. Before anybody could fully grasp the implications of what he had stated—that a roster would be posted the next morning in the community lounge—he left the meeting hall, returning to his rooms. A shocked silence gripped the room for a long time.

Lena had attempted to speak to Lard, but he would see nobody.

He had given the women one week to find suitable male companions, as he so nicely called it. If, after that, they had not done so, he would pick suitable mates.

The roster that assigned everybody their daily responsibilities was posted. Some of the women were given minor jobs dealing with tech organization, data processing and research, more secretarial duties—obviously an attempt on Lard's part to downplay their importance. There was so much to learn at this point, though, that such blatantly sexist assignments were almost laughable, and nearly meaningless in the long run. Lena's own designated job of researching the ship's medical information was a natural and logical use of her skills.

Lard and Mardi where the only ones without posted duties.

The dining hall was almost empty by now, but for a few late eaters. The woman opposite Lena was a slender-faced girl with blonde hair and shallow cheeks. Lena remembered the woman's name was Dilli Zor, and she had lived in the twenty-sixth century to the age of 318. It was hard to believe that this young, innocent-appearing woman could have been so old.

Lena smiled, trying hard to forget the public announcements Lard had made the night before. She was fighting an almost impossible battle to convince herself that in some manner, Lard Talor was the best man to command now that Grant was gone. Some of the women could have taken leadership, but everybody seemed to be in a state of shock. Perhaps the promise of immortality brought a heavy counterweight: fear of losing it. Yet they were almost assured of endless immortality, unless someone or something managed to crush it totally out of existence. Modern science could do just so much.

She tried to keep her mind away from the idea that Grant had been simply gobbled up for a quick afternoon snack by that horrid creature.

Why should she care? They hardly knew one another.

Turning her attention to the woman, she inquired, "You're Dilli Zor, aren't you?"

"Yes," the other admitted, looking quickly up at her. For a moment she seemed about to say something, then apparently changed her mind.

"How are you adjusting to all this?" Lena studied the woman's face. She meant it as a light attempt at social conversation, but it was obvious that Dilli Zor did not trust her. They were all strangers trapped on a ship on an alien world. All of them from different backgrounds, societies—almost different universes.

"Fine, I guess." The woman's voice was distant, controlled, almost calculating. "They have me doing data research on gardening right now."

"Interested in that?" Lena asked conversationally. "Sounds like you aren't too happy with—"

"Well, not my most challenging lifetime project. But here we have to use our abilities as best fit, I imagine. Mr. Grant would have handled things differently, I suppose."

"I'm sure of it!" Lena exclaimed heatedly. How she missed him. If only he was still alive.

The woman seemed to be studying Lena for several moments. Making mental calculations. Then she said, "Mr. Talor knows what he's doing, I would imagine. Executive orders are never loved by the underlings. And decisions have to be made by someone. After all, order must be constructed out of this...mess!"

There was something in the other's voice and manner which implied great doubts.

"There are other ways," Lena offered, rather flatly.

"I guess so. Always different ways." She took a bit of her mock-meat, and then shrugged. "But someone has to play King Exec."

"Or Queen? In my time it might have been a woman," Lena offered with a light, mocking smile.

"Yes, in mine, too. But why bother? If Lard wants the Royal Big Man Role, let him. As long as he gets results. I need time to adjust to this new life, new body, new experience!"

There was a long pause while both women seemed to be circling around the subject like boxers, sizing each other up. Then Lena asked, "What'd you think of Lard's talk last night?"

Dilli hesitated, laid down her fork and then considered Lena for a very long moment. "He made some important points. I have to give him that. But I'm not thrilled by his so-called 'Breeders' idea. I'm not a cow!"

The woman almost smiled at that, then shrugged and continued.

"I mean, it's really beastly. Mating off with a man like we were animals." Dilli sounded quite angry, on the verge of losing control of her finely constrained emotions.

66

"Birthing a child in such a coldly calculating union. Not my ideal of romance! But then, can we find romance in a place like this? At a time like this?"

"I suppose in time," was Lena's response.

Dilli nodded thoughtfully, then seemed to have made a decision to trust her. "From where I came from children weren't even...well, even a married couple couldn't have a child until the government gave them permission. It was a special thing, an event that people prayed would happen to and for them—as a loving couple. Everything was over-crowded. You just couldn't have babies like that! Population had to be controlled very carefully. Now, I just can't suddenly change a condition of three hundred years!" Her voice cracked and she repeated her first question. "Isn't there something we can do about this?"

"Not right now," Lena said in a somewhat uncertain voice. For a moment she felt as if she had gone too far with this total stranger. How much trust could she invest in any-body?

Dilli broke into her thoughts. "Mardi sure fell into step—and fast!"

It was an empty, almost catty remark, but starkly fac-tual. Lena nodded. "Mardi lived in a society which had dif-ferent norms from mine, far looser."

"Well, okay. That's fair. But sure opposite from mine, too!" Then after a moment Dilli asked, "What are you going to do about this...Lard thing? This pairing off?"

"Wait and see what happens."

"But in a week—"

"In a week a lot can happen!" Lena suggested a bit softly. But what that might be, she couldn't imagine. Maybe Grant would return from the grave to save all of them from a fate worse than death.

After breakfast Lena took a walk down to the lower levels of the ship, then into the airlock. There, just outside the ship, she found Flip Kord silently looking out at the river.

"Nice, isn't it?" she commented softly, coming down beside him.

Flip turned, and grinned in happy welcome at seeing her. "Oh, hello, Dr. Hitten. Yes, it is a nice sight. We'll have a city there someday, and we'll all see it grow and expand."

"Assuming we survive," Lena pointed out. "Immortality does not promise escape from death through accidental means."

That was one blunt fact that Grant's fate had hammered home to everybody.

Both of them were silent for a depressing movement, then Flip suddenly blurted out, "Why couldn't it have been Lard, instead of Grant?"

The statement struck the air like some shocking explosion. It was immediately obvious that Flip felt that maybe he had spoken too quickly, too bluntly. It was getting to the point where nobody trusted anybody else. The first signs of real terror were already evident in their little society.

For a moment Lena didn't say anything.

Flip added, "I can't help it. I've said it and...well, I don't buy Lard's dictates. It's not that I wish him dead, but nobody has the guts to debate him."

Lena shook her head. "We're all afraid. It is normal to fear misused power. Way back in the twentieth century, the German people during World War II were a prime example of that. Germans were conned, then controlled, then frightened. Lard likes power, needs it, and has it. How are we to stop him?"

"We outnumber him," Flip observed, but his voice revealed that he knew that this argument offered no answer.

"But he's armed. We're not. He has Whets and Jake. What do the other men think about his little announcement last night?"

Flip looked down at his feet. Finally he nodded. "I argued that unions should come about naturally, but the men came up with one grand agreement: Yes, I was right, but so was Lard. Wonderful! This is a new world which needed new rules.. Children must be the first consideration of every member of the colony. Because of that, Lard is right."

The road of least resistance was going along with the idea—less dangerous, even for the women.

She wondered whom she would be paired off with. Or should she pick somebody, perhaps like Flip? She decided that might not be a bad choice. She almost approached the subject then, but decided to leave it for another day.

Lena turned and then went back into the ship, found her room, and locked herself inside. There she sat back in the small lounge chair that was pulled from the wall, and tried to think out some means to use her intimate knowledge of what made Lard's mind work. The wall monitor, with its connection to the ship's main computer library, taunted her. Lena shook her head. This morning, she would start researching the medical libraries.

She needed to try to sort things out. There must be a way to turn things around before Lard really went too far. The morning conversations played out again and again in her brain.

There has to be a way to stop Lard without taking any personal risks.

She almost laughed at that last reality. Without risk? Life without risk was life without growth. Were they doomed to live an endless, unchanging existence? Safe? One did not grow being comfortable. And one did not win any rewards without taking deathly risks.

The bitterness that followed this thought sank her into a deep depression that only unconsciousness could release momentarily in dreams.

* * * * * * *

Terrible heat was pressing in around Grant when full mental alertness surged back through the cells of his brain.

He struggled to his feet. Swaying, he attempted to decide which direction to go. Obviously he had to find the river, then go downstream until he located the ship.

It was some time before he could clear his mind enough to reason several facts out. The sun rose in the west and set in the east. The ship had been on the southwestern side of the river. He had to go northeast on the assumption that the bird had continued to fly in the same direction it had started. If he were wrong, chances were that he might never relocate the ship.

Once all this was clear, the rest seemed fairly easy. Grant turned toward the northeast and started forward, forcing his feet to lift, move, fall, lift, move, fall. The army cadence sang automatically in his brain.

Grant's eyes attempted to keep alert for any sign of danger, but his dazed mind could only manage to avoid the trunks of trees, the larger branches. It was like a nightmare through which he had to cut in order to find sanity and reality.

By the time darkness fell he was still in the forest, still mechanically moving forward like some toy machine built to be placed under a Christmas tree for some young adventurous boy. Night had been around him for a long time before his mind recognized this fact. He found a tree and clawed his way up. Hunger and thirst were pains he now completely ignored. His shoulders were burning fires. He knew they were probably infected. He needed medical care, fast.

During the night Grant went into a feverish madness. His sleep became a disjointed black nightmare, filled with great winged creatures. Demons and devils taunted, huge beasts threatened his life. Several times he woke up screaming, his body dripping with sweat, his throat dry, his gut pounding with pangs of hunger. It was an endless state from which he could not find an escape route.

Once the sun finally came up from the west, Grant slipped from the tree. His actions were those of a sleepy zombie, eyes blank, lips parched and cracked.

His feverish mind slipped from the sane world. He became something less than man, something more than a whining animal. At times when his thoughts were momentarily clear, they would quickly retreat, shocked at what his hands were doing. Several times he was aware of eating insects, at others, juicy fruits. How he managed to escape death from the many creatures of the forest was a miracle. He did not know how many days the madness continued. When lucid moments came, it was to discover he was following the banks of a river. Once he became aware of splashing insanely in icy cold water.

Nightmare creatures flitted across his vision, like shadows in a dark dream: tall, six-legged, hairy brown, horse-like animals, with faces split by a double row of nee-

70

dle-sharp teeth; small, purple-colored snakes; large twelve-legged spiders inches long; bull-like blue muscular beasts that could attach anything that moved within their vision. And once a strange, greenish colored, man-like form carrying a spear passed him in the late evening. That night a storm struck the forest and he found himself running through the underbrush, screaming insanely. Suddenly he came upon a man-like creature much the same as the one that had passed him earlier that day. He stood over this creature, who was caught under a fallen tree, unable to move, hardly conscious. As if possessed by some other force, some other, more sane mentality, he freed the creature, then ran off into the forest night, frightened at what he had done. The next morning he hardly remembered what he now considered a nightmare dream.

The first clear event he became aware of was lying on the bank of a river, staring up at the double-size blazing sun. For a moment he blinked, then rolled over to see the rushing river splashing over thick moss-covered rocks.

For some time Grant lay there watching the river and not knowing if it was the right one, wondering where he was, how far he had gone, how many days had passed. After a long time he slowly became aware of the fact that his mind was clear, his thoughts sane and organized, his awareness of the real world somewhat normal.

With a gasp of relief, Grant stood on shaking legs and discovered he was totally naked. He noticed there were no tracks coming from upstream. Immediately he turned. Footprints in the sandy beach running downstream showed that he had been traveling in the wrong direction for an unknown period of time.

The first thing he did was dip into the icy waters, taking a careful sip of the refreshing liquid. It tasted clear, like melted snow.

Grant felt his shoulders, examined them as best he could, and discovered much to his amazement that they were already partly healed. Days, maybe weeks, must have passed. Or his young, new body had the ability to heal very rapidly.

He felt weak, but his mind was jumping ahead, al-

71

ready planning the next moves.

Then Grant started downstream. His eyes were now alert for any sign of immediate danger. He searched for materials that might serve to make some kind of crude spear.

Early in the afternoon, Grant found a patch of tall, thickly stocked yellow ferns. Upon investigation he discovered it would be an easy matter to break one of the branches off at the base, then trim away the leafy foliage. By late afternoon he had a six-foot pole with a point at the end. While working on the shaft, he had wondered how many of the nightmare shapes of his delirium had been real. The man-like creature he dismissed as a rank illusion.

He gathered fruit that looked vaguely familiar. He discovered it was sweet, with a minty flavor. He continued downstream, stopping as hunger gnawed at him to sample fruits that looked edible. He worked on the principle that he had apparently already existed on the fruits while mentally delirious.

During the next day his strength seemed to return. The healing of his shoulder wounds was remarkably fast. The only explanation to account for this was the fact that something in the food he was eating and the rebuilt youth of his body had sped up the normal healing processes.

Several times during his long walks along the river banks it was necessary to hide in the bushes while savage animals satisfied their thirst. A horned beast colored dark red and built much like the African rhino of Earth made a rush at him. Only by climbing into a tree was he able to escape instant death. While waiting for the beast to return to its drinking, Grant could not help remembering the stories of Tarzan he had read in his youth and feeling much like that savage jungle man. He had become a naked savage on a virgin planet. And he could not help wondering how much of civilization would have to be stripped from all members of the colony before they learned to adapt to this savage world.

A little later that day, Grant came across a herd of deer-like creatures that quickly turned and fled at his approach.

Sight of these animals built hopes that he might be near his destination, but this proved false. That night he again slept in a tree, weary from the long exercise. His new body, though youthful, had slept for hundreds of years in Deep Freeze, and this adventure was for the first time using these muscles, filling them out, grinding off all the useless fat that had subtly built up in their tissues.

The next day was hotter than the others before, and it was necessary to rest many times, bathing in the water in order to escape the burning anger of the sun.

It was then, for the first time since regaining sanity, that he saw one of the huge birds that had captured him.

When it swooped down from the sky, Grant had the horrible feeling that all had been for nothing. He leaped from the water, grabbed his spear and braced it against the ground with both hands.

CHAPTER SEVEN

Lard looked across the large table in front of him and the laser on top of it. It was part of his normal, everyday attire, plus the nice, nasty looking whip rolled up and attached to his belt. That last touch had been at Mardi's suggestion. The members of his colony were nervous, tense, their eyes gazing back with uncertainty.

A grim, satisfied smile formed on Lard's face. Did he read fear on their faces?

When the children feared their father, they respected him. And they obeyed their betters. Respect for leadership was important for the survival of their colony.

It was obvious that some of the paired couples may not be totally involved in Joyous Love! He laughed inwardly at that.

Though some, like Mardi, embrace my Free Love directive!

The men and women sat there like normal couples carrying on romantic affairs, though they were too reserved in their affection to reveal it in public.

The men were fools not to eagerly plunge into that sensual banquet and feast on all the delicious goodies offered up. Lard figured this decree of his would divide the men from the boys. But most importantly, it would break any possible reluctance on the women's part to join in on the fun! To say nothing about putting them in the submissive social position they so rightly deserved. A role designed by Nature to make human survival possible. What choice did they have? And why not enjoy the sensual side of life?

Some women, according to Mardi, really liked experimenting with their new bodies. Though most resented the

74

Breeder concept.

Making babies might be the practical excuse he had given all of them, but the erotic pleasures of life were of prime importance.

Give the children their toys and they'll be too involved in play to rebel against their governing leaders.

He smiled at the women, wondering what they would be like.

He would soon know all their secrets, but wouldn't dare share any of his with them—not the real ones. A leader had to be isolated, and mistrustful of everybody!

These men and women might be sheep, but could become dangerous if trusted.

Jake and Whets had reported resentment of his control over all weapons.

I'm not about to give them access to blast my back! he thought with savage determination.

Any serious objections to his decisions would be met with a public flogging of the perpetrator.

Lard hoped somebody would speak out of turn, give him an excuse to make an example. Power was delicious, and the use of it even more intoxicating than the pleasure of Mardi's love-making. Developing a private connection with Mardi had been a beautiful distraction.

Everybody was paired off now. But whether they were actively mating was the major question concerning him at this moment.

"Well, my friends," he stated in a rather pleasant voice, "we are finally becoming a real community. I hope you are all enjoying the new wonders of youth and immortality. I hope you are sharing fully with one another."

He hesitated, and his eyes found Dr. Hitten, who had paired off with Flip Kord. They were an unlikely couple, and he wondered if they were sharing. He looked forward to sharing with Lena Hitten.

"We must double our numbers. Then triple that. The ship offers immediate shelter and all the food supplies we need. Exploration of the planet is secondary to enjoying life and birthing. A few probing searches have been made outside the ship, but with care. Never again do we want to lose a man or woman."

He paused, then continued, "I hope all of you are as joyous with your partner as I am with Mardi Shores! But even then, I understand some of you may not be as fully delighted, so have come up with a wonderful solution that will be fair to all concerned. I have decided, in order to assure the greatest possible success in my birthing program, that a rotation of partners will be made every two months. In this manner anybody who might be unhappy with one partner will find fulfillment with another! And without the embarrassment of having to break things off. A safeguard. Plus a neat way to easily get to truly know one another!"

Immediately there was a burst of angry retorts sounding from half a dozen mouths. Art Rent leaped to his feet. "You must be out of your mind!"

"Hardly! Do you have a better solution?" But the question was not meant to be answered. "I'm looking out for my flock, here. I think I know what is best! And the best thing we can do is be fruitful and multiply! None of us are children. We're aged and experienced adults who enjoyed long, rich lives on a distant Earth. Now we must build our new colonial world to suit our new bodies, based on the new and freely giving concepts of love and care for one another."

"That's bull!" Art snapped back. "How dare you—"

"Dare I?" Lard picked up the laser that had been on the table. Whets followed his example. A murmur raced around the room like fire. "Dare I...what?"

Once silence had returned, Art Rent continued, "You can't get away with this madness."

"What madness? Offering a sound, realistic plan for the future?"

"Forced breeding is bad enough! But forced shifting of partners! That's inhuman, immoral—"

"By whose standards? Yours? We don't need to be wasting time," Lard announced. "Immortality set aside, the world out there is alien, and the sooner we start populating it, the sooner we'll conquer it."

"Oh, for God's sake—" Art broke off, then spat. "You're disgusting! I don't buy it! Who put you in charge?" He made a sweep of his head to take in the rest of the people.

"Who voted him Master of the Universe?"

"That is quite enough!" Lard motioned with his laser. "Whets, bring this man forward! It's time to set a standard! An example of Mr. Rents!" He fingered the grass whip attached to his belt. "Spare the whip and spoil the child!"

Lena Hitten stood up. Her face was indignant. "Mr. Talor, surely you aren't going to do anything violent!"

"Violent? I would suggest you remain seated, or you will be joining Mr. Rent." The threat in his voice seemed to hit home. All the others who had shown any signs of objecting now froze, their faces white.

"This isn't," he announced, "a matter for voting. It's a matter of who is in charge."

Art Rent stood there, dazed, his face tight and pale as Whets approached him. Like a robot, he stiffly let the other shove him forward, too proud to give resistance.

"You are a troublemaker, Mr. Rent. I am now going to make you far less of a problem." He grabbed the man's brief-on, ripping it down to his waist, exposing a thickly muscled chest and back.

"Jake," Lard said to a tall, slender-faced man who had proven to be an excellent underling, "you will use this on Mr. Rent. Twenty lashes." He handed over the whip.

Art Rent started to say something, but then seemed to change his mind. His eyes were fastened to the laser held in Lard's hand.

Lard observed the others in the room. They were on the verge of objecting.

"Get on your hands and knees, Mr. Rent! Now!"

As the man did as instructed, Lard decided to give the majority a rationalization which might calm their shock..

"I want you to understand one thing, all of you! I am not a cruel man. I do not like what is about to happen. But we must have total cooperation. We must make misfits like Mr. Rent understand there is no place for them in our colony if they don't learn to adapt. We are in a cruel situation, and there is nothing we can do but adapt to it. Otherwise, we will die! There is nothing personal in this action against Mr. Rent, other than to teach him that we will not stand for any arguments that might endanger the lives and safety of the majority. This is a warning to him, and anybody else who is foolish enough not to see the true state of affairs. I am looking out for everybody's interests! Mr. Rent will find himself in Deep Freeze for a few hundred years, where he can do nothing to interfere with our natural growth if he tries to make trouble again. One warning per person. Then Deep Freeze!"

Jake closed in on Art Rent, a blank, resigned expression on his pinched features.

"First, Mr. Rent," Lard said in a voice which could be heard by all, "I want you to understand the reasons for the demands I am making of all of you. We must have children, and if one man or woman proves unable to produce children, we will find some other occupation for that person—more dangerous activities. Those who can bear children we will worship."

Lard finally told Jake to proceed with twenty lashes. "And everybody watch! If I find anybody not watching, man or woman, I will see to it that they are next after we are finished with this man!"

There was a cold, heavy silence as Jake took his stance over the helpless man braced on his hands and knees like some beast.

A smile of rather grim pleasure curled Jake's lips as his right arm was flung back. A gasp sounded from several women as the whip swung down on the naked back, cutting a cruel welt across tender flesh as it connected.

During the next forty seconds, Lard kept his eyes on the people in front of him, ignoring the sound of the cracking whip. The muffled grunts of pain from Art Rent slowly grew louder.

Towards the end, Lard looked rather impressed by the tortured man's strength of will. He was trembling, blood splattering his back. But he had not collapsed under the whipping.

Jake strained and let the lash smash down even more powerfully across the torn flesh.

An even louder snapping sound was accented by the terrible cry of pain. Art's body went rigid. His arms shuddered. With each of the last three strokes of the whip, agonized, pitiful moans rang out through the room. It was obvious the man had gone beyond the limits of resisting agony. His body slumped forward on the last stinging blow, a terrible explosion of anguished air uttering from deep within him.

Then Lard looked carefully at the bloody back of the all-but-unconscious man. "Have Miss Hitten tend to his wounds."

With that, Lard twisted around and left the room.

* * * * * * *

The bird dived at Grant like some hellish demon jet.

As it attempted to reach his body with those huge three-pronged talons, the spear he held ripped deep into the left wing, near the shoulder blade. The bird angrily flapped its wings like giant fans, causing a torrent of wind to twist up dust, matted twigs, and leaves from the ground. With mighty force it ripped away from the spear, its huge beak snapping at the fire-hardened point. Then, hissing out its hatred, the bird haltingly retreated into the sky. For a moment it hung over Grant like a huge black shadow against the blue heavens, as if about to make another attack, then backed away a little higher, turned and flew off in a northerly direction, as if deciding that its victim was hardly worth the trouble involved to change it into a tasty mid-meal snack.

Grant let out a deep sigh of relief and slowly took up his journey. He hoped that at any minute a turn in the river would bring him upon a large grassy plain where he would see the Earth spaceship. But with each bend in the river came deeper disappointment. Not until he came to a point where the river joined a far larger one was it apparent that he had been following only a tributary river. Both his body strength and spirits dropped to a low ebb. The harsh sense of failure was like acid in his throat as he continued on the forced march. For the first time since regaining his sanity, he considered the possibility that it might never be possible to return to his companions; he might wander the forest world for the rest of his life. A sense of bitter loneliness choked at him. It seemed as if he were the only human in the universe.

Never before had he wanted to see the familiar steel jungle of Earth's Los Angeles Major, which now could hardly exist any more.

Events seemed to blur and stumble over one another without logical sequence. It was a nightmare through which he plunged like a blind man, helplessly driven by some invisible force.

Day blended into night, and once again he slept in a tree. The next morning, after eating a diet of fruit, he continued on this journey, which now seemed directionless.

His thoughts kept turning to the other human survivors on this world. They would consider him dead by now. Lard would have taken command.

Grant washed his face in the river to help clear his mind of such thoughts. It was getting late in the afternoon, the sun just touching the eastern horizon, spreading its hot rays into the cloud-covered sky in deep fiery reds and oranges. Color streaked the heavens.

As he looked at this beautiful sight, he felt his breath catch in his throat. A sense of smallness overwhelmed him, and for that moment it seemed all of Mankind was very small next to the totality of universe. His survival was totally unimportant to anyone but himself...and perhaps some Maker. Somehow that gave him very little comfort. Years in war had washed away the childlike belief in the God he'd been told about as a child attending Sunday school. He never found a solid replacement for that image. Man's brutality against all living creatures had left a gaping hole in his mind and soul. Let the Godmen deal with such matters.

Yet the reality of this planet, this place, this future, left room for doubt about everything that had been a part of his Earth-based belief system.

He shook off such thoughts and continued on this vaguely hopeless journey.

For the most part, time seemed to shift. Night and day blended. He realized, in a distant way, that some kind of fever was dulling his senses. It was difficult to clearly define reality from illusion.

In a half-world of uncertain reality, Grant moved downstream hoping to find a place to spend the night. Visual images seemed blurry, like a fog enveloping his brain.

Then suddenly everything sharpened, focused.

Like a man who has been jolted by an electric hammer, he stared in stark disbelief.

Not ten feet away was a deep impression in the soft naked dirt near the bank of the river he'd been following.

Even while seeing this, his brain clouded over and his body weaved. Straining, he became rigid.

"What's...illusion?" he asked. "What's real?"

Grant struggled to cut past the mental fog of fever, slice beyond the illusion to reality.

"Focus!" His eyes widened, narrowed, then widened again in their attempt to find reality. His breath sucked in, tight.

Vision cleared once again, and he wanted to run back into the mental gloom. Escape the implications of what he was seeing.

A soft trick of lighting.

The sinking sun was already beyond the horizon, and long phantom shadows blended into the darker depths of the forest. In this semi-gloom, it was difficult to be sure what was there.

Grant slowly stepped forward and then stood over the revealing impression at his feet.

Except for the size, this might have been a human footprint.

It took only seconds for the complete implication to sink in. The impression was almost six inches wide and just a little longer than his own foot. There was no doubt that this was a footprint of some bipedal humanoid.

He bent down over the print, fingers delicately tracing the outline without touching it. On close examination it appeared that the five toes were webbed. A mental image of the nightmare creature carrying a rough-hewn spear teased his memory.

For the first time Grant tried to hold the evasive mental picture. He had rejected that event as pure fantasy. Even now he was not sure as to its reality.

Then slowly a dim image formed in his mind, as if some photo were being lifted up from deep shadows. He was remembering things that had been fogged nightmare shadows before now. He was looking at an alien creature. Whether it was real or a quick invention of his mind was difficult to tell for certain.

The face had been large, with a hawk-like pointed nose, the mouth a great gaping slit cutting deep across hollow cheeks; large fangs hung over the thin lower lip. The head was covered with green fur, the skin a deeper greenish tone. The eyes were twice the size of a human's, set at forty-five degree angles from each other, which must have given perfect 180-degree vision with side vision reaching well beyond 230 degrees. The body wore nothing but a loin cloth of a leathery texture.

This mental vision shimmered in his mind and slipped away, only to reform. It was then that he felt, more than remembered, the vague dreamlike event of rescuing such a mad creature in the dark, storm-torn forest night. Instantly he rejected that as a fevered nightmare.

He looked at the footprint on the soft ground. A shiver slowly inched along his spine.

There was intelligent life on this alien world—primitive, savage man-like creatures. He could mentally picture grass thatch houses, primitive villages surrounded by virgin forest, tribal units spotting the full expanse of the world.

A shiver traced down his spine as he recalled a conversation with Lard. The other man's first instincts would be to conquer, dominate, or exterminate such an alien culture. Lard would use the ship's advanced technology.

Grant knew he had to find the ship before Lard found out about such aliens—before it was too late.

* * * * * * *

The jetcopter was coasting high over the trees when a large grassy meadow broke the seemingly endless forest. Whets and Jake were in the back seats, Flip Kord at the controls.

Lard, sitting next to him, pointed and ordered, "Land down there. Do it!"

"What'd you see?" Jake wanted to know.

Lard didn't answer. He merely kept pointing downwards.

Flip Kord landed the copter in the broad meadow. He stayed in the cabin as guard, as usual. He wasn't trusted with weapons. Jake, Lard and Whets made the exploratory search of the immediate surroundings.

"There's nothing unusual here," Whets observed coldly. "Don't know why you had us land."

Lard considered his answer before giving it. He had to be careful. "I thought I saw something move on the meadow."

They were some fifty miles south of the home ship. Most of the landscape had been thick forest, broken from time to time by narrow meadows. The public purpose of these expeditions was to get a better look at the world in which they lived. But Lard's reasons were more simply stated: find any evidence of intelligent life.

"We must make certain the planet is ours for the taking," had been his instructions to them in private. "We'll deal with any intelligent life forms in an aggressive manner."

So far, after several such missions, they'd found no evidence of anything other than savage beasts.

This morning, Lard was in the lead, Jake holding the micro-recorder.

He had seen something just as they were flying over the clearing. A startlingly human-like form had quickly disappeared into the forest. What caught his attention was the flash of light on what appeared, for a split moment, to be a spear point flying toward a small herd of deer-like animals who had been grazing in the grass. They'd scattered upon hearing the jetcopter's noise.

The meadow was covered with thick, foot-high grass, and it was not until Lard came within a few yards of his destination that he saw the animal lying dead on the ground. He stepped boldly up, the laser held tight in his right hand. His gaze quickly froze on the sight of the dead animal.

Sticking in the beast's side, half broken off, was the shaft of a primitive spear.

CHAPTER EIGHT

Lena smiled down at Art Rent, who was lying on his stomach in the low, comfortable bed. It had been a couple of days since the brutal whipping, and the wounds had almost healed.

"Our new bodies mend fast," she observed conversationally, a warm, friendly smile playing on her lips.

"You did a fine job, Lena." There was a soft, eager light in Art Rent's eyes as he gazed up at her. It was obvious what the man must be thinking, wanting. "In a few days I'll be well enough to take care of Lard—once and for all."

"What can you do? What can anyone do?" Lena frowned, worried. He was a powerfully built man, but had been almost broken by the beating. "I don't want you getting hurt again."

They had exhausted the subject over the past few days. In this room they felt safe to speak honestly.

She had told him something about Lard's need to be a Big Man. "He takes the idea of expanding our population and—"

"Turns it into forced breeding!" Art snapped angrily.

"In the long run it won't work, but in the short run, it is damaging."

"And that could run for a generation or two!"

"That's what concerns me," she admitted.

Their conversations had shaped a building trust between them, but no solutions. Nonetheless a bond of friendship had developed, and Art was beginning to reveal stronger emotions for her.

His eyes were probing deeply into hers. "You know how I feel—"

84

The voice was husky, the words filled with the kind of emotion she wanted to avoid.

"Art, please," she managed, attempting to brush aside what he was about to say. "I'm not ready for that. I like you a lot, Art. But—"

"But aren't lustin' after my body?" He laughed, as if attempting to joke the whole subject away.

"Put that way, well...you sure have one! Which I'll simply ignore!" She winked, then added, "But lusting isn't my thing right now."

"What a shame! And these damned bods are raging fires, aren't they?"

She merely nodded, totally aware of that painful fact.

"I guess," he continued conversationally, in a revealing thick voice, "we've been supercharged with some wonder biochem stuff to make us bursting with animal desires."

"Yes, I think so. Part of International's plans, no doubt!" she admitted. "After being dulled for countless decades, it seemed...well, we were old people when we went into DF. I guess our biological clocks had tamed the fires...and now we're painfully aware of youthful hungers. I'd forgotten what it was like to be a teenager!"

She actually found herself laughing at that.

Art lowered his gaze away from her, as if afraid.

She said, "I'm just not ready to push it...yet. Too many other problems."

"Sure."

"Well," she said, more professionally, "right now you have to get better."

"Then we'll deal with Lard."

"You're in no position—"

"We have to find some way." Then his eyes once again traced along her total form. "God, you're a lovely creature!"

That last remark was blurted out unexpectedly.

Then he added, embarrassed, "I'm sorry. But all of this is just too much...coming at us from all directions."

She started to say something, then decided against it. Instead, Lena let silence be her response.

What difference did it make? Having somebody

really care for her could be a big plus. Friendship bonding was necessary. If it turned to deeper feelings, it couldn't be helped.

They needed more time, space to adjust. Lard wasn't giving them even a moment to breathe free air.

Lena said, "I suspect our self-appointed leader has other reasons for his breeder program!"

Art nodded. "I suspect so, too. But—"

"Lard might even be right, in a perverse way, about a population expansion. It's his methods that I hate. But, in the long run the real question is this: Does it really matter how the children are conceived?"

"Even using a sperm bank would be questionable at best." Art retorted angrily. "Forced mating is beyond the norms of a sane society."

"I don't think this is Lard's real motive. I suspect he's trying to reinvent a primitive, male-dominated tribal society."

The man laughed at that. "I think perhaps you're right. Not such a bad idea from the male's point of view. Some men always liked their females barefoot and pregnant!"

She nodded, shrugging that off. "Not what one would call flattering to the women!"

"You know, Lena, maybe pairing off with somebody who cares isn't such a bad idea. At least—"

She bit her lower lip. "Maybe," she choked out, desperately avoiding her own confused feelings. "Right now, though, it isn't an issue. Perhaps things will be different in a couple of months."

She frantically tried to think of some way to change the subject, even while vaguely aware of a glowing churn in her own body. She stood there helpless, like a little school girl.

He pushed with, "I just wanted you to know, at least."

"Okay, I know. Now you settle down. Be a nice fella," she quickly stated, hoping to make a joke out of it. "It's just that...well, every man falls for his nurse at one time or another."

86

"It's not like that, Lena."

Suddenly the image of a handsome, grim faced young man formed in her mind. It took a second to recognize the features as those of Hal Grant. A choke lumped in her throat. Why should she think of him?

If Art were Hal, her reaction would have been different. It was a shattering revelation, and violently jarring. And too late! Hal was dead.

"We all need time," she almost whispered, not certain what those words meant to her at that moment. Time to adjust to the fact that Grant was gone?

"We, Lena, we all have to start with somebody. Quite frankly, I'd rather it be with you," he laughed, a bit too lightly.

"Well, better with a friend than an enemy," she admitted in the same light manner. "If that's the best solution."

After a few moments of silence, Art shifted on the bed, his eyes hardening, lips curled in sudden determination. "Somebody has to bring an end to all this foolishness!" He tried to sit, the muscles of his body rippling rigid. "Maybe if I could speak to the rest, they'll back me up!"

"No," she said, gently urging him back on the bed, fingers surprised at the steel hardness of his tensed muscles. Art Rents was a very powerfully built man. "They're all frightened after what happened to you. Even Grant would have had to stand alone!"

At that point the door burst open and Jake stepped in.

"Mr. Talor wants everybody in the lounge, including him, assuming he can be moved."

Art raised himself up, face twisted in pain. "I can do it," he announced stiffly.

Lena helped him to stand, and the two of them slowly made their way to the lounge.

Lena set Art in a chair in the front row. Lard had taken his normal stance in front of them, flanked by Jake and Whets, the desk like a barrier wall between speaker and audience.

"I have a startling announcement to make," Lard said once everybody was seated. "There are aliens on this planet—semi-intelligent beings!" He then told them the details of his startling discovery. "Jake here thought he saw a manlike shape in the forest."

He held up a roughly hewn shaft which was just a little over three feet in length. At its end was a remarkably modern spearhead. "Take a look at this!"

Stunned silence answered these statements.

"If you will notice this," he pointed out, touching the tip of the spear point, "it's of some rather sophisticated metal—nothing exactly like it in Earth-type culture. This suggests advanced and highly modern methods of manufacture. The shaft is rather painfully crude, apparently wood cut from a tree, trimmed and shaped. The point is locked in place over the end of the shaft, and there doesn't seem to be any means of binding."

One voice called out, "What do you make of it, Mr. Talor?"

"Of this, itself, I don't know. Obviously, the point was made by one culture and the shaft by another."

"Does that mean there are two intelligent alien cultures on this world?" another voice inquired.

"I doubt it. I'm developing a theory, and I believe there is only one primitive culture." He extended the shaft to the nearest woman. "Pass it around so those who wish can take a look. If there is some advanced techno society, wouldn't they have made contact? And wouldn't the ship's computers have discovered any evidence of such a civilization? So they are primitives."

Lena, who had sat quietly absorbing each statement, now stood. "What do you plan on doing about this? Make contact? Develop some kind of relations with them?"

"Relations? Sure. At the point of a laser."

"Is that...smart?" Her voice was unexpectedly shaky.

A gleam flashed in Lard's eyes as he leaned across the large desk and stared directly at her. "What would you expect me to do, woman? Make love to them?"

"I haven't given much thought to it," she admitted. "But—"

"Isn't that just like a female?" Lard laughed scornfully. Then, dismissing her with a wave of a hand, he turned his attention to the others.

"I don't know if you realize what this means to all of us. Lena, here, has voiced a question which no doubt all of you are asking yourselves. Well, I'll tell you this much—and this should be obvious to all of you! We must protect ourselves. It is simply a matter of survival.

"Any semi-intelligent life will consider us an enemy and will strike without warning when the time comes. There will be no quarter given. Primitives discovering strange beings on their planet, being unable even to guess our true nature, will become automatically horrified. To them, we are ugly monsters from outer space or some inner-space hell. Who knows what they'll think. Assuming they do think at all! Apparently they have not discovered our presence on this planet; otherwise they would surely have already attacked. This is to our advantage.

"It will now be necessary to restrict all normal activities outside the ship. Nobody will leave the colony—the ship—at any time without my consent!

"We have to consider ourselves much like the American settlers who came upon the savage Indians. We must now band together, as a unit, and discontinue this quibbling among ourselves.

"Oh, I know about that! You all hate some of my suggestions. Hell, I can't please everybody. But I'm doing my best to take care of you.

"Some of you are not doing your best to expand our population. I know that. I'm not dumb. But this will all be resolved, I promise you.

"In the meantime, we have this very serious problem. And I expect all of you to rethink your objections to my rulings.

"Grow up. See things as they really are. Stop whining like bad little children."

The words had exploded with unexpected emotion. And just as suddenly, Lard stopped, surveyed the startled faces in front of him.

"I'm sorry. But this is serious. We have to set aside our silly quibbles and work together." He spoke in an almost pleading voice. "You must understand this."

At that point he raised the spear. "This is real danger!"

There was a murmur of agreement from everybody.

"Good. We have to pull together as a family group, with one desire, one motive, one thought: survival! The time to unite is now! Are you with me?"

Half the men immediately leaped to their feet; then three women stood. Slowly all the rest joined them. Lena and Art Rent were the last to stand, a fact which Lard did not miss.

"Good!" he exclaimed. "Now it should be understood that we are at war, a natural war of man against the alien."

Lena fought back a nagging suggestion of sickness gripping at the lining of her stomach. She felt helpless. Lard's total victory was obvious.

An outside threat had squeezed them behind him. This was what he had needed to solidify the colony into unquestionably supporting his every demand. If he was to be stopped, it had to be soon. In fact it was probably already too late.

"Just why must we consider them enemies?" she demanded in a harsh voice.

"Because they will consider us enemies!" Lard explained in much the same tone he might have used with a small, foolish child.

"I don't agree. There is no reason to assume this, and—"

Lard raised his hand. "Lena, my dear child, you will refrain from disagreeing with your superiors?"

"I resent your words!" Lena exploded. "How dare you!"

Lard stepped around the table desk, stood in front of her. "You resent what, woman?"

"I'm not a child!"

Without even a visual warning, the man slapped her firmly across the face. It was stinging, but not brutal, just loud and effective.

Lena felt Art start to rear up and pushed him back with her right hand.

"You're what I say you are, dear child!" he announced, moving back between Whets and Jake. "You might

90

have been important back on Earth, but this is Larton. A new world. With new rules. New needs. New requirements for survival. And women must discover their place in this new society. So please don't make me do something I'll regret."

The treat there was bluntly obvious.

"What the men decide will count. And us men agree that these aliens are natural enemies and—"

To everybody's surprise, Art Rent blurted out, "I'm a man, and I have decided nothing. I don't agree with you, and believe it should be brought up to a vote after long and detailed discussion. There are people here far smarter than you and I, Mr. Talor." This last remark he directed to the rest of the room. Several faces were beginning to show doubt as to the wisdom of Lard's policy.

Lena clutched at Art's hand, but he yanked it away, sliding forward. His whole body was arched, rigid. "Dr. Hitten, above all, has a specialized knowledge that most of us lack—"

"You're pushing it," Lard warned in a deadly voice.

"You can't treat her like a child! And hitting a woman—"

"She's a breeder, and better accept that fact." The man ignored the last part of the statement as totally invalid. "And no greater tribute could be offered her—or any other woman here."

Lard's eyes swept the room.

"She's a doctor." Art growled, suddenly out of control. "How dare you!"

"I'll dare what I think best," Lard snapped, face drained of color.

"Then apologize to her, right now!"

Lena softly hissed, "Please, stop!"

"And apologize to all the other women here," Art demanded.

"One more word and you've had it!" Lard announced.

"I'm not afraid of you. What can you do that you haven't done so far?"

Softly, but with death thick in his voice, Lard ordered, "Have this man brought forward."

91

Art didn't wait to be brought. He stepped toward the man before anybody could move, murder in his eyes. It was obvious that the pain ripping at his body had been soothed by the rush of fury.

Lena wanted to stop what was happening, but knew it was too late.

Suddenly Art leaped at Lard Talor, his huge hands finding the other's thick throat.

It all happened so quickly that Lena could never reconstruct it in her mind afterwards. Hardly had Art's hands closed on Lard's windpipe before both Jake and Whets knocked him unconscious with their laser guns, using the weapons like clubs to batter the back of his head.

Lard stood over the other's stilled form at his feet, his breath heaving like a death rattle, his eyes filled with such a blaze of hatred that Lena was sure he would kill Art before another minute had passed. He finally said in a rasping, ugly voice, "I could have him executed for that!"

Flip Kord cried, "Men are too valuable here on this new world, Lard!"

After a moment's consideration, Lard nodded.

"Into Deep Freeze with him. It will cool the man off. By the time we revive him, things will be a little more organized, and he will see the error of his ways. I have to consider that he was unquestionably out of his head. Poor fellow." His voice lacked any pity for Art. Jake pulled the unconscious body from the room.

"Now, I want some of you to come with me on a search of the surrounding territory," he announced, once more taking command. "We will begin a series of A-Hunts. We will search out the enemy and destroy it without mercy. We will let the enemy know our mighty power before attempting any personal contact. And all this must be done before any resistance can be formed. There is no time to lose! Are you with me?"

With one voice, Lena heard the others shout out their acceptance of Lard's proposals.

"Who will come with me?"

Hands were raised high in the air, almost in symbolic salute to their new hero.

92

Lena recognized Lard's methods and shuddered. Hitler had used the Big Lie to lead Germany into World War II. Now Lard Talor, would-be dictator of twenty-three human souls, was attempting the same methods of leadership, without due process of a vote. Hate and the Big Lie.

It was obvious that all active resistance had disappeared from their colony. And there was nothing Lena could do now. The time for resistance had come and passed, bringing defeat. Now all she could do was await the outcome, hoping that their lives would not be forfeit.

* * * * * * *

The sun was dipping deep into the horizon as Flip Kord stepped out of the copter next to Lard. The plain was covered by a thin low fog resting some two feet over the ground. It was a moment of beauty on a world that had turned strangely ugly in the last few weeks.

Lard was talking to Jake and Whets, but Flip paid little attention to their conversation.

They were at the airlock when Lard shouted to him, "Are you coming or not?"

"Just taking in this sunset," Flip managed to say with a smile. He hid the hatred he felt for Lard.

"There's no time for such matters." Lard was angry because the day's search by jetcopter had been such a failure. They had covered miles and miles of forest, which seemed to stretch out over the whole continent in all directions, broken only by a high range of mountains and scattered grass-covered plains. A lot of animal life had passed under their flight, but Lard was not interested in this. He was now obsessed with searching for aliens and killing them.

Lard was just turning to enter the airlock when suddenly, without any warning whatsoever, a high-pitched screech sounded from the surrounding grass. Before any of them could understand what was happening, a spear flashed through the air, just missing Whets, who stood at Lard's right.

Flip Kord was the first to move, leaping toward the airlock, not looking back to see what was attacking him. Unreasoning fear coursed through his body, moving the muscles at fantastic speed. It wasn't until Whets cried out in terror that Flip's mind even attempted to reason out what had happened.

Lard was firing his laser gun as Jake disappeared into the airlock.

"Aliens!" Whets cursed as Flip passed him, leaping after Jake.

Now Flip turned, feeling momentarily safe within the ship. He was unarmed, but the urge to discover exactly what the enemy looked like was overpowering.

Heavy shadows raced across the plain. Darkness had fluttered down onto the world, creating a sudden blanket of gloom to obstruct a clear view of their surroundings. Forms that were all too human in appearance flashed quickly back and forth, appearing and disappearing against the fog-covered plain.

Lard fired wildly at the shadowy figures as another two spears reached out and barely missed him.

With a curse he leaped back into the airlock with Whets.

"Close it!" Lard screamed hysterically.

Flip was already in the process of slamming the door shut, swinging the wheel into place. A moment later the three of them leaned back against the wall, panting, sweat dripping down their chalk-white faces.

Lard was the first to recover, and after taking a couple of deep breaths, he asked, "Did anybody get a good look at them?"

"Just saw that they were human-like," Whets said. "Sorta human, that is. All I saw was shaggy shapes without any details."

"You?" Lard directed at Flip.

"Nothing." Flip shook his head.

"I'll report this to the others immediately. We'll have to take more care in our activities, be more alert. How the devil they slipped in around us like that, I don't know. In any case, this proves my point. I was right! So terribly right! Don't you agree?"

Even Flip Kord nodded.

Lard wiped his upper lip nervously. "They are quite hostile! Hostile monsters to be totally destroyed, wiped off the face of the Earth...I mean Larton! We'll have to deal with them in a very harsh and total manner! They're hostile! Don't you all agree?"

Flip found it difficult to reason an argument against the man's statements. Somehow he felt it was all wrong, but he was helpless to offer any opposition.

Lard Talor might be an unstable, dangerous man, but he was possibly right about the aliens.

CHAPTER NINE

That night Grant slept restlessly in a tree, his mind alive with speculation about the footprint discovery. If there was life here, then the humans would have to become friendly with it—or destroy it. An all-out war of extermination could not be won by humans.

Every movement in the forest became, in his imagination, the footsteps of awesome humanoid creatures. By morning he felt more exhausted than when going to sleep.

After a quick breakfast of green-colored, juicy fruit, Grant continued downstream, his thoughts whirling with the concept that Man was not alone in the universe.

He kept alert for any other signs of aliens.

That night he instantly fell into a deep, exhausted sleep. His dreams were haunted by vague visions of Lena, but they were illusive images. In the morning he awoke abruptly to the startling sound of what could be nothing other than a jet or copter. The sun was glaringly bright. He all but fell out of the tree. His spear was forgotten as he ran insanely out into the river, shouting, waving his hands. He was stunned by the fact that fellow humans could be so near. So deliciously near!

When he came within sight of the jetcopter, Grant fairly screamed.

"It's me...here...here!"

The copter was flying high above the river bed, at the tip of the forest trees. He screamed until his very lungs hurt, throat rasp raw.

It had disappeared by the time Grant realized the awful truth that they hadn't seen him. The crushing blow buckled his legs, as if they'd been hit out from under him.

96

Suddenly he was sitting in the water, tears unashamedly streaming down his face.

Many times during war he had been cut off from all human companionship like this. That wasn't a new experience on Earth. But here, on this alien planet, unknown light years from his mother world, totally isolated, alone, everything was starkly different.

The welling pain that ebbed through him now caused no shame. On Earth you could never be really very far from some fellow human, even if they might be a deadly enemy. He was gagged by the overwhelming hunger for human contact. This had been so close.

His very nerve endings hurt, desperately longing to be soothed by a human hand. It was not a sexual thing. It was raw loneliness, but the stark awareness of that erotic element teased his consciousness.

He suddenly longed for Lena's gentle touch.

What a thought. Strange. Compelling.

Yet the image of Lena Hitten held firm. He embraced it with almost wanton pleasure. In such a small community, romantic unions were to be expected. Given a chance he'd have made such a connection with Lena. He held that illusion like a starving beast clinging to a tiny morsel of food.

How long he sat there, trembling in rage, terrible pain, and anguished longing, it was impossible to tell. Slowly the focus on the woman's form, face, and being centered stronger in his mind, eating away the other thoughts.

Cling to that vision, he told himself. It was a harmless illusion, a more pleasant fantasy than the other nightmare horrors. Imagine Lena coming into your arms. Feed on that. Devour that image!

Much later, weary, mentally exhausted, Grant stood, and dripping wet, he took up the march. He forced one thought to predominate: The ship could not be far away!

Find Lena!

It was a mantra for survival.

Return to the ship.

He was going in the right direction.

But the world darkened without any sign of the other humans. That night he convinced himself it could not be much further. Sight of the copter had teased his mind with haunting images and an overwhelming need to bring this terrible isolation to an end. It was a long time before sleep faded over those tormenting thoughts.

And he dreamed of Lena Hitten. The two of them were almost touching. She stood, reaching out. But when he'd try to fold her into his arms, kiss those soft lips, the vision faded, melted, shattered into nightmare monsters. Then Lena surfaced once more to tease him with a seductive smile. He ran towards her, and for a moment it seemed as if they were clinging frantically together. Then the dream flashed away.

The next morning Grant felt somewhat dazed at first, bathing in the memory of that dream, experiencing a mix of guilt and pleasure. But the total effect was a sense of release. Perhaps there was hope. This morning he whistled happily as he continued downstream. He had picked up a large broken tree branch, which served as a club if he were in need of one, since he'd left his spear at his sleeping place the day before.

By mid-morning, Grant came to a bend in the river, beyond which the waters seemed to calm and spread out to about a thousand yards in width.

A harsh lump caught in his throat. The sun was flashing bright on distant metal.

Suddenly he was running, club flaying, arms high over his head. Illusion or reality, Grant didn't care or even consider. Madness took possession, mixed with the hope of days, the longing pain of loneliness. Whether this vision was a hallucination or not, he would fly into its arms.

He was an image of a madman racing through the thinning forest.

A long growth of beard covered his face; his hair had grown and become matted with mud. He was a frantic mad figure, screaming and waving his arms. As he came out onto the plain and saw the spaceship standing there, he could hardly believe that this was not some taunting dream. Too many days had gone by with bitter disappointment. And now it was there before him.

There was nobody in sight as he came racing up to the ship's outer airlock. His lungs were bursting; his heart

98

pounded hard.

Lena, Lena! His mind played over the name, then flushed it away. Dreams and illusions were one thing, but soon he'd probably be facing the hard reality of a woman who hardly knew him.

Grant beat his fists insanely against the airlock door, shouting wordless cries to get attention. Joy choked at his throat. Desperate tears ebbed in his red-rimmed eyes. The relief cramped the air in his lungs.

Suddenly the door swung away, and Grant found himself looking up into the point of a laser rifle thrust into his face. Then, just as quickly, the barrel slammed against the side of his head.

Stunned, he fell sideways to the ground, tried to rise, then lost consciousness.

Grant became aware of a blaze of bright light in his eyes.

A harsh voice said from his right, "It's coming out, Jake."

Grant moaned and opened his eyes. He was in one of the ship's rooms, lying on a bunk. Two men were in the room with him. Each carried a laser rifle, held ready for any emergency. They stood but a few feet away.

The tallest man suggested, "Maybe we should have shot him, Hicks."

"I don't know," Hicks replied, his small face contracting into a frown. "If I didn't know better, I'd say he was human. But that's impossible."

Grant asked, "Don't you recognize me?"

He slowly sat up in the bunk. The two men tensed as if they had just taken a brutal blow in the stomach.

"Take it easy," Grant suggested. "I'm not about to do anything."

His head hurt; he felt sick, dizzy. "I'm Hal Grant. What's happened here?"

The two men exchanged glances, unbelieving. If he had been a tree talking to them, they couldn't have looked more shocked.

"What the blazes do you think I am?" Grant blurted, coming to his feet and glaring angrily at them.

"Well," Jake, explained, "you can't be Grant. The general's dead...and you...well...if you are Grant, you'll understand our behavior...once you know what's been happening."

"Who—or what—the hell could I be?" Grant exploded, looking from one to the other.

"Maybe this is Grant," Hicks suggested, but he sounded quite doubtful.

Jake nodded. "Or some demon trickery!"

"A ghost?" Hicks mocked. But there was no humor in his eyes.

"What's wrong with you two?" Grant exploded, furious, frustrated. "I'm flesh and blood. Not some demon ghost!"

Hicks answered, "The General couldn't have survived that bird. Even if he did, it would be impossible to live so long in the jungle without weapons or food or...it's been two months—"

"What?" was all that Grant could say.

That long?

"Just be quiet until Hitten comes. If anybody knows Grant, she does," Hicks announced.

Grant felt a wave of relief. Lena was alive and well. He studied the two men, unable to believe that they didn't put it all together.

Who the hell could he be?

What had happened here to change things so completely?

Jake added, "And you better have the right answers to her questions, or we're assuming you're one of...them!"

"If you think I'm something—whatever it is," Grant stated, thickly, "why the hell didn't you kill me right off?"

Jake grinned, crookedly. "I guess you looked too human to just kill. So—"

Hicks cut him short. "Let's stop the chatter. I'm not convinced of anything...yet!"

Jake nodded, but there was a softer light in his eyes now, as if he might believe Grant.

The door suddenly slid open, and Lena Hitten stepped into the room.

100

She looked at Grant and then smiled. "Bring a shaver, Jake, for General Grant. You men can leave us. I'll be...examining him."

"Mr. Grant, Lena," he corrected her, feeling a burst of joy at the sight of her. Once the door was closed behind the two men, he added. "Hal to you."

For a moment it had seemed she was about to fly into his arms. How he wanted to hold her, feel the soft connection of that lovely form against his.

"What happened to you?" she asked, standing still several feet away.

"What's happened here?" Grant countered in an almost too commanding voice.

"It's a long, ugly story." She suddenly slapped her hands on her sides. "I can't believe it! Thank God you're alive! Everybody thought you were dead. It's like seeing a ghost. And you don't know how much we need you! Lard's taken control of things!"

"I would have imagined." Grant quickly told her of his escape from the bird and the long mad adventures which had followed. Then he explained about the footprint. She nodded, strangely alert to every word. He told about the figure that had passed him unknowingly in the forest. "I was still half out of my head with fever. Thought it was...delusion."

There was a moment of silence as that sank in.

"It wasn't," she announced. "We've seen signs, too. Some of the men have sworn they were exactly like humans—but that was hysteria. Your report is the only detailed description. Everybody will be excited to learn this. It's just about all we've talked about since Lard's discovery."

"How's he handling things?"

She bit on her lower lip, as if repressing sudden anger. She told him how Lard had taken over, then said, "Nobody crosses him—not after what happened to Art Rent."

An arched eyebrow questioned that last statement.

She quickly filled him in on the details, then said, "Lard had him put into Deep Freeze, to be recovered when things are 'organized'—maybe in a hundred years or so! That's his solution to troublemakers. Nobody will face up to him."

Granted nodded, grimly. "Not smart to debate an armed man. Unless you have a counter punch that's sure to win the day."

"What can we do?" she almost pleaded.

"Nothing, for now," Grant announced without hesitation. "Better a strong hand at the helm rather than a weak one."

She frowned at that.

"Dictators come and go," he pointed out with a quick wave of his hand. "The people survive, if they don't get executed by the Mad King!"

"Or killed by an alien monster!" She told him about the night attacks and A-Hunts during the day, as Lard called them.

"At this very moment he's with the some men, hunting aliens. They went out this morning, because of the attack last night." She then told him in detail what had happened while he was gone.

"How'd things get so outta control?" Grant wanted to know once she had finished.

"Lard claimed you'd want him in charge. Once he had the guns, well.... Now the alien scare has dulled further resistance against him."

"Why haven't you started building a settlement on the river bank?"

Lena said bitterly, "According to Lord Lard, a village is out. His message is fast pairing up and faster breeding! Mardi Shores is pregnant. Wonder of wonders, a baby Lard to help populate Larton."

"Larton? Are you kidding?"

"Oh. Yes. He's named the planet after...himself."

Grant thought that over and was about to say something when the door burst opened and Jake stepped in, carrying a shaver.

When the man was gone, Grant asked, "What's this about Mardi and Lard?"

"Like I said, couples are to pair off and breed. Immediately, if not yesterday. If we aren't pregnant in two months, that is—out the door to another man's bed." She shuddered.

102

"And the first switching is due!"

Grant felt a cold fury eat at him. "He's nuts!"

The door suddenly swung open, and Lard stood there, laser gun in hand, face set in hard grim lines. He motioned Lena out of the room, then closed the door behind her.

"Well, I see you made it back," Lard slowly said, coldly studying Grant as a man might examine a lion about to spring in attack. "I heard some of your conversation. And I'm not nuts! You have a lot of learning to do, Grant, a lot to catch up on. Things have changed since you were here. But first report to me what happened!"

Grant did so. All the time he watched Lard, wondering what the man would do next.

When finished, Lard nodded thoughtfully, then said in an openly frank voice, "I told everybody I was following your design for our colony."

The man hesitated, as if awaiting Grant's approval.

"This system is working well. It's best this way. But what I overheard of your conversation with Lena—you sound somewhat confused about things."

"Using women like cattle?"

"What else would you suggest? They are our breeders here on Larton. That's reality!" The man winked, chuckled. "Isn't it a sweet universe? All these lovely ladies...with their young bods...to serve us men!"

"And the women, what do they think?"

"They don't need to think!" He laughed at that, as if at some private joke. "Believe me, they're enjoying!"

Grant controlled his response. "Male-dominated society?"

"A tribal society must be male-dominated." The man was serious now, sounding amazingly reasonable. "Surely you see that. Women are caretakers. Homemakers and mothers and nurses."

Grant couldn't resist a bland interjection at this point. "Maids and submissive mates for their male masters! Right?"

"Well, of course. Now you have it. That's their natural place. And the men, well, they do the building, exploration, design, organization, government—as we've always

103

done in ancient times! Hunting and all warrior activities. Plus leadership. Of course! In a very practical sense that's how primitive human societies have survived in the past, and it's the way we'll survive here.

"All females must become mothers as soon as they're physically mature enough. That means at age twelve to fifteen. That's the schedule for the second generation. A harsh dictate, sure."

"Rather!" Grant inquired in a straightforward manner.

"Well, regardless, I need to have your support on all this!" He hesitated for but a moment, fingered the tip of the laser gun. "You understand that."

Grant merely stared back.

"Need your public, open support or...well, I'll just say this little adventure pushed you over the edge."

"Nobody will believe that," Grant stated.

"Maybe. Maybe not. But who's to debate my explanation? I'll dump you in DF. When you're revived, if ever, society will be two or three hundred or thousand years older. Be reasonable. Why debate the point? We can work together, can't we?"

Grant didn't hesitate to say, "Naturally, we have to. Just so we have a firm understanding."

"Then you'll be totally supportive?"

"Of course." He would be of no use in Deep Freeze.

Lard relaxed, even smiled. "Good."

The two men were quiet for a few moments, then Grant decided to play it very casual. He picked up the shaver.

"Tell me your plans." Grant started to shave. "Maybe you have a few points I can iron out in my own mind. This is still all new to me. And could we have something to eat?"

"I'll have something brought in while we talk," Lard offered in such a manner that it was obvious Grant was a prisoner.

"Okay, have the food brought in," Grant said blandly, as if he had totally missed the implication of Lard's statement.

It was about a half-hour later, and Grant was sitting at

the small table that had been pulled down from the wall, finishing his meal of computer-processed Meat & Potatoes. Lard Talor, having finished his long lecture, stood over him, laser dangling playfully in his beefy hands.

Grant ran the fork around the now empty dinner plate that had been brought earlier, attempting to buy a moment to consider his next response.

"Well," Lard said after a long silence, "what do you think now?"

Grant tried to look thoughtful as he said, "Looks like you have things working like the ol' well-oiled machine."

"Then you'll support me? You'll make a general announcement to the others this evening?"

Grant kept his voice flat, saying, "Sure. If you deem it that important!"

"Wonderful. Just wonderful!" Lard patted him on the back.

Grant observed, willfully hiding the sarcasm, "I see you've put a lot of thought into all this! You'd have made a dandy leader for many a nation!"

Lard beamed, totally unaware of the blatant insult. "I always thought I'd be good in such a capacity, but in my time a man didn't get a chance. My grandparents were workers buckled down to useless jobs, three hours a day, three days a week, and couldn't get out of the set strata the unions placed on them. It was considered better than having everybody on government welfare. I spent hours reading about better and worse times." He shrugged and raised his eyebrows. "Well, a man couldn't better his social position! I want to make sure this doesn't happen on Larton. Here we can become anything we want! That's the dream."

"And make a better life for yourself and your children?" Grant offered blandly.

"Yes, yes! I'm so glad we understand one another. At last. It is very important to me. You were a historical hero of mine."

"Really?"

"Sure. Didn't everyone consider General Hal Grant a hero?"

"I wouldn't know about my historical reputation after

being Deep Frozen!" Grant tried to laugh at that, to appear truly flattered by the man's attempted praise.

Lard laughed, too, and seemed to relax for the first time. "I'll have quarters arranged for you—or if you wish, these are yours."

"I could use a larger room." Grant surveyed the one they were in, not much more than a cubbyhole, with bedbunk, sink, and a wall table that pulled down.

Then he said casually, "Oh, and about Dr. Hitten—I would like her...well, as—"

"Your first lady companion. Wonderful choice. I'd have picked her myself." Then he winked, patting Grant once more on the shoulders. "But Mardi kinda grabbed at me!"

"So I heard," Grant managed to sound almost perversely pleased. He leaned forward, grinning as if sharing some man-to-man secret with him. "Well, I'd sure like connecting with Dr. Hitten. As you can guess, it's been some time!"

"Lena. They're all on a first name basis. Gotta keep them in their...proper perspective!" Lard laughed, almost hysterically. "Don't you agree?"

"Only if you can arrange things for her and me, okay?" He actually reached out and gripped the man's shoulder. Winking, he offered, "Kinda think she'd be a real challenge!"

Lard grinned, pleased with himself. "Yes, of course, Mr. Grant! But hardly a challenge. The women must submit, and they know it! After all, as one of the special supporters of my cause, you can have anything you want—as long as you continue to enjoy the fruits of our directives!"

There was a hard warning note in his last statement. "I'll be calling a meeting tonight, and you will make your public statement. Then Lena is yours to devour as you wish."

Lard slipped the laser into his holster. "I'll see you get anything you want—other than weapons, of course. I don't trust you quite that much, you understand!"

Grant bowed. "Of course not."

CHAPTER TEN

Grant felt awkward standing there next to Lard Taylor. The two men were behind the huge table-like desk separating them from the other members of the colony. At first it was difficult to pay attention to what Lard said, and he dismissed much of it as flowery rubbish concerning "the General's" amazing return to the flock. This he ignored, but was instantly attentive to what followed.

"We have now been together for two months. The fact that only two women have become pregnant creates some concern. Remember, it is our duty to build the colony's population as rapidly as possible."

The man's eyes went from one woman to the next. "This is your duty, ladies. So we start switching partners. It will be done randomly by the ship's computer.

"Whets, whose partner is pregnant, will have the right to stay with her or choose any women as his next two-month companion."

As Lard spoke, Grant watched the others for any signs of rebellion and was struck by their submissive response.

"Now, Mr. Grant wants to speak." Lard turned. Their eyes met. The man's gaze warned: Be smart.

After the normal hellos, Grant very carefully picked his words:

"It gives me great pleasure to discover you're all in grand health. Even Art Rent is healthy and alive in Deep Freeze. This is important. We must all survive, at all costs.

"Ultimately we can't depend on the ship and immortality to fulfill all of our human needs. As we all learned those first days here, the ship suffered a lot of damage getting us here. And while it is functional, and will probably remain so for as long as we need to make use of its technology, it's important to plan for the far distant future. A future independent of its shelter.

"We're safe in here, for now. Given enough time, it will be necessary to establish links to the planet, to produce our own food from the very soil of this world. In time great cities will spread out, flower the landscape—but only if we have a strong and healthy population.

"All past social norms of limited birth rates must be reversed here and now. Where it was logical on Earth to conserve on space and limit family size to avoid overpopulation, here we have unlimited space for the coming generations."

Grant hoped he'd clouded over his main message with a lot of flowery camouflage. Survive. Don't do anything to endanger that.

As Grant spoke, he found it was quite easy to make statements he could live with. It was important to say nothing that might backfire later, after Lard was deposed.

"The fact that two women are already pregnant is exciting news. We all must celebrate that. Who knows, we could be the last humans in the universe. These two babies are the first of a new Mankind."

He hesitated for a moment, noticing that Lena's face revealed only icy annoyance at his words.

"We must begin a program of cooperation. Lard has made some tough decisions. And he's determined to see these policies carried out. United we are stronger than when divided. Right now we few humans need to stand together.

"If there is any resentment concerning the present leadership, I suggest that open rebellion against authority is counterproductive—and foolish. Ending up in Deep Freeze gains nothing! At least not for the deeply frozen member of our community. Rather chilly in there. And no fun in the sun that way!"

He tried to act as if this was some kind of perverse joke, chuckling to see what their response might be. Some laughed heartily, a few merely smiled. Lena looked down, avoiding his eyes.

"In war, you fight to win. And most of the time it

isn't done with a sweet smile, but at the point of a sword."
He let that sink in before adding the cover-up. "We are at
war with the very elements of this new world. We are the
aliens.

"Survival is what this is all about. That simple. Don't
forget it."

Again he paused only long enough to let that sink in.

"Leadership is as strong as the support it gets, and the
tools it holds at its command. Perhaps some methods may, at
any given moment, seem cruel, but in the long run we must
adapt to reality...or die."

Then turning to the man next to him, Grant announced in a bold, firm voice, "And today Mr. Lard Talor is
that reality! Our present Leader!"

Lard was grinning with foolish pleasure.

After a moment, Grant finished with, "I'm certain
that Mr. Talor respects the lives of everyone here. I'm truly
pleased that under his strong leadership you have all survived."

Grant stepped back as the men and women nodded
and appeared on the surface to be quite pleased with his
statement.

Lard, still smiling, said, "Assigned companions will
be posted in this room tonight, and the women will move
into the men's quarters in the morning.

"Oh, and Lena Hitten, because of a promise made to
Mr. Grant, you will join our beloved General for a period of
two months."

Grant glanced at Lena and saw the woman go rigid.
She didn't look at him. Apparently his speech and Lard's
announcement had sent the right message.

Lard asked, "Are there any questions?"

Silence answered.

Lard quickly closed the meeting, turned to Grant.

"Your words are reassuring."

Grant smiled. "Believe me, I meant everything I said.
To the very last word."

Lard patted him on the back. "Well, perhaps we'll
make a good team, after all."

"Why, of course!" Grant held back any sarcastic rebuff. Hopefully, Lard was being hoodwinked.

* * * * * * *

Flip Kord sat in his small quarters, feeling a bit low. Lena had just left, and he was awaiting the arrival of his newly assigned female companion, Jeeni.

He hated losing Lena's companionship. A lovely, intelligent woman. He really liked her.

Flip's mind was running over several conversations they'd shared. It was an instant replay of impressions and memories, which just blended into a tangled sequence.

"Have you noticed," Lena had said one evening, "how none of us act like old people? Yet almost all of us were well past two hundred before DF. I have thought about that for some days."

"I guess all of us have," Flip offered, unable to hide his own growing attraction to her.

Lena noticed his gaze, but managed to ignore its implication in a very ladylike manner.

"How'd you get Deep Frozen?" Lena inquired conversationally, diverting the exchange to less personal matters.

"When death faced me," he offered, "DF seemed a pleasant ideal state. In my last years, age was eating my flesh away. Death seemed almost desirable. Yet we cling to life, even when it isn't good to us any more, even as the aging process dims our wits."

She sighed. "DF got me hooked, early on. I wanted to see the future."

"I simply wanted escape," he admitted.

"And DF offered it, too?"

"DF obsessed me, in the end. I did not believe in a life after death."

"Not the religious type?"

"Not the conventional one. I never believed we could know it all, that our brains were able to understand the answers. And any God that might be the First Cause could never explain it all in human words. Guess I couldn't buy into that system of blind belief."

110

"A difficult leap of faith for the scientific mind," she admitted. "Some of us are able to isolate the two arguments into different mental chambers. Science in one; religious faith in the other. Hence they can't conflict with one another."

"Well, maybe. For me the conflict was never resolved. But DF, it offered a way to avoid death. It was an alternative. At times I didn't want to live. And I was terrified of a death that offered no hope beyond ending life. It was the fear of death that caused me to DF."

"That's rather interesting," she laughed. "A lack of belief in life after death forced you into DF!"

"I couldn't believe it offered more than a slim hope. So I was taken into the ice of eternal hope. To awaken in this ship was quite a start!"

He paused long enough to study Lena's fine features, then added, "To be youthful in...every way...is a little startling. I'm not tired anymore. Seems that youth breathes on hope and dreams of the future."

"Yes. Our new bodies bring a lot of new feelings—perhaps old ones we've forgotten."

"You feel that too?" Flip inquired.

"We all feel it," she managed, avoiding his gaze.

"Is it only our erotic centers that are magnified? Or are there some deeper elements...that have been changed?"

"I really don't know, Flip," was her thoughtful reply.

One night, while trying to avoid noticing how enticing she was as a woman, he said, "You must have been popular...with the men."

"Not until I was out of college and had my degree."

"The degree made you suddenly sexy and desirable?"

She laughed, embarrassed. "No. Just no time. Then I dated some."

"Then you were married?"

"My, my, been peeking at my stat charts?" She laughed at that, as if reading his thoughts. Maybe the sense of envy was in his eyes.

Flip knew some couples were becoming lovers. He was already experiencing a strong need for intimacy. And he was strongly attracted to Lena.

The woman answered his question with, "Sure, married a couple of times. And divorced once."

"That's a hell of its own. Divorce is damnation!" Flip announced. "So I've been told."

"Very much so, and requires a total rebuilding of one's life."

"Like here?" he wondered. "Starting over with the past gone."

"No," she said, shaking her head in thought. "That's the point: Our past is dead forever. It is different here. We are different. Memories of Earth seem vague, distant. Maybe International did something to make the adjustment to our new lives a bit easier. And that's why we don't miss our families."

"Have children, then?"

"Several." She hesitated, smiling. "You know, I haven't thought much about that? Who knows, maybe some distant relative is in this ship, now. How horrible. I'd hate to find a lover here who was a descendant of mine."

Then another time Flip asked, "What're we going to do about the...Lard's...Commandment?"

It was as blunt as he could get on the subject, but felt it necessary to bring it up.

"I don't buy that breeders thing. I hope you understand. It has nothing to do with...you."

He merely nodded, feeling both disappointment and an automatic understanding.

She continued, stammering over words. "I'm not ready...to play that card. Not yet!"

"Not ever, his way. This is crude, rude and disgusting, if you ask me!" Flip announced furiously.

Lena laughed at that. "We're hardly children. We aren't virgins. We're old enough to know that the hard facts are to be fruitful and multiply. In a small society that Biblical dictate applies. In some cultures fathers sold their daughters for some sheep or tools that were considered far more useful!"

"But hardly as much fun!" Flip laughingly offered, letting his eyes sweep over her like a lustful beast about to devour a delicious morsel.

"Now you sound like a man in heat!" she offered. "Seriously, but—"

"Well, seriously, I'd find you a desirable woman, under the right circumstances," Flip admitted.

"Thanks. That's really very nice. And most of all, thanks for being a friend about this."

"Nothing to it, just my nature."

She patted him on the cheek and said, "I need time to adjust to all this."

He merely nodded.

Their relationship stayed at arm's distance. Both of them, actually, had needed the time to adjust.

Now two months had changed some of Flip's thinking. He'd become highly alert to his need for a woman. There was no other way of putting it. And his new partner was a lovely, somewhat flirtatious woman.

Jeeni had caught his gaze several times in the past weeks. Her manner was shyly reserved, yet somewhat direct in its curiosity. They had only a few polite verbal exchanges, but she'd gazed at him in a very probing manner.

The thought of being intimate with her sent a lovely wave of guilty pleasure through him.

Just then a timid knock sounded on the door.

"Yes?"

"It's me," came Jeeni's soft voice.

"Come in."

Before he could even stand, a dark-haired woman entered, the door closing behind her.

"Well, here I am, I suppose." She stood there very pert, her nice, firm body pressing against the soft folds of the brief-on.

"Welcome. Make yourself...at home. This is our normal three-room Super Duper Deep Freeze Flat." He tried to laugh, eyes lingering on the swells of her breasts. It all made him feel like a teenager on his first date. "Standard issue, so I'm told!"

"Can I put these things away?" she asked, indicating a small bag in her right hand.

He nodded.

"I think it best that we cut through the ice, don't

you?" She tossed that line off in such a casual manner that he wasn't quite sure what was meant by it. "Come to an understanding as to how things are."

"Sure," Flip replied.

"Why make it difficult?" She had an attractive, delicate way of almost gliding across the room. Her hips moved seductively, without any touch of vulgarity—surprisingly self-assured.

For several minutes he had a chance to consider her rapid entrance and exit. The manner of her total confidence was surprising. Not aggressive, not submissive, but merely straight to the point.

Returning, she said, "I guess we might as well make the most of things."

The woman looked so childlike. It was hard to believe she was over twenty.

She raised a delicate hand before he could respond. Noticing the surprised expression in his eyes, she laughingly said, "My virginity is long gone! Even if this new me looks virginal! Tain't so!"

Her total demeanor was both blunt and outspoken, in a bright, but boldly humorous way, and without question flatly seductive.

She struck a cute pose, hands on hips, as if silently asking how he liked her. "Hope we'll get on."

"I hope so, too," Flip assured her, appreciating the sweep of her hips, and the slow flow of exposed thigh. Just a wonderful, mature kid, in her prime of life. "What age were you before DF?"

"A wee bit under 200. Can you imagine me an ol' hag?" she announced with a great burst of self-mockery. "Was married many a time. So I'm a lady of some minor experience. Hope you'll approve!"

She stood in front of him as the relaxo-chair opened up to make room for the two of them. "This is really all rather exciting, isn't it, Flip? I'd been simply dead during those last years. Youth gone, beauty gone. And I didn't even realize it—I'd forgotten the thrills of being young and vital and actually raging with all kinds of roaring hormones! Just an aged old broad, I was! No fun that way!"

114

She sat down next to him. Now the woman seemed as uncertain as Flip felt. Perhaps it was the very intimacy of their sudden physical closeness, almost touching. "But all that maturity...doesn't bring any smarts to deal with this kind of situation, does it?"

The two of them sat there, staring at one another. He was beginning to really enjoy the experience. Their eyes met, and for a very long time he felt as if he was being absorbed in some kind of gently welcoming embrace. Strangers wondering about one another.

"I was really rather delighted, Flip, when I found we'd been paired for this two month period." She was sizing him up, attempting to reach into his very mind and read its innermost thoughts. "Kinda wondered about you."

"I'd wondered about you, too."

"Now I guess we'll find out." It was quite direct, without being coy or brazen. Then finally she said in a small voice, "But it is a bit scary, isn't it?"

"I suppose we're all a bit scared." He started to reach out to touch her. Then his hand froze and fell to his side.

She saw, merely blushed, turned away, as if aware that this opening gambit had been, perhaps, almost too grand in its boldness. "Don't get the wrong idea about me, Flip."

"In what way?"

"I'm just your normal, red-blooded female who has turned suddenly young! That's really something to suck up so suddenly."

They were silent for some time, each aware of their own troubling thoughts. Flip realized that the impact of DF and immortality had effected everybody differently. This woman seemed to be pretty open and up front. It was very appealing.

Abruptly, she faced him again, and in a somewhat serious manner, said, "I know you work closely with Lard, Jake, and Whets."

"Yes," he answered, uneasily. The statement had come out of left field.

"What kind of men are they? I assume they're delighted with this arrangement with us ladies."

"Yes. They are."

"And you?"

"I'm finding it more inviting by the minute," he admitted with a swift smile.

"Well, I assume that's a compliment!" She managed a quick smile, then asked, more bluntly, "What I wanted to know, Flip, is how and where you stand. I mean, you work with these guys."

"Yes. Does that make a difference?"

"No. But...you're not one of them?"

"I'm a male. I like women. I fly the copter. That's about the limit of our mutual sameness," he stated.

"I was wondering about those expeditions. Do you think the aliens should be killed?" The woman shivered, then looked away and hugged her arms, as if trying to hide a chill.

"Heavens, no. But...I'm not in charge."

She nodded slowly, once again meeting Flip's eyes, as if trying to read his thoughts.

"And this stuff?" She indicated the room, him, and shrugged. "This kind of arrangement makes you uncomfortable, I suppose!"

"Not quite sure," he admitted.

"Mardi calls it Free Love," she shrugged, eyes still studying Flip's. "Nothing's really free."

"True. But it is nice to be intimate in a caring way. With somebody you care about."

"I agree." She sounded very secure and serious. "I really do."

"This is bloody awkward, at best! Isn't it? No room even for illusions."

"You're an idealist. I like that, Flip. But idealism is not always workable." It was a statement of fact. "Heck, darlin', what choice do we have? Ignore the obvious or simply relax and enjoy?"

There was an awkward moment, then she offered a cute smile and shrugged helplessly. "And if we don't do the expected, we're in deep poop!"

They both laughed at that. Suddenly they had leaped across an awkward gap. The rest would be easy.

At that point the sound of Lard's voice came out of the very air itself: "Flip, report to the copter bay."

116

Jeeni looked a bit startled, then frowned in mock-pain. "Well, no lovin' this morning."

"Guess not," Flip countered. "Guess we're outta luck!"

They both laughed at that. Then she moved close to him. Taking his hand, she said, "I really do want things to work out right between us."

Her fingers were warm in his. "Okay."

She surprised Flip by kissing his cheek. "There, see? Won't be all that difficult."

Flip felt a warm edge of desire ebb through him.

Her lips turned up in a small smile.

"I'll be waitin' fer ya." She giggled and patted his cheek, then opened the door. "Out ya go, honey! Bring the bee back to sting the queen!"

She winked up at him.

He started to slip close to her, wanting a goodbye kiss. But she pushed him playfully away through the door. "Later. We'll dance all night together!"

"Just dance?" he inquired, in mock-horror.

"You'll like my fancy steps!" Her eyes flashed with honest warmth.

As he moved along the corridor on his way to the copter bay, he felt a very real sense of excitement. Dancing with Jeeni sounded really promising!

* * * * * * *

Jeeni stood there looking at the door. Flip seemed quite nice. And there was a little boy quality about him she found quite appealing. She could accept the man as more than just a bedroom tumble. It might be very nice with him.

Intimacy was unavoidable in such a confined, small society. But forced mating was unnatural. That was a mixed passion dish to swallow.

During the last weeks with Cag, it had been okay enough. In the first days she'd been somewhat under shock, confused. He was a sweet man and didn't attempt to push matters. They had talked a lot about the intimacy issue before anything actually happened. She found him to be a gen-

117

tle lover, a caring human being.

In the last week or so she'd been studying the other men, with a growing realization any of them might end up as her next partner. It was a strange, uncomfortable realization. Yet some of the men were quite appealing, even desirable—everybody was young and physically at their prime.

Well, Jeeni told herself, with some sense of honest pride, I've never been a wallflower.

She'd always enjoyed her lovers. Even extramarital affairs were not uncommon in the world she and known. But they were kept politely private. Her religious upbringing had always underscored a sense of values and moral ethics.

She had totally accepted, as a personal conviction, the engraved quote at the entrance to the church her parents had gone to: "Love must be the Center of Our Total Being." Then inside, on the wall, was a plaque upon which was printed:

"Seek those who fill the voids in your life. Recognize that all humans are weak and needy. Accept the promise that is yours for the taking! Don't limit your choices. Let your inner being rejoice in the bliss of love. Don't resist that inner call. For love is the very center of our being, the gift to share with joy and ecstasy."

The minister of that church had been her first lover. Yet it was only in marriage that she found real freedom and love.

Great voids were present in the best of her marriages. Jeeni had known for a long time that pure romantic idealism was childish fantasy. And she had never been without a lover during her prime years. The last decades, though, had been empty of real intimacy. An aged body attracted few admirers.

But here, on Larton, with this newly revived youth, it was just wonderful. How delicious to be admired by men, to have them want her.

As Flip so obviously wanted her. He'd been unable to keep his eyes from revealing that hunger.

She knew he'd be a nice caring lover. She really looked forward to the coming two months.

With a deliciously contented sigh, she started to ex-

118

plore the small quarters. A living room to relax in, a kitchen to snack in—since they all ate together communally—and the bedroom, of course.

Jeeni decided to prepare herself for the evening. She wanted to make it as perfect as possible. Delaying intimacy was silly. And totally undesirable.

* * * * * * *

It was already late evening. Flip Kord was at the controls of the jetcopter. Lard was sitting next to him in the co-pilot's seat. And as he swung the copter to the left, he tried to drive his thoughts away from Jeeni.

She was, in a very bluntly subtle way, quite seductive. And he looked anxiously forward to being alone with her.

If only it had been that way with Lena, his mind teased him.

He wondered how beautiful Lena had been on Earth. International had, in some cases, added to their clients' natural beauty. And why not? While rebuilding an old body into a new one, it was an easy matter to make things better than ever. Nobody could live for two or three hundred years without gaining a smoothness of personality, a sharpness of wit.

Flip's mind snapped back to the copter at Lard's shouted cry.

"There! Look! Down into those treetops—near the river!" Lard was waving his hand like a flopping rag.

Flip sudden saw what Lard was shouting about. They swooped down, following the course of the fleeing figure of an alien far below.

Lard reached out the window, laser in hand.

He fired.

Blazing flame burned a trail behind the running alien. The creature tensed, mouth opened in screaming pain, as it limped into the cover of the forest.

Lard bristled with anger, his eyes gleaming savagely as he looked at the laser in his hand. After a moment, he said, "I guess that's enough for the day. It's beginning to darken. Otherwise we'd go down and get that bastard!"

119

Flip felt a shiver shoot down his spine. There had been no reason for shooting the alien.

But he said nothing. Silence was a habit by now. Nobody wanted to follow Art Rent into DF. And with Grant supporting Lard there was nobody to take up the sword against the man.

For a moment Flip puzzled over Grant's statements, and a sense of wonder touched him. Exactly what had the General really been saying? Suddenly he wasn't quite sure. His mind attempted to remember the exact words, the long statements, and weed out their real meaning. Nothing made sense.

It had been very unlike Hal Grant to submit so completely to Lard—not unless the man had changed a lot from the famous general the history books had recorded.

Lard's voice cut into his thoughts. "Well, back to the pleasures of the night. Right?"

Flip turned, annoyed by the man's question and manner.

Their eyes met, but he didn't respond.

"Who're you matched up with for the next months?"

"As if you didn't know!" Flip muttered.

"Quite frankly, I don't. The computer made the pick. Jake posted it. I had other matters. So...who is she?"

Flip wanted to tell him it was none of his business, but simply muttered, "Jeeni."

"Yes. Nice. Very nice." Lard nudged him with an elbow. "Enjoy, Flip. Enjoy! Life is sweet, and long. Ain't it nice? All these beautiful ladies just for the taking. I tell you, every woman is just as anxious and willing to enjoy as my Mardi! Father Lard has blessed his children with permission to enjoy the fruits of their youth!"

The man laughed hysterically at this, then patted Flip on the shoulder.

Damn the bastard! Most of all he resented the fact that the man was bloody right. He could hardly wait to be with Jeeni. His body surged with startling desire.

"Just enjoy, my boy! I demand it!" Lard's brazen laugh mocked him.

Flip was very careful in his response. "Yes, of

120

course. You're right. I'm going to enjoy."

"Good! It's important. I kinda got the impression that you and Lena weren't really...enjoying!"

Flip avoided the man's eyes. "What makes you think that?"

"Just not as dumb at you might believe. Lena seems kinda standoffish, a bit of a snob. Poor Grant. I do believe he's gonna be a bit disappointed in her!"

"Hardly," Flip said in a controlled even voice. "She's a very nice woman."

"And not easily pushed around. Well, we'll take care of that—next time around. Unless Grant orbits her bod." Then changing the subject, he added, "Luck with Jeeni. I do believe she's a bit on the cooperative side."

Flip had to control the impulse to smash the man's face. But instead, once again, he played it very safe. "Sure. I'm sure you're right. Looking forward. Enjoy."

He forced himself to laugh, making it sound blatantly coarse.

"I'm really glad you're adapting! Means a lot," Lard announced, suddenly very conversational. "Really pleased, Flip. Maybe you'll be converted despite yourself."

Flip just nodded.

"It's a man's world, Flip. As things were always meant to be. Male dominance made homo sapiens Masters of Earth in ancient times." Lard laughed at that pun. "And here on Larton, we'll have immortality to enjoy the fruits of...."

The man continued to rattle on, and Flip managed to simply nod correctly at the right moments. His mind just centered on images of Jeeni. He hungered for the intimacy she had so nicely promised. It had been a long time since knowing the soft warmth of a woman's body melting against his own.

CHAPTER ELEVEN

Three days had passed since Grant's arrival and public statement in support of Lard Talor, during which time he had silently observed the pattern of the Larton colony. One of the important elements was the vidscreen in each suite, connected to the ship's central computer and memory banks. All historical, scientific, and information libraries were at their fingertips. He spent long hours searching through the ship, getting a feel of things, and making plans for ultimately overturning Lard Talor's rule.

Only Lena knew about his real plans. But it had been difficult to convince her.

That first evening, in the new quarters allotted both of them, Lena had at first been icy cold, uncommunicative as she sorted out the few personal possessions she had accumulated during the last few weeks.

After several minutes silently watching her at the small table, Grant said, "Lena, I want to explain something to you."

Whipping around, facing him, Lena snapped, "You don't have to explain anything! I think you did a grand job a little while ago! Just a grand job!"

"That's what I want to explain to you," he told her softly.

"What's there to explain?" she demanded in a bitter voice. "It seemed quite clear to me that you think Mr. Talor has been handling things just right!"

"At what point did I make such a statement?" Grant countered, continuing to keep his voice calm and soft.

It took her some while to react to his question. She was sitting on one of the two chairs. Her face changed ex-

122

pression. The anger shifted to amazement, then to disbelief.

Now she slowly stood, facing him, tensed like a coiled spring about to unwind with explosive force. "You said it with every word you spoke!"

"I don't believe that's correct," he told her in that same quiet voice. "If you consider everything that I actually said, I believe you'll discover it was the kind of speech I might have made even if Lard were not in command."

"What?" she gulped. Her face blanched. Her fists clenched tight as she stared up at him in wide-eyed shock.

"First, I pointed out that I had returned to the ship to discover that everybody was alive. I said that this pleased me. I admitted to the evident truth that reproduction is of prime importance to our colony, a fact which nobody in his right mind would deny. I never said that I agreed with Lard's methods of forcefully mating couples!

"I advised everybody to submit to Lard's rule and implied as indirectly and subtly as possible that when a man has a gun, you don't argue!

"I pointed out that the most important thing is for all of us to live through this, and that time would finally change all things. Time was on our side, if we but waited.

"What is demanded of us now will not be fatal, anyway. We are going to become a very tight family group before the first year is over. Lard is forcing close relationships immediately—merely quickening the normal. His methods are wrong, that's all. In time, a natural coupling-off would have occurred. If we wait him out and don't attempt to put ourselves in a position to be killed—or put into Deep Freeze, which won't do anybody any good—in time things will change for the better.

"He cannot last long, Lena. He wants personal power at any cost. There is no room for such a man here. We have to pull together and work together for our common need.

"Now if you just think it over, I believe you'll see that I never once said that I supported Lard's methods. By implication, I only advised against doing anything impulsive and dangerous. I advised waiting and protecting our personal selves from harm. No victory has to be total, and no defeat has to be lasting. A good general always learns when to pull back his forces so that he can fight another day with what he has left, rather than struggling with nothing. Obviously, to this point, no real lasting harm has been done against anybody, other than hurt pride and a few unpleasant weeks."

"You didn't see Art Rent's back after Lard finished his little public flogging!" Lena spat back.

"In war, people get hurt. Art served the purpose of showing that open revolt will get nowhere. Lard will take any measures necessary to get his way!"

"Why didn't you speak out against him? The others would have backed you!" But Lena was beginning to sound doubtful.

"Because Lard would have killed me instantly, which would have served his purposes, not mine! And I doubt very much that anybody would have backed a dead man!" Grant pointed out explosively.

"But you made a deal with him—about me!" Her voice quivered, and she lowered her eyes to the floor for the first time. "And I guess you will take your rewards."

"If you mean you and me," Grant said with a gentle laugh, "you can stop worrying. I only wanted to protect you from being forced by some other man who wouldn't respect your wishes."

Lena nodded, thanking him, but said nothing more on the subject. He insisted she have the bedroom, while he slept on the couch in the lounge room.

But each day it became more difficult to avoid a closer intimacy. A growing sense of mutual trust and desire was becoming more evident. An accidental touch sent silent signals between them. Lingering eye contact communicated far more than words. While real feelings were budding like a beautiful rose, they were unable to grab the prize: casual intimacy was not their style. Both of them had, over the years, become somewhat selective in their choice of lovers.

During this time, Grant learned that only a few select trusted men carried side arms. Others were to be given weapons only if necessary on A-Hunts. He had turned down two offers to go on copter hunts with Lard, claiming to have had enough forest adventures for the time being.

Jake or Hicks were almost always within sight in the

background, silently monitoring his actions. This made his informational search of the ship far more difficult. He tried to appear casual about such explorations. At night he would once again find Lena in their shared quarters, more alertly aware of the very strong desire building inside him. How long could he continue to hold back his real feelings? They generally carried on casual conversations as if Lard were listening in the next room, although it was obvious they weren't being monitored. That first night's exchange would have brought down some very rapid reaction from Lard & Co. By the third day he decided to have a real, uncensored exchange with Lena.

After the communal dinner with the others onboard the ship, he suggested to Lena, "Let's take a look outside. Together."

She glanced across the table at him, at first surprised, then saw the serious expression in his eye. "Yes, I'd like that. A romantic stroll around the ship?"

"In the evening on a moonlit night," Grant offered, as they left the room and started down the hallway.

Why did he suddenly feel a flush of excitement? It wasn't romance he sought on this walk, but information only she might have. Yet a sense of something different ebbed though him as they started towards the lower levels where the airlock was located.

* * * * * * *

Mardi Shores was thrilled by her pregnancy. What had startled her most was how different she felt about things. The stark change was unexpected. Of course, on Earth she'd never been able to have children. It had been the only defeat in her life.

Now as she considered the quarters she shared with Lard, a sense of fulfillment settled over her. Even though he spent too much time in the "King's Lair," their relationship had turned into a pleasant enough one. Lard had leadership duties and an office to run them in. These quarters were their private love nest.

The man who had fathered her coming baby, while

125

strange and sometimes terrifying, was like an overpowering jungle beast that totally captivated her sexual needs.

She'd always enjoyed sex, playing the male animal like some magnificent musical instrument. It was so easy to make them fairly groan and moan with ecstatic pleasure. She could cause any man to sing the passion song like a marvelous tenor.

That first day she had entered this room, two months ago, had been rather fun and exciting.

Mardi had moved without hesitation, sure of herself. Men like Lard Talor could easily be handled with a little feminine skill.

She dumped the small bag in the corner, then took a drink Lard offered.

"To us." He saluted her body.

"How nice and inviting."

"I'm a generous host!" It was a rather controlled and coldly stated line.

She sat in the chair opposite him, across a small table. "Well I hope you'll be generous. I want you to like me, you know."

"I will. Assuming you're all that's advertised."

"Oh? You saw my ads?"

"What ads?" he countered, somewhat puzzled. "You have them?"

"Well, come to think of it, not here. Back on Earth."

"You weren't in my century," he announced. "Not even in the history books!"

"Shame. Perhaps you missed something...very nice."

"Oh?" An eyebrow arched dramatically.

"I was quite popular in my day and age. A big star," she proudly announced.

He mocked her with a frown, asked, "Star of what?"

"ErotoAdvents," she explained, leaning across at him. Not only a star of Advents, but the producer, writer and director of some of the most successful VRs in history. "I was the vision of all men's fantasies concerning the most desirable woman in the universe—I suppose!"

"Really? All that? Sounds rather promising, I must say."

126

"Yeah, perhaps. On Earth I had my fame and success. Isn't that what it's all about. Success and power?"

"Fame? Success? Power?" The man chuckled, eyes feasting on her like some wild animal. His gaze swept her body as if physically caressing it. "Famous? Were you?"

"Very. I made men want my bod."

"How many did you make?" he demanded, glaring at her. The mood change was stark.

"ErotoVids or men?" she inquired, carefully watching the man.

He shrugged like a brooding little boy, obviously unnerved. He spat out, angrily, "What's the difference?"

He's the jealous type, she mused, pleased. "Hey, hon, don't get mad. You'll break the mood of this scene."

That line startled Lard. His eyes widened. "What scene?"

"This one. You. Me. Here." She patted the table, just missing his hand—purposely.

"Oh?" The man sounded puzzled.

"Gotta follow the script, otherwise the mood just flickers away!" She snapped her fingers. "Just like that. Snap-snap!"

The startled look in the man's eyes was almost amusing.

She raised her arms high above her head, enjoying how the man's eyes followed the lift of her breasts. "Gotta go with the flow from one point to the other."

His eyes were all over her, devouring every curve.

Her lips parted, smiling sensually at him. "See what I mean?"

Mardi smothered the attempted to mock him. Men were really so basic. "Like what you see?"

His grin was almost evil.

Let him look good and hard. First he must see a powerhouse lady to conquer. And she'd been just that on Earth.

Just follow the script as you invent it, Mardi!

A wiggle here, a smile there, an exposed shoulder, a quick peak of breast, and they were like little boys wanting to play with every new toy in site.

Mardi's job required more than simple show-all. The

ErotoAdvents demanded a real sensual experience. That couldn't be faked. The electronic sensors recorded every sensation. Now she was revving up the old engine. Warm desire mellowed to hot waves of lush need. Layer by layer, Mardi dug deeper within the sensual erotic chambers of her body. It was like some inner beast was savagely screaming to be released. She grabbed control of this powerful new bio-engine and slowly focused on the man.

He just stared wantonly at her, blatantly obvious. She matched his mode. "Bet I know what you're thinking, hon."

"Don't 'hon' me," he muttered, very annoyed.

"I was thinking of the historical Huns, dear man!" she quickly announced, quoting from another famous script. "They were the warrior beasts that raped Europe in Roman times—and totally dominated everything that came into their control. Especially the women."

Nice choice of words, Mardi admitted. They fit perfectly.

"So you're educated." Was that contempt, annoyance or amusement in his voice? It was difficult to say. Then almost in a threatening manner, he added, "But just how smart are you with a real man?"

She let the tip of her tongue just barely run along slightly parted lips. "Smart enough to know better, I suppose."

Laughing brutally, he said, "Does a woman in your profession really need to...know...better?"

"I wasn't a whore, if that's what you mean," she announced with a bit of annoyance. "I'm passionate. And made it work for me—I just used my natural talents and became very famous. Do you consider me a naughty lady? Are you a bad little boy?"

"Come closer and I'll show you," was his simple retort.

"Nope. Not yet..." Her gaze lingered over his body. "Ya gotta let a gal burn a bit."

What Advent's script did that come from?

He actually chuckled, "Just don't burn to cinders."

"But first let me rev up, Lard!" Mardi made the line read a bit harsh. This man wanted to dominate, so she'd set him up real good. "Wouldn't you like to know more about the real me?"

He stood, and she immediately did so too.

"I don't like games!" he announced, threateningly.

She felt a delicious wave of deep pleasure.

"No. No game playing." Real wanton passion raced through every nerve.

"Better not! I'm not in the mood."

"I just want you to know I required a special kind of lover! A very special one," she announced, teasing him with a pat on the cheek. Frantically she wanted to move things rapidly to a quick union. But Mardi knew better. She winked, ran a fingertip down his shoulder. "Do you think you can be special for me?"

"Why not?" He actually shivered and flushed with desire.

"Well," she stated in a very soft, throaty manner, "prove it!"

The expression that twisted his features was almost frightening. He grabbed at her, brutally drawing close. "I don't have to prove anything. Not here on Larton!"

"Oh, really?" Mardi's eyes hardened to hide the very real fear ripping her guts. She laughed brazenly, managed a wicked wink. "With all these delicious young males running around loose?"

That last line had shattered some invisible wall, entering space that was deathly violent. It had been a dangerous play, thrusting through his defenses.

Mardi never knew exactly what happened next, or how it was that he savagely slammed her bodily against the wall. The brutality of his act, coming without warning, was physically stunning. She felt lightheaded, deliciously floating on the raw edge of ecstatic pleasure. She almost lost control, shivering with lush desire.

"Don't even think about them!" he spat out furiously.

Her lips managed to murmur, "I'll play who I wanna play!"

"Not while you're with me!" Once again he violently smashed her against the wall, hands clawing her shoulders, fingers like talons.

For a long, painful moment she struggled with the mix of fear and raw lust gutting her mind. Then slowly endless scripts lifted up from ancient memory. Picking the right line and attitude was instinctive.

"Why, Lard, babe, you sure are a deliciously jealous male animal!"

"Demanding," he warned, pressing firmly against her. "Very demanding."

She could feel the rippling tremble of his beautifully hard muscles and let her own frame shiver in delight.

"My, are you the powerful Hun!" She surged against him, squirming, squealing. "I love a strong man. Domination-sex can be so enjoyable! Don't you think?"

He merely snarled at her, "I can be very jealous...and dominating."

"Prove it! My big, brutish Hun!"

Without warning he swung her downwards like a rag, laughing in pleasure. "Time to play, then!"

She screamed in delight as he smashed her to the floor, his body brutally crushing against hers.

"I mean it!" Then a bit softer, "Total loyalty while we're a couple. Okay? Later, well, that's another matter."

"Sounds real nice, I can promise that."

"That's better! I'd hate to hurt you."

She tried to claw at his back, but he twisted his hands around her wrists and smashed them to the floor above her head.

She laughed in delight and arched up against him, thighs parting in blunt invitation. In the next moments it was impossible to tell who was the aggressor, or the seducer. Neither of them played submissive.

She thrilled inwardly, skillfully directing the man with her body, her movements, letting her own mind slip to a lowered state of consciousness. All thoughts centered on the physical connection of his flesh united in her growing needs. He was easily driven down her chosen pathway—one designed to control his inner erotic switches. He might be dangerous if crossed, but deliciously, laughably malleable in her expert hands.

Mardi found it simple to respond to the man. This

130

new International-designed body was a prime machine with highly sensitive nerve endings.

She let all thought focus on the physical connection between them. The wild beast burst alive like an explosive force, deeply thrilling in its intensity. Her whole being dived furiously into the raging passion quickly sparked by his very maleness. Automatically she embraced him, totally, greedily enveloping every delicious movement.

The responses racing at every nerve were overwhelming. Never had she been so deeply aware of every cell in her body. The continued pulsing thrust of pleasure was like hot lava burning her flesh. The throbbing rhythm overwhelmed all awareness beyond the continuous boiling waves of fire bathing over her again and again.

Mardi felt the universe close about her as she drifted on one layer of pleasure after another, each more intense, each deeper in its envelopment of her total being. Time simply vanished, spreading out beyond the limits of consciousness.

When it all ended she wasn't even aware.

At some point she was breathing again, almost gasping.

A great weight lifted from her body.

For a dreamy moment she let herself continue to drift, vaguely remembering.

Then sound and light jarred into being.

She felt isolated, abruptly abandoned.

Panic started to slap at Mardi. Then she looked up at the man. He was standing over her like some demonic nude David, grinning with shameless pleasure. His eyes swept brashly back and forth over her totally conquered body.

"Any of your ErotoStuds do that to you?" Lard demanded, preening like an overstuffed rooster. "I thought I'd killed you!"

Yes, she remembered. All too many had been delicious, wonderful lovers. She'd been lucky.

Lard, for all his crude brutality, was beyond anything she had experienced before—but was it him, or her own flesh, her own new body?

She could hardly wait to share intimacy with the

131

other men at the colony. In time that would happen. But for now she had to deal with Lard in a very sensitive manner indeed.

"No, dear man. Nobody drove me that far over the edge."

"I can almost believe you," he laughed hysterically. Then without even a warning, he smashed his hand across her face. "Don't bull me!"

She didn't need to ask him, but did so, anyway. "Why?"

"Why not?" The man actually laughed, good-naturedly. "I figure a woman of your quality deserves a good spanking from time to time."

She hugged herself, and let a very real mocking laugh join his. "You'd be surprised, my dear delicious Hun. I've done it all. And enjoyed it all! I think you are such great fun. I want more!"

"Yeah, sure. Later. Get dressed! Then fix things pretty in here. I have important matters to take care of."

And having thus coldly dismissed her, he left the quarters.

She stared at the door, annoyed and somewhat puzzled. Lard was all she'd expected, though a bit more complex. It might take some doing to keep him in line.

A smile played on her face as she slowly rubbed, then caressed, her arms. "How nice that all was."

She considered the room, and decided to offer up what he demanded—playing house lady. Maid and mistress. The rest was quite easy.

Her mind shifted to the present.

This new world demanded new solutions to survival. Mardi had always been a smart, progressive thinker, and successful because her mind was sharp enough to use what elements the world around her offered up.

She smiled to herself. "With this much time, what's the hurry?"

Then finger tips touched her flat belly, which would soon swell with motherhood.

"This comes first," she admonished. "Then maybe I'll take on nursing—the beginning course towards motherhood. Raising children might be as rewarding as controlling men had been. A different kind of human control. I think I'll like that!"

CHAPTER TWELVE

The moment Grant and Lena stepped outside the ship a sense of amazing relief settled over him. It was early evening and the sun was blazing red against the horizon, the air still sultry and hot. There were strict orders to return before complete darkness.

They had left the airlock arm in arm, taking on the outward appearance of two lovers. This was the show for others, but a show which Grant found highly enjoyable.

The soft nearness of Lena was breathtaking. Once outside, and away from the airlock, their attitude changed only slightly—not enough for the vidcams to notice, if they were monitoring them.

They talked in low whispers, as might befit lovers on an evening stroll. But the conversation was brutally serious.

He asked, "Exactly how do the women accept their subordinate position? Especially this...forced intimacy issue?"

"That's hard to answer. We all come from different social backgrounds.

"Mardi Shores adapts. During her life the first ErotoAdvent production companies became popularized. You saw and heard, and you felt what the actors were supposed to feel. For the men it was a replay of the obvious porno. For women romantic fictions were produced to satisfy their emotional needs. Mardi was a natural for those VRs and became popular even in soap versions. She's a free spirit, calculating, and a survivor.

"In Lard's time, the religious conservatives dictated their idea of morality into law. The Universal Conservative Party crushed liberal thinkers into dark holes. Lard lived a

134

structured life in a society that did not allow for social, sexual or work freedom. Every action was mapped. You did what your father did before you. Married the woman your father picked, and you had children when the government gave permission. He rebelled, hating things. Now he wants to fashion a world to his own liking."

"Can't blame him," Grant admitted. "We all want our own freedom of choice."

"Flip came from a society with no laws to restrict adults from a free choice. But the morality was love. It was a perfect setting for the more romantic ErotoAdvents to develop sometime later, far after he went into DF. When that happened, the world was exposed to a sensual revolution never known before in our histories. After that the blue noses screamed and laws were snapped back into place—very restrictive ones. Controls brutally enforced.

"This is the mishmash!" She shrugged, smiling. "There is no simple answer to the intimacy issue. But women do need time, or it won't work. There are alternative solutions to population expansion. If there were no men, we'd use the sperm banks International supplied us with. Something Lard is deathly quiet about."

"Lard's forced two-month partner switch will smash any resistance to his ideas!" Grant stated, angrily. "We need some basic standards acceptable to all!"

"Easy, big fella!" She touched his shoulder, as if to calm him. "Under normal circumstances, in a very short time, our small band will adapt its old customs. It'll all happen as a result of the natural reactions and behaviors of...well, all of us. It'll evolve out of our interactions. We'll adapt a workable new system, leaving the old ways behind. We just need the time."

He considered that and said, "But Lard won't adapt. Stopping him is my first priority."

She frowned, concerned. "Just don't take unnecessary chances."

"I don't plan to," Grant assured her.

They were silent for a long time after that. Grant never knew when her hand touched his. But for some time, he felt a deep pleasure holding her soft, small fingers.

He wanted to draw her closer.

She broke the long silence with, "Our children must be raised in a loving atmosphere."

Her fingers tightened against his. It seemed to Grant that the two of them were locked in a wondrous embrace.

She started to say something, then drew slightly back. Without a word, Lena pulled her hand from his, staring at it as if it were something disconnected.

For only a quick moment those eyes met his, and he saw the silent pleading that merely reflected his own confused feelings. Then all that simply clouded over and vanished, as if by an act of will.

"Grant, we can't live like this," she stated rather blandly. "It's all wrong."

He said nothing, uncertain, exactly, what she was actually meaning.

"The way Lard wants things.... How can we develop the proper love-bond with children who are the product of rape? We have to stop him!"

"I know," was Grant's only comment.

With sudden passion she blurted. "Our species survives through a healthy bonding -and our superior brains. Physically we're weaponless—no claws, no fangs. I feel so helpless!"

"Don't know about those claws!" he chuckled, desperately trying to lighten the subject for just a few moments. "Women have always managed quite well."

"No. That was seductive controlling, not real claws!" Her eyes flashed flirtatiously. "Another subject!"

Suddenly the desire to be all business had vanished. The silences were lingering moments filled with the sharp awareness of her very nearness.

They were now halfway around the ship, and the sun was beginning to dip lower and lower against the horizon. Reds bathed the dramatic cloud-splattered sky.

Lena suddenly said in a playful manner, "Then there's our immortality. How will it impact that ol' romantic ideal! Can you conceive of being with one person for eternity?"

"Never!   Not   possible!"   he   chuckled.

"Well...realistically speaking."

"Who wants to be realistic on a lovely evening like this?" She laughed and, taking his arm, urged him forward. The mood had changed, become amazingly intimate. "I don't!"

Then she hugged even closer. "Imagine a thousand years from now. Hal, will we know who is our great-great-grandchild?"

It was stunning how completely she'd managed to say so much without really saying anything at all. In such a simple way she had changed their relationship forever. They weren't two friends talking together, but lovers taking a romantic stroll through a strange and wonderful world.

The early evening glow of red-gold spread darkening shadows across the sky.

They were just rounding the spaceship's far side, not more than a hundred yards from the airlock, when a sudden high-pitched whining sound cracked on the evening air, coming from the direction of the forest.

Grant's body went into automatic action. A soldier learned in battle not to question the unknown, but to react as if it were a mortal attack. He saw running figures racing toward them, while at the same time his own muscles were in the process of pressing Lena toward the airlock.

"To the ship!" he shouted, fairly shoving Lena in front of him.

His eyes were already searching for something which might be used as a weapon.

But already the racing alien figures were cutting them off. Grant's eyes swept their immediate surroundings. There was no place to hide, nothing to use as a weapon. He cursed Lard's personal ambitions, which had caused the weapons to be locked up.

Suddenly they were totally cut off, with the greenish alien natives between them and the ship. There was no way to go but back the way they had come. He already knew there was no hope of escape.

A moment later a circle closed in on Grant and Lena. They became ringed by strange humanoid creatures, huge eyes staring at them, large mouths gaping. It was impossible to tell if the expressions were hateful or victorious.

Grant felt that struggle was useless, but was still prepared to do combat with his naked hands.

But before he could even strike a blow against the first native, he felt the shaft of a spear slam into the side of his head. Stars sputtered like a supernova. A scream slashed through the air. Then black silence closed around Grant's brain.

CHAPTER THIRTEEN

First of all, Grant could not believe he was alive. Just awareness in a black sub-space. Just consciousness. The last thing he remembered was facing certain death. The black became richer and a sense of sound penetrated its gloom. He lived. Slowly his mind accepted this fact as his senses pressed the evidence home. The side of his head pulsed with dull pain. The aroma of burning wood filled the air.

His right hand attempted to reach up and examine his head, which felt as if it were two inches too big all around. Not until then did he realize that he was bound hand and foot.

Soft voices spoke in the darkness around him, and Grant realized that he was lying on the cold, damp ground, propped up against what felt like a rough pillar. As he opened his eyes, he saw that night had descended. Dark shadows flickered across the little clearing in the forest, created by the small fire some ten feet away, around which squatted three half-naked aliens warming their hands.

Those weird alien faces with greenish fur-covered heads seemed like something out of a mad dream. The angular hawk noses drooped down to sharp points, thrusting like spears toward their bony chins. Yet there was something about their huge eyes, suggestive of an insect's, that seemed more gentle than cruel. One had the impression that the aliens could almost see behind them because of the obvious wide angle of their vision. Their body structure was much the same as Grant remembered. Their human-shaped chests, shoulders and arms were muscular. In a subtle way, their faces suggested caricatures of devil creatures. If horns and tails were added, plus a washing of the greenish tint to the

139

hairless flesh, it would not be hard to imagine that these were inhabitants of Earth's mythical Hell.

A quick search of the surroundings revealed Lena as a bundled-up shadow on the opposite side of the fire, leaning against the bole of a huge tree. Her eyes were bright as they stared across at him. She was bound in much the same manner as himself.

Relieved at seeing her alive, Grant's attention shifted to the immediate problem of their captivity. Instinctively he struggled against the bonds that gripped his wrist—a useless effort. Even if escape were possible, where would he take Lena? In the first place he had no idea where he was. He could hardly guess in what direction their captors had gone. How would they find the ship, let alone survive a journey in the forest? His own survival and return to the ship had been dumb luck. Yet Grant would rather risk that danger than what might be facing them now.

Again, uselessly, he strained against the firmly clamped grass rope holding his wrists, then angrily muttered, almost soundlessly, "Forget it!"

There was no escape! A sense of total defeat pressed in around him. They were helpless.

What kind of fate is planned for us? he wondered bitterly. Hardly as a feast cooked up in a huge metal pot.

It was amazing that these creatures even existed. The idea of other intelligent life in the cosmos was still somewhat mind-boggling. Yet these aliens were living, breathing, thinking creatures on a world of their own—no doubt with their own set of ethics, morals and concepts of creation.

And that fact staggered him to the core.

These creatures sitting before him obviously existed, but they seemed at a very primitive level of cultural evolution, hundreds, maybe thousands of years behind humans. Their conversation was a high-pitched squeak splattered with short silences. Every once in a while one of the three would nod in either his or Lena's direction, as if making some comment concerning them. It all seemed insanely human to Grant, just like so many of his own military experiences sitting around camp fires. Soldiers talked about the women back home, children, complained about the army food, made

140

the normal nasty cracks about the prisoners. The pattern here seemed much the same. The three aliens, like countless humans in very similar circumstances, warmed themselves against the icy cold of night in front of a hot fire. Were they making casual conversation about war, or about home, or about the prisoners they had taken in battle? Very likely. At least that was the illusion their actions seemed to indicate.

Perhaps these aliens were not as totally inhuman as they appeared.

Their weapons were a strange mixture of semi-modern and primitive, at least from what he could make out of them in the flickering firelight. They carried at their sides two-foot knives with curved, flat metal blades. Spears lay on the ground in front of them, as if ready for use in any emergency. Piled to one side, slightly away from the fire, were what looked like bows and quivers of arrows. The aliens gave the appearance of being a primitive hunting party, and for all their weird physical appearance, they did not seem so wantonly cruel as merely simple savages. Their huge eyes picked up the flames of the fire and, like small mirrors, reflected its image in miniature detail. As they talked, their wide mouths quivered open and shut with amazing speed. It was some time before they seemed to tire of their conversation. Two lay down next to the fire; the third stood, taking his spear in hand. He moved over to Lena and examined her bonds. She casually accepted this without any outward sign of horror or repugnance. The alien's lips drew back wide for a moment. Then it turned and moved over to Grant.

"Hello," Grant offered, knowing how useless the greeting was. Yet for some reason he had not taken the time to analyze, it seemed a natural thing to do.

The touch of those long fingers was gentle as they checked the grass rope that held Grant's arms and legs. It stood over him for a while, staring down, the expression on that alien face quite unreadable. The lips moved, and the high-pitched sound that came from the throat seemed harsh to Grant's ears. He had noticed that each hand had three long fingers and two opposing thumbs. Slowly it turned away and hunkered down next to the fire, eyes moving easily from left to right, gazing out into the forest.

Grant's mind began to speculate on exactly what the aliens were planning to do with them. Possibly a slow death by torture. Yet the alien had been startlingly gentle while examining the ropes binding him.

Why weren't they killed right off? Grant mused. Of course, torture until death might be some primitive religious rite for which they were being saved. Yet there had been an intelligent gentleness in the creature's eyes.

"Are you all right?" he called softly to Lena.

"I'm not hurt," she assured him in a slightly trembling voice. She sounded exhausted and near the point of losing control of her emotions.

"How long were you conscious?"

"From the beginning. They knocked you down, then grabbed me. Almost immediately we were dragged into the forest and bound. Then the rest of them went on ahead, leaving these three to attend to us. They're very strong, carrying us like empty sacks over their shoulders." Now her voice was stronger, as if the fear had drifted away.

The alien, who had been watching them as they spoke, now moved close to Lena. The long knife was in its hand. Lena broke off with a choking sound of fear. Grant tensed helplessly against the ropes.

The alien leaned down and placed the flat of the knife blade across her mouth. He seemed to stare into her eyes for some time. Then he moved to Grant, repeating his actions.

The meaning was obvious.

For some time Grant lay there thinking, his back propped up against the tree. So far no real harm had been offered. That was the only fact that held hope, other than the possibility that a search team might be organized by Mr. L. Talor & Company.

Lard would prefer him dead.

Such was the blend of his thoughts, as exhaustion slowly blurred them out. Sleep crushed away awareness.

Then the blackness was shattered by blinding sunlight. His eyes snapped open, and he saw the aliens cooking a small bird-like animal over the small fire.

They conversed in spurts.

The smell of the cooking food caused Grant to realize

how hungry he had become. Thirst made his mouth dry. Every muscle was cramped.

Lena was already awake, and he nodded to her. "Good morning."

"I've tried to get them to understand I'm hungry." She laughed nervously. "But they don't get the point."

"Forget it," Grant suggested. He felt a sudden hopelessness in the face of their captivity and the almost impossible problem of communicating with their captors. They could die of starvation or lack of water.

One of the three aliens drew its knife and covered its own lips. He turned to Grant and Lena. The action was meaningfully direct. They both lapsed into silence.

After the bird had been half eaten, the aliens approached Lena with the remains. They placed it in front of her and waited to see what she would do. One reached around and unbound her hands.

"Slowly!" Grant warned.

One alien covered his own mouth with a hand, staring at Grant. The warning was enough.

Lena inched her hands forward, then slowly rubbed circulation back into her fingers. As she reached for the remains of the cooked bird, she looked up at Grant, her eyes frightened, questioning. The food could be poisonous for them. She looked at the aliens.

They stared back at her, then talked among themselves. One of them disappeared into the forest, the other two coming over to Grant with the meat, extending it to him after untying his hands. They were alertly watchful of Lena while at the same time studying what he might do.

Grant looked at the meat, studied it, and decided to take a chance. He considered the possibility it might be deadly to them. Yet during his feverish wanderings through the forest he had survived on unknown insect creatures, fruits, water. The chance of this food killing them was almost zero. He grinned, picked up the food and took a small bite, hunger deciding the issue. For a few seconds he allowed the meat to simply sit on his tongue.

Lena gasped, her eyes on his face.

The meat tasted slightly bitter, but he gulped it down

without so much as a shudder. The second bite went down even quicker. He had to resist finishing the meat. As he was extending the small remains of the bird to one of the aliens, the third returned with purple fruit. Grant recognized the fruit and nodded to Lena.

After she had eaten the fruit and what was left of the meat, they gave Grant one of the purple heart-shaped fruits, which he quickly devoured.

The three natives chattered among themselves, apparently pleased they had solved a puzzling problem. Then they rebound Grant and Lena's hands and, after gathering up their weapons, scattered the remains of the fire. One came over to Grant and lifted him up, throwing him over a wide shoulder. A second did the same with Lena.

Grant became aware of a harsh acidic smell, which he realized was the natural odor of the creature carrying him.

They moved through the forest at a quick pace, sometimes along what looked like game trails, at other times cutting their way through footpaths that had apparently not been used for some time. The sun beat down upon them like fire, even through the thick ceiling of forest trees. Once, in the middle of the day, they rested by a small pond, refreshing themselves with water. Grant was highly relieved when they offered both himself and Lena a drink from small shallow cups they carried in a pouch. After a short rest they continued on their journey.

Just as darkness was floating over the world, they came to a clearing in the forest which opened up into the face of a high cliff.

Immediately they were surrounded by dozens of other aliens. Some were only slightly smaller than their captors, while others were tiny, thin, frail naked things that leaped and ran around, chattering among themselves. Grant saw several strange blue-gray structures lining the edge of the clearing and running up against the face of the cliff, but did not get more than a fleeting look. This revealed little, suggesting just enough to spark his imagination. A moment later, he and Lena were carried through an opening, beyond which all was total darkness. Grant guessed they were either in a cave or some building. Their two captors carried them for some time in the darkness and finally stopped. There was a grating sound; then they were taken to the right, gently deposited on a hard floor, and left alone.

"Are you all right, Lena?" he asked.

Lena's voice sounded directly from his right, not more than a foot away. "Yes, I guess so. A little cramped and sore. Wish they'd untie these ropes!"

"I'm sorry about this," he told her, knowing that his words sounded foolish. "I didn't put up much of a fight. Not that that would've helped."

"Lard's to blame, really. Weaponless...what could you do?" Her voice was unafraid now, filled with bitterness. "Did you notice those buildings as we came in?"

"I noticed some kind of structures, but couldn't make them out."

"I got a good look, Hal. They appeared to be made of some kind of metal, and were old and worn. At several places it appeared that huge chunks had been blasted away." Her voice was filled with a sense of puzzled awe.

"Maybe you imagined it."

"No, I don't think so. I got a good look for a moment. We're in such a building."

"I wasn't sure. Could be some kind of primitive cave, for all I know."

"That's what you would expect," she observed.

Silence followed. He could hear her heavy breathing in the dark. A sense of helplessness attacked Grant, becoming a constricting coil winding painfully inside him. How he wished he had some kind of weapon—or at least some way to get her out of this death trap.

"Afraid?" he asked.

"No, I don't think so. Not as much as I was."

"Well, don't be. Fear can be a bad enemy, worse than the reality that might face us."

"What do you think they're going to do with us?"

"I couldn't begin to guess. If this was Earth, it would be easy to come up with some kind of answer. Here, who knows?"

She said thoughtfully, "It's funny, but I should be scared silly. Yet, for some reason, I can't help believing

145

they're not as savage as they appear. And, in any case, maybe the fantastic fact that they even exist is far too interesting to make them completely terrifying. On Earth, in my time, scientists would have been willing to die for this kind of evidence of intelligent life in the universe. The way these...creatures have handled us is quite civilized and...well, gentle, I guess, would be the right word. They act as if they were a little afraid of us, being careful, not cruel."

"It's hard to tell. Our reference is human," Grant pointed out. "They might think they are being very cruel. Possibly to them this is some form of torture, being confined in total darkness." He hated himself for having said that. It was stupid and would only serve to frighten Lena. He quickly added, "Yet I doubt it. Possibly their eyes can see quite well in the dark. I would guess that's the real reason for the lack of light here."

"You know, Hal, another thing I noticed: the weapons. They are a combination of primitive and modern. They seem like American Indian weapons, better than Stone Age weapons, in which the point of a spear or arrow was chipped out of rock, then attached to a roughly cut shaft of wood. Here the metal is advanced, and appears to be manufactured, even sophisticated, while the shafts are of rough wood. The implications are...troubling!"

"At the very least. And too fantastic to develop any theories." Grant was about to say something when a grating noise sounded, then footsteps, and a high-pitched chattering came from the darkness immediately in front of them.

Hands touched Grant; then he was pulled to his feet. A moment later gentle fingers had untied him. For a long while the chattering voices continued, and there was silence. The quiet dragged on for some time, until it was hard to believe they were not alone. Yet he was sure several aliens were still standing but a few feet away. A sharp exclamation cut the quiet for a moment. Then footsteps approached, and light flooded around him.

They were in a small, smooth-walled room with half a dozen of the aliens crowded around them. One, the tallest, was dressed in a loose-fitting red robe that clung to its shoulders and dropped to its feet. There was a white border along the seams at the bottom and top, with strange figures that looked like some kind of writing.

The alien looked at them for a while, then reached out and slowly examined their bodies with its fingers. After this examination had been completed, it gave a quick jerk of its right hand. Another alien stepped forward holding an oval box, and set it down in front of Grant.

Puzzled, he looked into the box, finding a mass of cubes, balls and strangely shaped black blocks.

Those around him waited, expecting him to do something.

Lena broke the silence. "I think," she said in a whisper, after gazing into the box, "this is some kind of intelligence test."

Without a word, Grant accepted her statement as fact and knelt down on the smooth floor, reached slowly for the box, and carefully turned it over, allowing its contents to fall free. Then he waited.

The aliens immediately began chattering excitedly among themselves.

So far, so good, Grant mused, slowly scattering the metallic pieces over the floor.

He looked up at the robed alien, making sure that nothing he had done so far had startled or caused alarm. The expression that peered back was blank, as if awaiting his next action.

Then, moving with extreme care, he began puzzling over the blocks and balls, placing them in various positions until they began to reveal a pattern. It was childishly simple once he reasoned it out. For the most part, two pieces would fit snugly over one ball, leaving room to place balls on all four sides. It was necessary to place other angular pieces around each of these balls. In a short time he had constructed a solid oval block about a foot long and six inches high. Once it was completed, he looked up at the aliens.

They chattered among themselves for a moment. Then one of them picked up the block, which was now held together as if by some magnetic force. Grant had not been aware of such magnetism while assembling it.

The aliens then filed out one at a time. The last alien

hesitated, spoke to someone outside, beyond their line of vision, and then left, closing the door, leaving them in total darkness again.

"Can you imagine that?" Lena cried, amazement thick in her voice.

"I wouldn't have!" Grant admitted. "An intelligence test. Fairly smart of them. I wonder what's next."

Soon the door opened, and light flooded the room again. This time it was a strange round bulb that glowed brightly. The alien laid it down on the floor. Two other natives entered carrying trays of food and water that were placed beside the bulb. A moment later Grant and Lena were once more alone in the cell.

Grant immediately examined the light ball. When he attempted to raise it, the ball flickered out. Releasing it, Grant grinned as light flooded the cell.

"They aren't taking any chances. It's too light to be used as a weapon—and as we have seen, it goes out the moment it's lifted from the floor." He stared at it momentarily. "Since they apparently can see in the dark, I wonder what the blazes they use this for." Then, without another word, he faced the smooth wall, examining it to see what it was made of. "Metal of some sort. Hard. Glassy."

Lena was looking over the meal that had been brought. "The same as what we ate in camp."

"They are using extreme intelligence with us and taking no chances—at least no more than necessary," Grant observed, sitting down beside Lena and beginning to eat. The bird meat didn't seem as bitter as the night before, and hunger made it taste almost good. "They have apparently guessed that we cannot see in the dark. Thus the light, which was probably improvised from something else. What has me going is this: Where did they get such advanced gadgets? And the intelligence test—as if we were the lower creatures and they were of an advanced culture." He shook his head. "It beats me!"

Lena's eyes gleamed brightly. "I only hope we find the answers before anything happens to us. How fascinating and exciting! Just think what we're seeing, learning, discovering!"

148

Grant reached out and patted her hand. "I don't think anything is going to happen to us. They've been thoughtful keepers and haven't hurt us in any way!" After finishing a bite of the meat, which was served on a small, lightweight platter, he mused, "That trimming on the robe looked like writing."

"What do you really think, Hal? About all of this?" Lena asked after they had finished their meal. "Don't hold back! Consider me as just—well, another guy."

Grant laughed good-naturedly. "That would be quite impossible."

"Please. I mean—just be blunt. I'm not afraid to die. Once having died in DF, it doesn't seem quite as bad."

"Except this time it would be forever—for real!" Grant commented dryly. He repressed a shudder, for the idea of death frightened him. Immortality had offered far too much to have it snatched away. Though at that moment he didn't feel the least bit immortal.

"I mean, Hal, I am trained as a scientist. Now what do you make of all this?" She gazed into his eyes with intense seriousness.

Hesitating only a moment, Grant decided to accept her offer. "Well, first, we aren't apparently in any immediate danger of being killed. They are approaching us much as scientists would approach alien creatures captured on Earth: with care, intelligence and gentleness, where possible. Apparently the robed one was some kind of leader or officer. Maybe a scientist. Maybe a witch doctor, if they have one. Who knows, really, for all our points of reference are human, and the facts keep changing from moment to moment. Last night I was convinced they were low on the evolutionary scale, about where we were during the Stone Age. Now I don't know."

Lena nodded, looking tired. "Possibly there's a simple answer."

They were silent for some time after that, taking in this stunning information of the last few hours.

Then suddenly Lean yawned, stretched. "Maybe if we get a good sleep, we'll be able to reason it out better."

Without another word the two of them lay down on

the hard floor. Sleep came quickly for Grant.

He was awakened by an alien bringing new food. After eating, they once more began talking about their situation and the strange combination of facts they had learned about the aliens. Shortly the door opened, and two aliens stepped into the cell. With one swift movement, one of them picked Grant up. Then, after waiting for him to regain his balance, it gently pushed him toward the door, indicating that he was supposed to leave the cell. The other alien had done the same with Lena.

They were escorted down long corridors. One alien carried a fiery torch to light their way. There were doors on either side of the corridor every ten feet or so, all closed.

Finally they came to a chamber in which were gathered some twenty aliens and strange saddled animals. These mount animals appeared much like the wild deer-like herds Grant had seen on the plain around the spaceship, but had thicker bodies and shorter, more powerful legs. Their hides were a deep purple, with red stripes running across their backs. The heads were large, with gaping mouths set with two rows of squared teeth. Small eyes moved nervously from side to side. The saddles were nothing more than little cushions attached by strips of leather, which were strapped around their bodies.

Grant and Lena were taken to two of the mounts and lifted onto their backs. Sitting comfortably in the padded saddle, Grant observed their surroundings.

The room was apparently cut into the side of a mountain. It was a beautiful and expert job of engineering. The walls were carved with intricate designs, which might have been a form of writing, or merely created for their beauty alone. The floor was hard-packed dirt. Several of the aliens were dressed in red robes, and these mounted the other six riding animals. Then, as if directed by some hidden hand, all eight mounts formed a single line, with Grant and Lena in the center, and started filing out through an archway in the back of the cavern. For some time they continued down a darkened corridor, making several turns until they finally came out upon an open plain, the sun blazing down from high in the sky.

150

Crossing the plain, the small caravan entered the forest beyond, all the riders continuing in total silence.

The movement of his mount was so smooth that Grant found himself merely swaying slightly from side to side. The rhythm finally had a hypnotic effect on him. How long they continued on like that he wasn't sure, for at one time he fell into a light slumber. It was late evening when the caravan came to a stop by a small brook. Here they made camp. Grant and Lena were gently helped from their mounts and fed fruits gathered from the forest.

They were not bound that evening, although a guard was always on watch to see that they made no attempt to escape.

Grant accepted the fact that they were helpless to do anything other than wait and see what the aliens had in mind. It seemed unlikely that death faced them in the immediate future, and events might change their chances of escape. They had to cling to hope, even if it was minor. Where they were being taken was a mystery he did not even want to dwell upon. It was a matter of taking it a day at a time.

CHAPTER FOURTEEN

The copter's radio cracked with static.

"We've found some kind of camp. Apparently this is where the aliens spent the night."

Lard recognized Jake's voice through the crackling interference of the speaker. He pressed a button on the control panel between the pilot and co-pilot seats. "It's getting late, so let's put up camp there. I'll have Flip zero in on you. Is there a clearing large enough to land the copter?"

"Not here, but a short way back. Whets says he'll take a couple of men back to meet you, sir."

Lard turned to Flip Kord, whose thin face was hard-set, the jaw like rigid iron, the lips and eyes frozen with grimness. The man looked a lot older than his features would have suggested. Everybody in the colony had changed slightly. But Flip was showing an edge of rebellion. That would have to be taken care of later.

"Track for location. We'll find the clearing and land, then wait for a guide."

Flip pulled a contact switch in front of him, activating the tracking bug for the ground search party.

Lard sat there outwardly calm as he gazed at the expanse of forest below, but he was still fighting the inner battle that had needled him ever since learning of Grant and Lena's disappearance. Lard's first reaction, upon learning the truth, was to write Grant off. He might have gotten away with it if Flip had not spoken up. For that, Flip would pay heavily the first chance Lard found an excuse.

His mind replayed those events:

Everybody had gathered in the lounge room to await his orders. It was about 2000 hours when he took his place behind the large desk.

"As you all know, Mr. Grant and Lena have disappeared." His eyes surveyed those of the people before him.

"A search party has revealed very little. Apparently there was some kind of struggle. A rough guess is that it was an alien raid. Whets has reported they were taken by surprise and then dragged off. It is foolish to continue the search beyond the end of the flat plain. We can assume they're dead."

Flip Kord stood, his face drawn. "I would like to volunteer for a search party to follow any trail though the forest."

Other voices immediately joined his, half the men standing.

"We have to be sure about them," Flip continued evenly. "I won't believe the General dead until proven otherwise. Look how he survived two months in the forest. While there's a chance, we can't give up hope."

Lard held back a sharper retort, merely saying, "I never said not to hope—but we have to be realistic!"

"I'm being realistic."

For a moment Lard look at the people in front of him. They were buying Flip's argument.

"We have to protect each other," Flip continued. "What if that was one of us here? I want to know for certain. We can't afford to lose one person."

To Lard's shock, Jake, one of his staunch supporters, agreed. "I'm willing to join any search party."

Whets nodded. "Us men can be replaced. But the women, that's another matter. What if Lena is alive?"

The implication was obvious. The loss of a woman was considered a serious issue.

"It could be dangerous," Lard warned, carefully watching the men in front of him.

"So what?" one man asked. Other voices added to the sudden outburst. It was impossible to ignore this protest.

."If we don't stick together we're lost!" a male voice shouted.

"What if it was you out there?" a woman challenged. "You'd want us to check! They might be alive...and depending on us finding them!"

153

Flip added, "Maybe you better reconsider."

Lard slowly held his hand up, but Flip continued, "We can't leave them out there to die—"

"Assuming they're still alive," Lard pointed out, his right hand squeezing tight until the fingers ached. Flip Kord had become a problem. "I still don't like the odds. I think they're already dead."

"We won't assume that," Flip announced. "And if they are, we'll deal."

Whets grinned. "I'm for teaching them aliens a bloody lesson!"

Jake nodded. "Either way we'll blow the monsters outta existence!"

"Is that how everybody feels?" Lard demanded, trapped. The answering cry proved that Flip had won the argument.

"As Grant has said," Flip pointed out, gently enough to sound, on the surface at least, respectful, "the most important thing here is to protect each other. Now's the time to put that policy into action!"

Grant had skillfully planted the seeds of rebellion. It had been a mistake to let him make that speech.

Wanting to limit the extent of his defeat, Lard offered a tight smile and said, "You are, of course, right. In the morning we'll begin a fully armed search, and revenge will be ours."

And as promised, the search began that morning, as soon as the sun was high enough to reveal a trail. One party went by foot, under Whets' command, following the well-marked trail the aliens had left. The second party went by copter with Lard, flying in wide circles, attempting to discover any signs of Grant.

By late in the afternoon, they found a camp where the aliens had been. They began their search the next morning with the early sun. Flip was sent back to the ship with the copter, with orders to tell the others what had happened. Lard did not trust Flip enough to arm him, and had decided this was the best solution to the problem.

Late that afternoon, as the sun cast long shadows through the forest, they came unexpectedly face to face with

154

a tall, spear-carrying alien. It just stood there in the pathway, staring at them, unmoving in the beginning. Then its mouth opened, hands lifted towards them.

Lard was the first to react: He aimed his laser and fired with one movement. The alien froze; then, as hot smoke billowed from its chest where the laser beam had burned its way through naked flesh, it crumbled to the ground without a sound.

Lard motioned to the others as he stepped over the dead body without even a glance back. Now they moved with great care.

As darkness settled, Lard heard the chattering of high voices in the distance, mingled with sounds of movement that might have come from a village or camp.

He pulled the party into a tight pack and whispered, "We move in and surround the camp, or whatever we find. Shoot to kill when I fire. We want every alien dead as quickly as possible. Then search for Grant and Lena."

Without another word, they silently slipped through the underbrush and came upon a clearing that opened up in front of a high cliff. Small fires were scattered throughout the camp. Figures gathered around the warming flames.

Lard felt a hot flash of excitement burn through every muscle, eating its way to a feverish point at the back of his eyes.

Motioning his men to spread out, Lard watched the alien village from behind the cover of surrounding under- brush. Once he was sure that the others had fanned out as widely as possible, he stepped forward, laser gun in hand, aimed, and fired into the closest group. The attack was so swift, so unexpected, that the aliens did not have a chance to defend themselves. They sprang to their feet. Some ran to- ward the tall cliff, where a large opening cut into its surface, but were quickly cut down as several laser beams were fired at their retreating bodies.

Lard's laser cut from left to right like a long fiery blade, slashing across leaping figures, large and small alike. His lips pulled tightly across his teeth as low-throated laugh- ter pulsed through him. Never in his life had anything been so thrilling. Not even the arms of a woman could create this kind of pleasure. His face twitched as the laser beam burned across a female alien holding a child in her arms. Laughter pushed his mouth wide open. He cut at the legs of a fleeing warrior, then let the laser beam race up the creature's spine.

Moments later, only seven men stood in the clearing, surrounded by a mass of scattered, charred bodies. The putrid smell of cooked flesh wafted on the night air.

It took several seconds for Lard to control the gasping action of his lungs. Sweat was dripping down his face and covering his body. The hand that still held the laser at the ready was trembling uncontrollably. For the first time since waking on that planet, Lard wanted a drink. He felt like celebrating, shouting to the skies, screaming to the gods the sudden greatness of power that surged through him.

Finally his eyes focused upon his surroundings.

"Be careful," Lard warned in a steady voice. He motioned that the search for Grant and Lena should begin.

Within an hour they had explored every structure, every room, each inch of the alien village, including a huge cavern cut into the cliff, and had found only a few surviving aliens, which were shot down without mercy. But there was no sign of Grant or Lena.

A man named Barry came up to Lard as he was walking across the clearing to one of the small cooking fires that still burned dimly in the night.

Excitement made Barry's gaunt features take on sharp, angular lines against the firelight. "Did you look at this, Mr. Talor?"

Barry was indicating the structures that surrounded the clearing.

Lard grunted, irritated. He didn't like the man very much. There was something about the eyes which haunted him. They were too bright, too thoughtful. "An alien village. That's all. The enemy camp. Wiped out."

"I'd like to take time to look at those structures, study them thoroughly. I have a feeling they are very old. You see, before I was a scientist, I studied archaeology in college and went on several field trips. This is an incredible find. Do you know what this implies? Can you imagine what—"

"In the morning we leave," Lard announced coldly,

ignoring the man's enthusiasm. "We return to the ship with the news that Grant and Lena are lost. They've probably been devoured, eaten as a tasty snack for those horrid animals! We don't have time for unnecessary speculation or study of the degenerate works of some savage beasts!"

He was looking forward to making the announcement of Grant's death. The loss of the woman was bad, even though her mind had always bugged him, but it was worth a "breeder's" life to have been rid of Grant. Now there was one less voice that might speak up against his authority, the only voice that might have reversed his designs for their future.

"Mr. Talor," Barry insisted, "I request that we stay a while to study these structures. We might learn something about the aliens and—"

Lard interrupted with an angry wave of his laser. "There's nothing to study here. The only thing we need to know is that the aliens die on the point of a laser beam. This is only the beginning of our war. They will fall back now, once others learn what man can do. We will rule this world like gods, once they have come to understand that we have the power of life and death over them!"

"But, sir—"

"That will be all! Tomorrow we leave!"

Barry stared up at Lard, his face revealing the shock that announcement created. "Then I'll make some studies tonight," he stated flatly.

Lard was about to deny him that right, then changed his mind. "You do whatever you want, just so you take up the march tomorrow. You'll be left behind if you can't keep up! Understand?"

Without a word, Barry turned and moved to the nearest alien structure.

Lard followed the man with his eyes, aware how easy it would be to kill the guy right then and there. The idea sent an erotic wave of pleasure though him.

Such life and death power was like a drug. Lard enjoyed the sensation. He withheld a giggle of delight. Such power was quite delicious.

His eyes focused on one of the shadowy alien buildings. It looked very old, even in the weaving fire light, as if age had marked it not in years but in centuries. They were long flat buildings with squared corners. At many places huge chunks had been melted away. Lard stepped over to one wall and touched it. Some kind of hard metal, smooth as glass.

A shiver laced up his spine, clutched his mind. His thought recoiled from speculation on this evidence. The blunt, frightening implications were beyond consideration. He rejected all thought of an alien culture above that of savages and blanked the buildings out of his mind.

In the morning he wanted to put as much distance between himself and this horrid village as possible. Best to not focus on the implications of an intelligent, semi-civilized alien species.

* * * * * * *

On the second day, Grant noted their caravan continued on the same routine as the first. During a rest period, they were allowed once more to sit together while eating a small ration of fruit. Their comments were limited to the morning's events. The forest was already beginning to thin out slightly, and a more hilly topography came into being. It was at this point that the caravan detoured around a herd of giant elephant-like blue animals. Neither of them had gotten a good look at the creatures, since the herd was too far away for them to see details clearly. But their captors apparently held the animals in great respect. He could see that in time the Earth colony would have great sport hunting these big game—assuming humans survived.

That night, they made camp near a small river. No real socializing took place among the aliens. Almost immediately after the evening meal they rolled into sleeping skins. Two guards watched the camp and captives.

Lena and Grant talked little, both being exhausted from the long journey.

The days that followed had a similar pattern.

Only the land itself changed, becoming more rugged. Occasional attacks from wild animals broke the boredom.

Once, while going around a huge lake, one of the planet's giant birds swooped down from the skies. The caravan leader made a high-pitched whistling sound with its mouth, and the bird immediately changed course, returning to the skies and disappearing toward the setting sun.

On the fourth day they came to a range of tall, snow-capped mountains and entered a pass which rose quickly to a level where snow was sprinkled over the ground in scattered patches. The air was now thin and cold. There they were attacked by a catlike beast that reminded Grant of a reddish lion. For but an instant he saw the massive head with broad horns protruding from its forehead. It all happened so fast that Grant saw very little else. The aliens dispatched the creature with a graceful skill and speed, quite calmly going about the business of killing. Without any ceremony at all they tossed the dead body into the canyon below.

It was the almost machine-like quality of the aliens' automatic counterattack that impressed him. From his vantage point it was impossible to see any real details. But he was impressed by their obvious skill, cooperation and killing ability.

Days drifted slowly by, and they came out on the other side of the mountains to a bare hilly country that stretched to the far horizon. In the distance, Grant saw a dim, broken line against the setting sun that vaguely suggested a city skyline. For a moment he felt a pang for Earth, Los Angeles Major, New York, Space Central, San Francisco, London, Berlin, Torbor, Paris—all that had been a part of his life.

As they continued down from the mountain pass, the view became more limited until only the grassy plains of the nearest hill were visible. Once in the foothills, the caravan made camp. The next morning they started forward at renewed speed, and Grant realized their destination must be quite near. By late afternoon they reached the top of a high hill, and for the first time Grant got a good look at what had appeared to be a broken line of rock in the shape of a city skyline.

In front of them was an expanse of flatland, as if some huge hammer had angrily pounded all hills away. In their place was a ruined city. There was no mistaking the arrangement of broken shapes. Streets suggested themselves through the rubble of charred, crushed ruins. It looked as if some crazed giant had raged through a modern city thousands of years before, attempting to destroy every structure within reach. No vegetation grew in this region. It was a place of death. Grass, trees, brush retreated away from the crippled sight, as if shy of an evil spirit lurking deep within the mass of metal and stone.

The caravan made its way toward the ruins at a slow, majestic gait, each alien seeming to grow taller on its mount as they got closer to the outskirts of the ancient city.

Grant's mind was drowning in seemingly unanswerable questions. For the first time it seemed brutally cruel that a language barrier existed between them and the aliens. What story could they tell? Maybe none. Maybe some fantastic tale that would be impossible for any Earthman to swallow, let alone understand.

They moved toward the center of the ruins, toward a high tower that revealed fewer signs of outward damage. Now and then they passed half-naked aliens moving along the cleared roadway. The nearer they came to the tower, the more aliens were seen moving along the road in much the same manner as humans going about some daily business activity that had become dull routine. Some females carried large metal jars on their heads; others had babies strapped to their chests. Children played in the streets, chasing one another among the rubble of shattered buildings.

As the caravan approached to within a hundred yards of the towering pillar of glassy metal, it came to a stop, and the aliens dismounted. Grant and Lena were pulled gently from their saddles. Now, with two guards on either side of them, they were escorted toward the tower, where robed figures moved out briskly to meet them.

Their leader and a robed alien from the tower exchanged a hurried conversation. Then they were escorted to the entrance archway and ushered inside, where hand-held lanterns revealed the way.

The corridor in which they found themselves was colored dull blue, with pictures of marching ranks of aliens

160

garbed in red robes, each carrying what could easily be some kind of rifle. Several doors opened at each side of them into large, unlit rooms from which came the sound of busy voices and shuffling footsteps.

Finally they were taken into one of these rooms. It was a large, high-ceilinged chamber, lined along two walls with low benches. At the far end was a throne-like platform, behind which stood a solid wall of amber metal broken by a series of buttons and switches. Scores of red-robed aliens crowded before this wall, conversing in quick, high-pitched voices. They turned. Conversation came to a stop as all eyes stared at the two humans. The silence was broken only by a soft hum which filled the room like an ominous whisper.

Grant and Lena were escorted to the front of the room, near the paneled wall that stood like some mystical computer machine.

During the next half-hour they were probed and poked, caressed and generally examined by each alien in turn. They were obviously a curiosity to those present.

As in the village, Grant was again presented with blocks and balls, which he quickly assembled. Then Lena was given her first chance to do the same. During this time all was silent as the aliens observed every move. Once they had finished with this intelligence test, a series of objects was put in front of each of them in turn. In the beginning there were such things as knives, spears, bows and arrows; later, there were different pieces of colored cloth. The procedure involved placing objects in front of them one at a time and holding each one there for several seconds, at least long enough for them to get a good look. Balls, cubes and oblongs followed the clothing display, each in different multicolored patterns. Then two aliens went through a series of motions and poses, sitting down, walking, talking, waving their hands, making every possible action their bodies could achieve. They repeated these several times in various positions, forward and backward.

At this point two aliens brought forth a pedestal and placed it in front of Grant. Lena was moved to one side so that she could not see what was going on. A large book was set on the pedestal, and an alien who stood to Grant's right

161

opened the book. Printing filled an off-white page. The lettering was strange angles and curves, running downwards. Grant was allowed to look at this for some time before the page was turned.

He found himself staring at a picture of a battle scene that was marvelously detailed. The picture at first appeared to be a color photograph, but after examining it further, he realized it was a finely detailed piece of art reproduced in full color. One of the most amazing things about it was the fact that hundreds of alien soldiers were fighting not with primitive weapons, but with what could be nothing other than modern projectile-shooting rifles, handguns and cannons. In the skyline were indications of explosions. The setting was a hilly, mud-covered battlefield, reminding Grant of his days at war for the United Nations during the twenty-first century.

A shiver of disbelief choked at him. The implications were devastating. Yet this might be nothing more than some artist's imagination conjuring up a fantasy war, much as sci-fi artists in his day illustrated stories of a far distant future.

He tried to convince himself this was the case, but the argument was flawed. Grant finally rejected all debate on that subject. Wait for information. Too many times in war, officers made the mistake of acting on limited information. The game of war was always liberally sprinkled with bluffs and lies. Years on the General Staff had taught the well-earned lesson to reserve final action until all facts were in.

Next came a picture of strangely shaped, multicolored flowers. A series of alien animals followed, including a bird like the one that had taken Grant to its nest as an evening meal some two months before. Rivers and mountains, plains and oceans flashed by on different pages; the planet's sun and moons, the heavens; aliens, both fully grown and tiny babies; platters of food; then a picture of a modern city.

Grant gasped in surprise. "Lena! Take a look at this!"

Immediately a gentle hand was placed over his mouth, then a moment later was taken away. Lena had been held back.

The city was beautifully laid out, with exotic gardens, slick white roads spotted with what looked like ground cars.

In the sky was an oval flying object. The buildings rose high, pillars rounded at the top. No windows were in evidence. Roadways reached across the tallest of the buildings, high above ground level. He didn't get a chance to do more than take in the full sweep of the city before the page was turned.

Next was a drawing of the city in which they were now located, appearing much the same as it did now, although possibly not quite so ancient. Again the page was turned. Now he was shown a series of paintings, going from realistic to modern and finally abstract. This continued for some time, until the art began to take shapes that suggested machinery. Then came a series of photographs. The shapes were unmistakably those of machines. Machinery of odd shapes, jagged designs, and unknown functions stared at him from the pages. A few were obviously ground cars, others flying objects—all windowless. Then followed a series of pages which were puzzling at first, until he began to see an unmistakable pattern reappearing. This pattern was much like Earth mathematics. After some time came a cutaway of an alien, showing organs, blood vessels, and bone structure. He was not allowed much time to study this, for the alien suddenly closed the book.

Gently he was urged away from the pillar, and Lena moved to his place behind it. Now the whole process was repeated. When she was finished, platters filled with food and drinks were brought into the room and set down on the long benches lining the walls to their left and right.

After being taken to one bench close to the machine wall, which Grant now guessed might be some kind of computer (though the idea still seemed fantastic), they settled down to a meal of fruits and a small portion of bird flesh, food the aliens had apparently decided was safe for them. The aliens themselves gathered along the benches before platters of steaming stew-like soup, all but ignoring their human captives.

"What do you make of all this?" Grant stared at Lena, ignoring the food.

"I'm afraid to guess," she admitted. "Did you see that city? I'll bet you it's a picture of this city before, well, before some natural or unnatural event destroyed it." She picked up a piece of fruit.

"I'd guess war destroyed this city," Grant offered, finding it hard to force the words out. His mind was staggering under all this new knowledge about the aliens.

She nodded while taking a bite of the fruit. "I don't think they're showing us this for our pleasure and information," she observed thoughtfully, squinting at the wall where all the switches and buttons displayed themselves. "You know, that looks more like a computer than anything I can think of, fantastic as it might seem. And those pictures in the book!" She took another bite. "I can't help wondering—no! It's too fantastic!"

"What?" Grant demanded, anxiously gazing into her eyes.

"Well, you'll think I'm out of my mind. But look at it this way. How would you learn to communicate with an alien? There are several ways. Teaching him your language is one. You put objects in front of him and repeat your word for each object. This is the common method used on Earth. But what if there was another way? Like telepathy?"

"Telepathy? You must be kidding. If they'd had telepathic powers, they would have used them already!" Grant felt disappointed.

"No! Not the aliens. But what if a machine could be developed that could, among other things, truthfully read the impulses of the mind? It's not too farfetched. Earth science, during my time, was not really too far from that—though no real serious research was developed along those lines. The ErotoAdvents certainly were a form of the process in reverse. The machine went into your mind, and you experienced all the sensations pre-recorded for your pleasures and entertainment. The next step might be such a process as I'm suggesting. So let's assume a culture could develop such a method. What would be the easiest way to communicate with an alien?"

"Okay, through telepathy," Grant admitted. "And although I should be able to swallow almost anything by now, I don't believe—"

"No, not telepathy as it is commonly thought of. I mean some kind of translating machine. You speak words,

164

and the machine picks them up and translates them into the second language, speaking a translated form of the message. Well—what if this machine was able to pick up our brain waves and then correlate them into an electronic pattern? Now a study of that pattern would develop another pattern, a new one, in its memory banks, which it could compute with its known patterns for the language of its program makers. In other words: It would learn the pattern of our thoughts by observing what electrical patterns take place in our brains while we look at certain objects, correlate them with what they know its maker's patterns are, and then develop a form of translation of these two symbols—mating them in its memory banks."

"And you believe that's what's been happening here?" Grant probed thoughtfully.

"I don't know. But it's a fascinating idea. Take the fact that International was able to teach us a common language while we were in Deep Freeze—and unconscious! Beyond that, I believe my theory would certainly fit the activities that have been taking place here. They approach us one at a time. Thereby they gain a cross-reference and develop a mathematical equation which fits as closely as possible. At first it might develop only a crude means of translating, but that would be enough to get basic ideas across to some degree, at least." She was thoughtful for a moment, then asked, "Can you think of any other reason for what they've been doing?"

"I guess not. But there could be a lot of reasons that don't make sense to us, to Earthly minds. We are thinking from our own point of reference. What would we do if—"

She nodded slowly.

"These are primitive savages—judging by the way they live in the forest. If they had a culture of science behind them, would they have not rebuilt their city?" Grant offered carefully. "It could be possible that whatever scientific gadgets they have are from another culture, built by other beings." But he could see holes in this logic, and he just did not want to admit them.

"They have some advanced culture," Lena put in, tapping out the points on the tips of her fingers, "or at least

165

have been exposed to the remains of an advanced culture that was wiped out by some accident of war—as you suggest. They apparently are aware of what they are doing. They've gone about it in a very logical—I might say scientific—way. They haven't done us physical harm, and have treated us with gentleness. They are seeking information studying us as we might study them, if things were reversed."

Grant shook his head slowly, fighting a mental war within his mind. "I'm a simple man. I'm not a scientist. I know how to move people, to organize a group into one united effort. This," he swept the room with his large hand, "is hard for my twenty-first century brain to accept. Yet I have to accept it, because the evidence is here. And what evidence is it?

"A primitive culture of savages, living in the forest. A ruined city. This room with a wall lined with buttons and levers. Books with reproductions of paintings and photographs in full color. It dazzles the brain!"

Sudden confusion in the room around them brought conversation to a stop. The aliens were leaping to their feet. They hurriedly gathered around Grant and Lena.

Grant braced himself, expecting the worst.

At that point an eerie thought sounded in his brain, one which he had not put there:

"Alien creature, stand. Walk to wall computer!"

CHAPTER FIFTEEN

Grant repressed a chill. A moment of terror cheated his control, then passed. That mental instruction to stand had not originated in his own mind!

Telepathy from a damned machine? How long has this alien technology existed?

This machine might have been built thousands or millions of years before the birth of Christ. What would the early Christians have said about this? How would they have fit it into their theology? Or, for that matter, any Earth-based religion? Buddhism? The followers of Islam?

In his time these were the prime movers in a world seething with endless variations of religious belief systems. Since Roman times, the One God of the Western world did brutal battles with Eastern variations. Whatever the raw Truths or Divine Insights enveloped in such belief systems, they were honest human attempts to understand the universal question: Why? What concept could be conceived by this alien civilization and culture?

Which God was the God of these aliens? One and the same? Or something totally devoid of human comprehension?

The questions raced through him like a flood of unwanted demons.

Grant felt suddenly very small, unimportant.

For a moment a mental chuckle of ironic humor touched him: Lard had planned on terrorizing the aliens with Earth's advanced technology.

"You, called Earth man," registered in Grant's brain. "You opposite-talk language-hear language-sound language. If understand, raise arms."

The form was highly crude, but the meaning was obvious.

Grant lifted his right arm.

The alien in front of him placed a metal cap on Grant's head.

Immediately the world in which he was standing flickered out of existence. A mass of impressions shot before his eyes, visual images which came into being and disappeared too fast to consciously react to them. It was like an endless flowing of colors flooding into one another in a torrent of visually indefinable forms. He was aware of only the rampant static aftermath. His senses were all being pummeled at once, and he heard sounds like whining music thundering beyond the scope of human ears. The sense of smell was dammed by over-stimulation. And every nerve in his body raged in such devastating overload that he knew nothing but a sense of tortured numbness. How long this lasted Grant did not know. Suddenly the room returned, and the cap was removed from his head. Another alien removed a similar one from Lena.

His whole body was trembling, the muscles jarred, the nerves shattered. Then slowly all that simply flowed away, as if bathed by some soothing drug.

A short silence followed. Then words formed in Grant's mind. Apparently the computer had just completed its knowledge of their "mental" language and was ready to communicate:

> Those you call aliens are the Ladda. The name of this world is Addoria. The Ladda have existed here for ten thousand Addorian years, having come from the heavens on the hands of their god, Addor. Addoria was built into a modern world of cities, each city containing the Voice of Gods—what you think of as a computer. The Laddian culture was highly scientific and warlike, and great nations used their knowledge to bring ruin from the skies. Addor, Great Creator of the Universe, decreed that such ruin would never

again come upon Its people, that a culture would now take shape which would respectfully worship, but not use, scientific knowledge for war. Out of the few survivors of the Great War developed the cultures you now see on Addoria: the Scientists and the Followers. Until now, there has been no cause for war, no cause to take arms against another. The Ladda are a peace-loving race, wishing only to live their lives without strife, without hatred.

You of the planet Earth are still in a primitive scientific state of cultural advancement compared to what the Ladda had achieved before total war wiped out their vast civilization. Emotionally, you are more primitive than your science. You have advanced weapons that can kill those of our people who are themselves armed only with the primitive spear, knife, bow and arrow. A war with your people, if allowed, could cost many lives, and make necessary the production of weapons to match yours. It is the wish of the Ladda, and the highest order of the Addorian culture, to forget the devastating horror which modern warfare demands. It would be easy to wipe out your people in one violent act of war. It is not the wish of the Ladda. We would live in peace with all living things, loving those who in turn do not attack, killing all who would endanger lives.

We bless all living intelligence, small or big, and wish not war and killing. Yet it is recorded here that the village which took you captive has been attacked and killed to the last female, male and child. Such brutality will not be allowed on Addoria. Such violent creatures are hunted and killed—not in retaliation, but in the interest of survival.

I, the Voice of Gods, have told you

this so that you will understand the cultural problems you have created. Our people are few, numbering only in the 50,000,000 scattered throughout the world in small packs. We can retreat from all contact with your people, or destroy them to the last female and male. We can give up a great land to you, or stand our ground, demanding respect and understanding between both our cultures. We find that the simple solution would be to eliminate the problem with one merciless attack. But our people have forgotten the old ways, and they have no wish to relearn them. Such a solution is less desirable than peace.

The thoughts faded away, and the stillness of the room seemed oppressive, threatening.

Grant was stunned to learn what Lard had done to the alien village. Such slaughter seemed insane, pointless; yet war had always lacked sanity.

It was vital to find the safe middle ground to avoid an all-out holocaust.

Grant knew that the threat to destroy the Earth colony might be nothing but a sophisticated bluff. There had been no hard evidence of modern weapons, other than those pictured in the book. It was even possible that the only surviving "weapon" of the once mighty Addorian civilization was this one computer.

An alien handed Grant a small red band, and showed with gestures that he was supposed to put it around his forehead. Lena was handed another band. They both did as instructed. The aliens in the room placed similar bands around their own foreheads.

The alien in front of Grant said, "This, which you now wear, is a loop of speech, which connects all to the mighty Voice of Gods. Consequently, it grants the ability to communicate and have our words mentally translated."

He hesitated before continuing. His eyes studied Grant in a very intent manner.

"Earth man, you have heard the Voice of Gods

speaking to you. It has always spoken the truth. We who live on the world are the inheritors of the ancient knowledge it contains. Only those in this room know that what it has said this day is the truth. It is our way to forget as much of the past glories of science as possible, living a peaceful and, in your terms, primitive tribe-like existence. We have no modern weapons now. But they can be made, as the spear points and arrow tips and knife blades are made by this machine before you. In its memory is all the knowledge of past civilizations, but locked in there is also a block which makes it impossible for it to give us any scientific knowledge which might be used to take lives, unless there is a threat to our whole race. This threat is now offered in the existence of your colony on Addoria.

"We have spoken to you, but have not heard from you. Speak, and give us a solution which can please all and bring peace to our world." He stepped back and waited.

Grant did not hesitate, for he knew that any hesitation could be thought of as weakness.

"I'm horrified by the announcement of what my fellow man has done to the Ladda. But this horror is tempered by the knowledge of the history of my people, which, like your own, has been filled with strife and war. It is the nature of man—and I would think of the Ladda—to seek survival at all costs. Man, nation, world, family, all seek personal survival, some kind of immortality. All creatures who do survive as a race will have this instinct of survival as a prime motivating force. The strongest or smartest survive in the end.

"I have seen, on my own world, pointless wars, pointless killing, all in the name of survival of a nation or a people. I have been a part of the mass murder, but in being so involved with it, I learned how pointless it all is. War does not solve anything. It brings only useless deaths—for today's allies are tomorrow's enemies, and today's enemies become tomorrow's friends. All die for peace, but peace eludes us, as blind self-interest becomes the only motivation considered proper and moral. Yet there are times when it is necessary to kill, to war upon others, because there is no other road to survival. The wise will avoid war and embrace peace when

171

and where it is possible.

"Like the Ladda, I tire of war, of killing, and wish nothing other than peace on this new world. When I say this, I cannot speak for all the members of our colony without qualification, for the obvious acts of aggression and war already enacted would make me a liar before I even spoke. But I can and will state this: My people do not wish war. Our present leader is attempting to create a state of war, believing that you are nothing but savages, primitives who would be frightened by our scientific weapons. He would enslave you and be the ruler of this world. There are always those who wish their own survival, for purely personal motives, at a cost which does not justify the rewards. I have spoken against this and believed it wrong from the beginning, even without knowing the true nature of the Ladda. Now, knowing the great past which has been yours, I find it possible to state that my people are more than willing to cease hostilities.

"There is much that our two cultures can share. Each of our species surely has much knowledge that can be offered in a friendly exchange.

"The act of my people in attacking your village was brutally inexcusable—just as your attack on the ship was an act of brutal warfare.

"I say to forget the past, and reach out our hands in friendship."

The alien spokesman said, "Those who attacked your ship have been punished. They were young, radical, frightened. They attacked out of ignorance, but they did not kill. Your attack was wanton, murderous."

"It was an attempt to rescue the two of us," Grant pointed out. "You had taken us by force, against our will, and held us prisoner. That was not an act of peace, either."

"It was in order to learn, to talk together as we are now doing. It was the only way we knew. The old way would have been to attack, destroying without mercy."

"Then let's be peaceful. Let us be friends, in the new way of your people," Grant offered grandly.

"While the Ladda wish no revenge, there is still a matter of justice, which they demand. Those responsible must be punished for their mistakes and crimes. Those who

172

killed the Ladda must in turn be punished, as we have punished our people for attacking you."

"We are few," Grant explained. "The man who gave the orders is responsible, and he alone. This man will be punished."

"We demand that he be turned over to us, or there will be no choice other than to find your words of peace but false sounds."

"We will punish our own people—and not ask that you turn over to us those who attacked the ship," Grant countered flatly.

There was a silence. Then the alien stated, "What kind of punishment would this be?"

"Punishment we feel is suited to the crime."

"Death for death?"

"The punishment will be decided upon by the new voice of our people—and I cannot at this moment speak for all the people of our colony," Grant announced without hesitation.

"We must decide. You will be confined to suitable quarters, fed and guarded until a decision has been made. If we agree to your terms, then one of our people must be present at the sentence and punishment of the man responsible for the attack on our village. If we decide against your offer, then death will follow immediately. And your colony will be attacked and wiped out. Take them away."

The alien waved toward those around it, then turned, standing before the computer.

Lena and Grant were quickly taken out of the chamber and down the corridor. In moments they were alone in a small windowless room brightened by one of the light globes. There was no furniture in the room; only bare walls of metal, shining like polished glass, and the door, which was bolted from the outside.

Immediately Lena came into Grant's arms, trembling. During their captivity he had almost forgotten that she was first a woman, second a scientific mind of great brilliance. His arms went around her slender form, and sudden emotion choked him. Suddenly he felt terrible helplessness. There was nothing he could do but await either the announcement of death or the offer of friendship and peace. In the meantime, he would hold her close, in the illusion of a protective embrace.

Grant was conscious of slowly sinking to the floor, and for the next hours they merely held one another in the way only real lovers can. Her movement into his arms had seemed so natural, normal, as if they'd been intimate for a lifetime. Grant couldn't help realizing how totally their relationship had so fully developed. And yet this was their first moment of such closeness, physically, mentally and spiritually. In a cheap popular romance, it would be the moment when they would pursue some seedy sexual union. Yet life created many forms of real connection. Some people might seek erotic union. But for them, at this moment, at this time, and at this place, this was their silent commitment to on another. They merged gently closer for what could be their last moments of life. This sharing was the ultimate intimacy, far beyond any mere carnal fusion.

They sank into a deep sense of one another, and nothing else seemed to matter. How long it was before he heard the door opening behind him was impossible to tell. Suddenly Grant was aware they were not alone.

Lena gasped, and he turned to find half a dozen aliens standing there, fully armed.

CHAPTER SIXTEEN

Jake stepped into Lard's office suite and said, "It's Barry again, sir. He insists on speaking to you.

Lard's fingers tapped the metal desktop as he gazed blankly at the door. "Barry is becoming a problem. The same question, I would guess."

"Flip Kord is with him this time, sir." Jake shrugged. His right hand touched the laser strapped to his side. It was an instinctive gesture, not meant as a threat. But the move was not lost on Lard. "They asked for an audience with you."

"Well, let's get it over with," Lard decided. "Go get them—and you remain present."

Immediately, Jake left.

Lard picked up the small stack of papers from the shallow basket next to his desk. The papers were his notes and ideas on what projects might be undertaken by the colony.

In the last days since returning from the alien village, Lard had kept much to himself, ostensibly for the purpose of making plans for the colony's future. But he actually needed time to sort out some very conflicted feelings.

He locked himself in the office suite that was set aside for the colony's leader, isolated even from his Mardi. That woman had shared some wickedly delicious nights with him. Yet even she wasn't to be totally trusted.

Lard felt dangerous threats to his authority from all sides.

Of course the aliens were the greatest threat. Killing them had been smart business. And highly enjoyable. He'd actually experienced an erotic jolt in the killings.

"Can't take any chances," he fairly shouted at the

175

walls. "Thinking monsters? Damn all you bastards!" He cursed at the walls. "Lucifer be damned! I won't let this defeat my purpose!"

He felt a shadow of cold slither down his spine, as if some supernatural demon had reached in and become part of his very soul.

A moment of panic made him stand, trembling. Then he cursed under his breath. "Don't go delusional on me!"

The room itself seemed to weave dizzily. Then he slapped his face and stood rigid. "What's wrong with you, Lard?"

An inner voice answered. You can't trust anybody. The aliens, even the colonists, are dangerous.

Again a shiver shook through him.

Lard relied on reports from Jake and Whets. These were the only two men he could depend on, at least for now. They enjoyed the power he had given them.

With a chuckle of pleasure, he remembered a line from a book he'd read:

"I am the power and the force and the Mighty Moshia, destined to bring his people to paradise," he announced to the room in a strong, powerful voice.

He was the Moshia of Larton. The Prophet Lard Talor who would lead his flock of sheep to Universal Peace and Immortality.

He felt almost godlike in this realization.

And he wasn't about to give it up for some monstrous aliens. Even intelligent ones.

"I do believe," he muttered, "this planet is too small for both species!"

He laughed hysterically at the very banality of the statement. A surge of pleasure rushed through him.

A jarring knock on the door snapped his mind out of the black pit.

Jake's voice sounded, "I've brought them!"

"Door, open!" Lard commanded, and as it responded to his voice, the two men entered the room, followed by Jake's form, which stayed just behind them.

Both looked somewhat determined.

Barry started to say something, but Flip cut in. "We

176

both believe that a study of the alien village's structures could be of great interest and advantage to us," Flip announced in a matter-of-fact voice. "Barry here claims there are signs of advanced culture and scientific knowledge."

"Means nothing!" Lard interrupted, his eyes hard on Flip. It was time to make a powerful point with this man. "I don't want to waste colony time with such useless studies."

"I don't believe they are useless, Mr. Talor," Flip said rather coldly.

"I don't care what you think!" Lard stood, fists clenched.

Unimpressed, Flip continued. "Such a study would give the colony some useful activity and an investigation to occupy its time."

"You can't be serious. We have more important things to do. We must stop the aliens before they become a serious annoyance!"

"You can't fight a shadow enemy," Flip cut in harshly, "and such a study might give us some indication where to look and—"

"Mr. Kord, you are becoming a troublemaker. I don't like your tone of voice. I don't like your attitude. I don't like—"

"Don't you think this is bigger than personal likes?"

The question startled Lard so much that for a moment he had nothing to say.

Flip continued in the same even tone. "We've been chasing around the territory for days, finding nothing. Barry has brought to light some very interesting information. There's a great possibility the aliens had—might still have—a higher culture. Here or somewhere. Now or in the past. But certainly it must have existed somewhere on this planet!"

"Forget it, Mr. Kord! There's no civilization! The ship's robo-brain would have that information in its memory banks, and would've revealed that the first day! The very idea of these alien savages being from an intelligent, advanced culture is a bad idea -dangerous.

"A: There is no indication that it has given them any modern weapons.

"B: It does not change the fact that they are at a low degree of advancement at this time. Which means?

"C: We can crush them. That's all that counts."

"We request permission to go to the village site and make a full study of the structures Barry claims might reveal—"

"Permission denied," Lard spat out angrily.

"Then we'll go without your permission!"

"You do that, and I'll have you wishing you had never been reborn. You'll serve as a public example—and Deep Freezed that quick!" His hands slapped loudly together.

"You can't put all of us into DF," Flip countered, his face stubborn.

"No, that's true. But once they see what happens to you before DF, when they hear your screams of sheer agony, whimpering for mercy, they will think twice. As you might start doing, right now. Just get out of here!"

Flip started to say something, then closed his mouth.

Barry said, "But, Mr. Talor, what harm does it do to let us—"

"It's useless," Flip announced, pulling Barry with him to the door. "Best we accept defeat."

When they had left, Lard said to Jake, "Follow them. If they try anything, lock them in quarters, and then report to me. I think that Flip Kord is up to something. And it'll be a pleasure to publicly prime him for DF!"

Once alone, Lard sat down, gazed thoughtfully at the far wall, his mind ringing with Barry's last remark: "What harm does it do to let us—"

Man was the King of the Universe, and there could be no greater intelligence.

Angrily, he withdrew from such thoughts. Maybe it was a good idea to begin building a village near the river. It would be busy work, at least. And it would certainly keep people focused on something other than themselves and the aliens.

And an easy target for attack!

With a heavy sigh, Lard tried to blank his thoughts. He would deal with such matters the next day. For now, he needed rest. He thought of returning to the quarters he shared with Mardi, then decided against it. He really did need rest.

* * * * * * *

Jake tried to appear casual as he watched Flip Kord and Barry enter the lower section of the ship, but a sudden shakiness played at the pit of his stomach like ice tracing along the lining.

Jake had uncertain feelings concerning the aliens. His emotions were mixed as to the rightness of the slaughter. Never before had he been so involved in such violence. Oh, sure, in his life on Earth there had been the ErotoAdvents, but that was not real, only fiction. Then at the World's Fair in '77, there had been the *Ersatzes*, androids you could hack to pieces for twenty points against your Credit Allowance. They were a wonderful way to dissipate one's violence.

Right now he wished he had a few Ersatzes to pound to death.

Jake had felt a sense of restlessness right from the very beginning, or rather, the first few weeks out of DF. Sure, he went for Lard's dictates about the women. Very nice to have them easily in their place. There were plenty of advantages to this "Breeder" idea.

He'd really enjoyed his two months with Hadi. She'd been hesitant at first, then later boldly passionate. That had been a pleasant surprise. And now Ryanna. A nice surprise. Publicly she'd expressed shock at forced unions. But in the privacy of the bedroom she turned on like a laser beam: hot and all-consuming.

Boredom was a harsh reality. Lard was trying to give them some direction, but it was not enough. Exactly why, Jake did not know.

And the man had withdrawn somewhat in the last days. Maybe it would have been different with Grant. He really did not know.

Even the two women he'd enjoyed so far could not replace the gaping hole of a life without the woman he'd been married to for so many years on Earth. Deep Freeze had robbed him of her.

Where might she be now, if still alive? Had she been taken off to some other strange alien world? Or was she sleeping away centuries with death-memories, dreaming of being reunited with him once again in some distant future?

International had given them false dreams and hopes.

Anger cut hard at him, burned raw at his guts.

He forced himself to return all attention to the present necessities.

Silently, he followed Barry and Flip Kord though the lower section of the ship and was surprised to discover that they were headed for the copter hangar. The two men whispered softly, then stepped inside. For a moment Jake had been afraid they might see him following them, but they were too involved in their conversation and activities to notice anything else.

Jake quickly covered the distance, reaching for the laser with his right hand. As he came cautiously to the half-closed entrance, he heard Flip speaking.

"Lard's insane! Where does he think he's taking us? Right from the beginning he's done everything wrong. But you'd think, like Grant pointed out, time would change things. A man has to have more than just a selfish survival instinct. When Lena was here, I could at least depend on her, but now, this blind, unreasoning refusal to make any studies of those ruins is insane, without logic. We must do something. But what?"

Barry's voice was high, thin. "I don't see what can be done. Those structures were built by a highly advanced civilization. They were old, very old, maybe several thousand years old. I could make some tests and discover exactly, almost to the exact ten-year period, what their age is. It's maddening! What a discovery. What a place to spend weeks in study. Those ruins could tell me enough to fill books. It's like reading history, like an experience you can't imagine until you have—"

"Yes, yes, I know. We've gone over it again and again, and there's nothing to do but wait for our chance. First chance we get, we'll let the others know how we feel. Lard knows he can't go up against the whole colony. If we strike hard at the right time, Lard will be helpless to divert opinion.

180

But it has to be timed right. Wait until the boredom sets in a little harder, wait until the unrest has built to a peak. Then, bang! What could Lard do?" He was silent for a moment, then said, "If only we could take this copter. Maybe. We're not children!" There was another short silence. Then Flip said in a disgusted voice, "Well, let's get out of here before—"

Jake stepped into the room then. "Okay, don't touch a thing. Lard won't like this. Nobody goes anywhere against his orders."

Flip stood there in front of the copter, one hand touching its door, as if he were about to pull himself up inside the cabin.

"What are you talking about, Jake?" Flip cried.

"You know. You were warned about using the copter without permission!"

"For God's sake, Jake, you can't be serious!"

"Cut the chatter!" Jake warned coldly.

"Come on. You can't be that blind. Lard hasn't given a sane order since he started and—"

"I'm warning you, Flip! Cut it!"

"Look, Jake, can't you see?" Flip questioned in a more calm, controlled voice. "The colony is going to pieces because there's not enough to do. I mean, there's plenty to do, but Lard's vetoing every suggestion. What harm would it have done to give us his blessing? We have to live, all of us, in a way that will give purpose and direction to our lives. Our own purpose and direction...or the proper and intelligent purpose of a sane leader. Lard just isn't—"

"One more word, Flip, I mean it!" Jake threatened, his eyes hardening.

Flip started to say something. Then, instead, he leaped at Jake—but far too slowly. Jake rammed the laser into the pit of the smaller man's stomach. As Flip sank to the floor, doubling over in pain, gasping for the breath that had been smashed out of him, Jake threatened Barry with the gun. "Are you coming without a struggle, or do I give you the same treatment?"

"What's gotten into you, Jake?" Barry questioned in amazement.

"Just shut up and do exactly as I tell you!"

For a moment, as he looked at the other man cowering before him, Jake wondered what he was doing. He experienced a surging need to strike out at someone, anybody. If there had been an ersatz in front of him, he'd have violently murdered it without hesitation.

Since being revived on the ship, he was stunned by the intense rush of unexpected feelings that surged through his body. Everything seemed magnified.

On Earth, he had lived a quiet, dull life with the woman he had met at the age of twenty-two. They had given birth to six children over a period of a hundred and six years. When she died, his life had been empty, aimless. He had gone into Deep Freeze simply to be revived with her. Bitterness ached in his gut. International had given them immortality, new bodies and this world upon which to survive. And a male utopia with the women as property to serve the men's total desires. His wife, Marsha, would have been shocked. But she was gone forever.

The ache burst like acid in him.

He would miss her for a very long time. But the reality of this world made all that past life merely a dimming memory of the meek, dominated male he had been.

Here on Larton it was different. In fact he never remembered having felt so turned on to the physical side of life. And the marvelous surge of personal power. Lard fed into those new needs. That was harsh reality, right or wrong. The man deserved total loyalty.

He would have to report Flip and Barry's actions.

He stood over Flip, waiting for the man to recover, feeling a sense of helpless guilt. It was too late to turn back now. He had to go through with it because something deep inside him screamed that this was the only way to ensure his own personal survival, his own sanity, away from tormenting thoughts of a dead wife who could never be returned to him. For a moment he felt the urge to kill himself, take the easy way out—and he rejected it as he had so many times in the past weeks.

Any means of survival was better than death.

"Okay, Kord, on your feet and out the door. We'll see

what Lard has to say about this," Jake said with a hard, tense grin on his thin lips.

CHAPTER SEVENTEEN

The forest was tropical, the sun beating down like fire, burning through the thick room of interlocking giant trees. Only the lack of flying insects made the day less miserable.

Grant's mind was swimming with endless rejected plans of operation. For almost fourteen days they had been making their way from the alien ruined city, over the brutal cold of the mountains and then into the scalding heat of the forest.

Gattia, the leader of his twenty-warrior escort, had told him that summer was now hitting its peak and would continue to do so for the next twenty-seven days, after which a swift drop in temperature would bring more tolerable weather to the lowlands.

Grant, before leaving the city with Gattia's escort, had inquired on the possibility of obtaining some more sophisticated weapons, such as the Ladda claimed to have. Gattia had simply said it was out of the question. The agreement was that Lard would be punished by the rest of the Earth colony, and then friendship could come into being; otherwise, open warfare would follow, and Lena would be first to die.

Gattia had told him this morning that they should reach the ship late in the afternoon. The two of them had become friendly in a formal sort of way. During their evening meals, they passed many hours exchanging information about their cultures.

"It is legend," Gattia had told him one evening, "that the Ladda came from another place, on the Wings of Gods, settling on this world and building great cities. It is believed

184

that the Ladda were splintered into many different political groups from the very beginning. Over the centuries these groups lost track of one another. Only during the last five centuries of the Great Civilization was contact made, followed by war and conquest. The world broke up into four major groups: the Dor, Katta, Lortai, and Yates.

"We came from the latter nation, and we believed that peace should be made between all nations. The Dor accepted our ideals, but were pressured by the Katta at their borders and the Lortai to their South. Political pressure grew to the explosive point, and it was necessary to go to war. This lasted thirty-seven days and wiped out all that was civilized in this world. All the government and military centers were completely demolished. In time, the few survivors who were spread out across the world managed to communicate through the Voices of the Gods. A dedication against all war became our governing policy. Hundreds of our years have passed since then, and no war of any kind has come upon Addoria."

Grant asked about the fact that Gattia believed the Ladda had originally come from another world, and the alien nodded thoughtfully, the flickering firelight reflecting in its huge eyes.

"There is a legend handed down over the generations which revealed much about our past."

He then chanted:

"The Ladda broke from their Home,
Came away through the void of black.
Saw a land of virgin forest.
And, lo, the new world was theirs!
The Mighty Pruning Eye of life,
Hotter and bigger in this sky,
Rose in reverse,
The moons were not two, but three.
And, lo, this was Addoria,
Our haven of peace,
Giving escape from the Dark Void."

Then in a more normal tone, Gattia explained. "At first it was considered a mere myth. Then we discovered it was rooted in truth. There is no evolutionary evidence that the Ladda evolved on this world. There are aged books, which were copies of copies of more ancient text that referred to things unknown here. And above all, there is another distant world in this night sky of ours, which scientist believe is our original home. Our astronomers had their magnifying tubes. "

"Telescopes?" Grant was stunned by Gattia's statement. It took a bit of explanation before the alien understood.

"None exist today. There are records of such in the Voice of Gods. Someday, perhaps, you will have to come and study with us. If we can find a solution to our mutual problems. There is much which the Voice of Gods might reveal to you. And with your immediate knowledge of the universe, I would believe it possible to prove conclusively that this legend is based on honest folk memories."

Grant's mind jarred to the present as the caravan came to a sudden halt. He was in the middle of the column of mounts, and Gattia came riding swiftly back to join him.

"We have arrived at the place where your people live. Have you decided how you will keep your word?"

Grant had already told Gattia something of the problems which faced him in any attempt to regain control of the colony.

"I have found a way," he assured Gattia as he followed the other to the head of the column. "We can hope that my way will prove successful."

Gattia continued on with Grant until they had reached the edge of the forest, still hidden behind a thin layer of underbrush. It had been agreed that it was best for Grant to approach the ship alone; the next day Gattia would send one of his fellows to the ship. If Grant had failed, that failure would be revealed by the reception the Ladda received.

Grant felt an urge to shake hands with Gattia, or to say something that could reveal his respect and liking of the other. But there was nothing to say that had not been said. They were members of different species. They had become friendly, but war was likely to follow. Such war would end

186

all human life on this world. There was nothing more to say.

Grant dismounted, then turned away from the forest and the Ladda.

He moved onto the plain and in moments saw the huge spaceship sitting peacefully on the grassy slope. Slowly he walked forward, so that anyone spotting him would have a chance to see who he was before firing.

* * * * * * *

Lard got the report within seconds after Kern, the man on guard duty, spotted the figure emerging from the forest. Immediately he left his quarters, heading for the main lounge room, where wall screens would give him a perfect view of the surrounding territory.

This was it. For days they had been awaiting signs of the aliens. His fingers flexed against his side, and hot sweat covered his body as he stepped into the main lounge. Several others were already present.

Lard moved up to Kern, who was talking to Whets.

"Well?" Lard demanded, looking at the screen. It showed a small section of the plain and a figure making its way forward.

Whets turned. "Just the one. I gave orders to await your arrival."

"Enlarge it!" He felt wild power surge through him. This was the thing they had all been waiting for.

Immediately Whets moved to the panel under the screen, and the figure loomed larger.

A gasp sounded from those close to him, seeming to echo around the chamber. Lard felt a shiver of eerie fear. There was little questioning the fact that the figure was Grant—Hal Grant, once more back from the dead.

Sick anger choked Lard. Hot frustration muted his voice.

Would he never be rid of this man? he thought bitterly.

"Whets, Jake, go out to the airlock and bring him to my quarters immediately. Don't let him say a thing. If he attempts to speak, knock him unconscious."

187

Kern asked, "Why, sir?"

The man's eyes were haunted, like all the eyes that looked at Lard nowadays. The public flogging that had made Flip Kord and Barry screaming masses of broken flesh had served the purpose of stopping all rebellion against his total rule. Barry was still confined in bed. Flip was Deep Frozen and out of the way.

"We don't know this is really Grant. Might be one of those monsters acting like him. And if it is him, well, we don't know what kind of condition his mind is in. I'm not taking any chances. Until I know, nobody else is to see him."

Lard turned and quickly made his way out of the room. In minutes he was in his own quarters, shaking uncontrollably. He pulled the laser from its holster, checked the charge, then went to the wall cabinet and grabbed a bottle of home-brewed liquor, which had been one of the projects he had put the others to work on some days before. With modern gadgets, they had been able to make a fairly strong and decent liquor within hours. He gulped several swallows, then sat down behind the desk, trying hard to control the shaky sickness inside his stomach.

He sat there wanting to scream.

Grant, it was always Grant—disappearing, apparently dead, and now coming back once more to plague him.

Grant had been dead too many times, and the colony had survived. Maybe it was time to consider a final solution this problem.

* * * * * * *

Whets kept pace with the taller man, thinking about the amazing fact that Grant had survived once again, not only the forest, but the aliens. What magic did he possess? What mystic charmed his very life?

Jake said, "Wonder what happened to Lena."

Whets merely grunted, shrugged. "Who cares. Just another breeder!"

As they left the airlock and moved towards Grant, Jake suggested nervously, "Better get our lasers out!"

Whets shrugged. "No need to play tough unless

there's some sign. Just be ready, in case. We don't know if this is really Grant, and I don't mind saying that I hope it isn't."

"Why?"

"Conflicts and power plays. Can't have two leaders in a group like ours. There will be conflicts. Either Grant or Lard would have to die. So it might be easier if this turns out to be some trick."

"What kind of trick could it be?" Jake wanted to know.

"How should I know? In my time on Earth they had *Ersatzes*—androids. Who knows? Maybe this is some illusion. A fake. Maybe we should kill it now! Before it's too late."

"You're buying Lard's claim," Jake observed. "I think it's Grant, all right. But I'm not taking chances."

They were now only yards away from Grant The man's face was burned dark from the sun, his eyes hard and serious as they met theirs.

"Get the colony together," Grant instructed in a demanding voice.

"Quiet, Grant," Whets warned.

"We're all in danger," Grant snapped back, his jaw revealing a grim determination.

"Quiet. No talking. We have orders," Whets commanded, his right hand touching the laser.

"Don't be a fool! We're all in danger of being wiped out and—"

Whets' laser slapped into his hand and slammed out at Grant's belly, stopping short. "Cut it, and fast."

For a moment nobody moved.

"What do you mean?" Jake questioned Grant.

"He's not supposed to talk," Whets warned, glancing at Jake.

"What harm?" Jake countered. The laser in his right hand moved just slightly toward Whets, then returned to point at Grant.

"Orders are orders."

Grant blurted out, "The aliens!"

"One more word, Grant, and I have orders to knock

189

you unconscious. It's up to you!" Whets' laser rammed firmly against Grant's stomach. It was not meant to hurt the man, only to stop him from talking.

Grant stared into Whets' eyes for a moment, then shrugged.

They started toward the ship in total silence. Only the soft murmuring of the evening breeze through the grasses around their footsteps broke the quiet.

* * * * * * *

Lard looked up as the door opened and Jake and Whets shoved Grant into the room.

"You can leave," Lard ordered.

Neither he nor Grant said anything until the door had closed behind the two men.

"I see," Lard commented, "that you were cooperative with them."

Grant nodded. "I tried, but laser guns speak loudly, don't they?" He grinned lightly. "I see you're still ruling with an iron hand."

"The way things should be ruled!" Lard offered briefly. The laser gun lay on the desk in front of him. For a moment he was tempted to pick it up, but decided it was not necessary yet. As long as Grant remained at a safe distance, there was no cause to push events to a head.

"I hope things have been running smoothly," Grant said conversationally. His eyes moved to the laser for only a moment, then returned to Lard's eyes.

"No real trouble, if that's what you mean. A couple of the men got a little out of hand, but we handled things smoothly enough."

"Mind if I ask who?"

"Flip Kord and Barry."

No reaction showed on Grant's face. He merely nodded. "Then I take it all has been okay otherwise. No deaths?"

"No. Nothing to report of interest." Lard cursed silently to himself. What game was Grant playing? "Well, what about yourself? We were convinced you'd been killed by the aliens."

190

"No such luck," Grant offered evenly. "But a lot has happened. I think I'd better tell it to you from the beginning."

Lard nodded and listened in silence as Grant told of his capture, their night at the alien village, their trip to the alien city, and finally about the offer of peace between the Ladda and the Earth colony.

"But," Grant concluded seriously, "there's one catch."

"Oh?" Lard raised his eyebrows. His right hand edged to the laser. Every nerve tensed. So far he was not convinced that Grant was sane, but it did not matter.

"Yes. I think it might be a good idea to tell the colony as a whole," Grant stated matter-of-factly. His attitude was too casual, too friendly.

"I don't see any reason to do that. You tell me. Then I'll decide what it is best to tell the others."

"Well, Lard, I want to point out one thing. They are of an advanced culture, and they do have the ability to strike at us in one swift blow. You do understand this, don't you?"

"I understand this is what you have told me. Did you personally see any of these weapons?"

"No. But there were plenty of pictures in the book. And the computer was obviously from a highly advanced scientific culture. Those light balls I was telling you about are used in night hunts to attract certain dangerous animals, either away from a camp or into a trap. They are able to see quite well in the dark, but the Ladda didn't take too long to realize this isn't true of human beings. They showed a great amount of active intelligence in their handling of the two of us." Then he added as an afterthought, "But of course they didn't show us all around their city, so I can't claim they don't actually have advanced weapons already in existence."

"But you didn't see any such weapons—nothing other than the primitive weapons we already know about?"

"Nothing. But I do want to point out that they can be manufactured, much the same as their arrowheads, spearheads and knife blades. You have seen the spearheads. They are made of an advanced metal, not of stone or—"

"Does that prove anything?" Lard demanded stubbornly.

"I'll put it this way." Grant's voice was silky. "It's enough to indicate they can do exactly what they say. There is no evidence to support any theory to the effect that they are engaging in a smart bluff."

"Of course, I have to take your word for this, don't I?"

"I don't understand what you're driving at," Grant said innocently. "After all, we're on the same side."

"Well, you've been against dominance over the aliens from the start. How do I know you haven't just gone off into the forest and hidden away with Miss Hitten, then returned with a fantastic and unrealistic story? After all, we found no sign of you in the alien village."

"I believe proof could be offered, quite easily at that. All you have to do is go with me to the city. By copter it shouldn't take more than a day. Then you'd have all the proof you need."

"If there is such a city, and if you were captured by the aliens, and if what you have told me is true, it could still be a trap. How am I to know they haven't robbed you of your mind? How do I—"

"Then you won't believe me?"

"I didn't say that, Grant. I simply pointed out that there is no proof, and as the leader of the Earth colony, I have to look out for the lives of everyone here. I guess it didn't occur to you to consider that fact," he finished bitingly.

"That's what I'm looking out for, Lard," Grant snapped back, for the first time showing emotion.

"Then, to get back to this condition of yours—what is it?"

"I would rather tell it to all the others at the same time, if you don't mind."

"I do!" Lard swept up the laser and leveled it at Grant's chest. "Now tell me first. I'll decide what's best to do, understand?"

Grant sighed, then took a deep breath. "Tell me Lard, what do you think is more important: the whole or the parts?"

192

"What's that mean?"

"Is anyone's life here at the colony so valuable that it wouldn't be worth sacrificing for the lives of the others?"

"That would depend on the circumstances," Lard countered very carefully.

"Would you say that my life would be worth giving up to save the rest of you?"

"Is that the condition?" Lard grinned.

"I didn't say that."

"Then what is the condition? Stop stalling!"

"The Ladda are upset about the slaughter of the village. They are a peace-loving race, but will not tolerate such violence."

"What the devil are they going to do against laser beams?"

"Far more than you can imagine, Lard. We're outnumbered, outclassed, and on their world! We are very few; they are very many." He spread his hands wide, as if making the obvious point.

"So you say." The man's tone revealed dislike more than distrust.

"So I know! They'll have it their way, no matter what!"

"I don't know if I agree with you. The condition for a peaceful way? What's the trap? What do they demand?"

"The man who is responsible for that slaughter is to be punished, publicly, in the presence of the Ladda, so they can believe in the word of the Earth colony." Grant stood there, legs slightly apart, arms at his side, eyes focused on Lard. He looked like a man about to spring forward in attack.

Lard tightened his hand on the laser.

"So you mean, in simple terms, you made a deal. To save your own necks, you would attempt to turn me over. Is that it?"

"No! Not our necks. The lives of every man and woman here. In any case, Deep Freeze would probably be all that's required. It's not death."

"You're out of your mind, Grant. And even if you aren't, don't think for a moment that I will allow Earth men, human beings, to crawl before primitive savages. As far as

I'm concerned, you're mad."

With that Lard stood up and started around the table, the laser still leveled at Grant's chest.

"Lard, you can't fool around with the Ladda. This is a serious threat. They mean what they say. If we don't do as they demand, it will mean an all-out war of extermination, and it's a war we can't possibly win. Don't you understand?"

"I understand that you're insane. That's all I understand, Grant."

As he started to move past Grant, the other leaped at him. The move was catlike, so swift that it was impossible to react immediately. But swift as Grant was, Lard reacted, fast. The distance was too great; the move was made in desperation.

Lard brought the laser forward, hitting the other man in the chest. He felt something strike his shoulder numbingly. His left fist shoved hard into Grant's face. Then he struck with the butt of the laser, hitting the other's head.

Grant slumped. Lard kicked out at the man's side, and Grant was flung across the room. He smashed against the wall and fell silent.

Lard's laser raised; he aimed; his finger pressed lightly on the firing button.

A thought fluttered across his mind.

What if Grant is right?

It was insane to believe him. Yet as long as the possibility existed, it didn't hurt to wait.

CHAPTER EIGHTEEN

Grant, when he came to, felt a sense of sick defeat. Everything he had done and said to Lard Talor had been a drastic mistake. Now it was easy to realize this. It would have been better to have lied. Yet the need to impress upon the other man the necessity to seek a peaceful relationship with the Ladda, the belief that even this man would realize how pointless it was to battle a superior force—thus endangering every human being on the planet—had motivated his actions.

Then doubt came. Some men would let the whole world sink rather than accept personal defeat.

Grant cursed himself for having been a fool, for making the mistake of misjudging the enemy. His only hope lay in the fact that Jake and Whets knew something of his mission and might put pressure on Lard. If only he had been given a chance to speak to them on his way to the ship. Lard had thought of everything. His chances of getting help from those two men were admittedly weak.

How long he was confined in the room before the door opened, Grant could not guess, for he had no idea how long he had been unconscious.

Lard and Whets entered the room, each armed with a laser.

"Come quietly," Lard warned, "and nothing will happen."

Whets stepped around Grant and shoved the laser in his back.

"Don't be a fool," Grant started to say to Whets.

Whets' laser struck the side of his head. It was a painful, but not a stunning blow.

Lips pinched tight, Lard commanded, "We don't want any of your insane mouthing. There's trouble enough here without you sounding off!"

As they entered the corridor, Grant saw Jake standing there, armed. For a moment their eyes met, and Jake's revealed a vague uneasiness, as if the man wasn't sure they were doing the right thing.

Grant was shoved down the corridor in total silence. They passed nobody else. It was as if the ship were deserted. Finally they came to a stop before a small room, into which he was shoved. The door slammed shut behind him. There was a sound of the latch clicking, then silence.

Slowly, Grant settled on the small bunk that was hinged to the wall. He considered these first weeks on the planet. Hundreds of years to get them here, thousands of years of evolution from cavemen, only to be defeated in a few days by one man's crazed superego.

Exhaustion finally claimed Grant, and he slept. He was awakened by the door opening.

Whets stepped in, carrying a small bowl in one hand and a laser in the other.

Grant immediately slipped his legs over the side of the bunk. "Whets, you're a reasonable man—"

"Shut up!"

"You don't know what you're doing, Whets. We'll be killed. All of us."

"Shut your mouth." Whets cursed between tight lips. The laser was leveled at Grant's chest. "I have my orders. If you try to speak, you'll be killed. I've given you fair warning."

Grant shrugged.

Whets laid the bowl on the small table to Grant's left. Then he turned and moved to the door.

In that instant, Grant had a wild impulse to leap at the other, but before he could do so, Whets turned slightly while opening the door, and it was too late.

Grant ate his food—a light-colored stew—slowly, forcing down each bite, while his mind attempted to devise some means of escape. Now a sense of panic overwhelmed him. Something had to be done before it was too late. His eyes took in the bare room. There was only one blanket, a pillow, the table, a chair and a bunk. No objects that might serve as weapons. The bowl was of a hard but light plastic, the spoon made of a flexible soft material. Neither could serve as an effective weapon.

The brief-on, which he still wore, was of a type of material that could not easily be torn by human hands.

He felt helpless.

* * * * * * *

Lard awoke in the middle of the night, screaming, sweat soaking his body like some oily slime, hot and sticky.

For some time he lay in the oppressive dark, shaking, his breath coming in hard gasps. He felt the softness of a feminine hand touch his shoulder.

"What is it?" Mardi Shores soothed. "Everything is all right."

"A dream," Lard managed, shaking her hand off. "A dream."

"I know. You were shouting something about—it sounded like Ladda—about them crawling all over you."

A shiver shook Lard. He remembered all too vividly. The dream had been terribly real. The aliens had been small insect creatures, marching like ants toward him. He was cornered in a small room, and suddenly they were crowding in all around him, and then over him, into his mouth and nose, across his eyes. Then he had screamed.

"What are Ladda?" Mardi inquired.

"Nothing. Nothing!" he said, laying back in the bed. "Leave me alone."

He felt her body move to the other side of the large bed. Silence filled the room around him. He lay there for a long time, his mind caught in a deep swirl of snarled torment. Once he had found himself on the verge of calling out to Mardi, about to tell her everything he had learned from Grant. Finally he slipped from the bed, reached for his brief-on, and dressed. He grabbed the laser and snapped it around his waist.

"What are you doing?" Mardi's voice called out from

the darkness behind him.

"Can't sleep," he mumbled half to himself. "Be back later."

He slipped out of the room, stepped down the corridor, hesitated in front of the door to the room where Grant was held prisoner, then walked past. A few minutes later, he was in the main lounge, standing before the huge monitor screens, the eyes that looked out upon the alien world surrounding the ship.

He switched on the cameras and set the controls below the screens so they could see into the darkness. Two of the moons were high in the sky, and the view was beautiful in an eerie way. Nothing moved upon the plain. It might have been a lifeless world out there. How he wished that were so! If Grant was right, aliens were waiting in the cover of that foliage below those giant trees.

Doubt plagued him.

Lard thought about his child, who would be born soon. Mardi would be the first mother on Larton, which was quite an achievement for a woman who during her Earth-years had been something of a tramp.

He tried to picture the child, but the image blurred, shapeless and vague.

Stepping over to a chair, he sat down and fingered the laser. His eyes stared blankly at the monitor screens. The thoughts that raced across his mind had little form, but carried the thin trace of nagging fear that had plagued him ever since talking to Grant that evening.

At one point consciousness slipped away. The sound of movement to his left suddenly jerked him awake.

Lard turned to see Jake's tall form step into the room. The man appeared surprised to find another person there.

"Well...hello!" Jake greeted him, sitting down opposite Lard, his long legs dangling out in front of him like awkward, broken poles.

"What're you doing up in the middle of the night?"

"It's morning," Jake announced. "I woke early. Had plenty of sleep." He seemed nervous; his eyes kept moving aimlessly around the room. There was every indication that the man had barely slept during the night.

"Oh," Lard managed lamely, "guess I lost track of time." He felt suddenly embarrassed, ill at ease. He wanted to be left alone with his thoughts.

"What's on the schedule for today?" Jake's voice was unnaturally sharp.

"What?" Lard stared at the man, noticing his blood-shot eyes, haggard lines around his narrow mouth, and sunken cheeks.

"The schedule, sir. You know. Like every day!" His voice was high-pitched, biting. He hesitated, then blurted out, "Yes, like every day. We get up, have breakfast, then sit around, talking pointlessly, then organize an A-hunt; back for lunch, more aimless conversation, another trip outside to explore away more hours of time, and back for dinner. After dinner, conversation which leads nowhere, and then bed. You know the schedule. Any changes? Or is it the same end-less nothing? When are we going to do something of impor-tance? When will we start building a village? When—"

The man shrugged, looking at his feet.

Lard was shocked by the words. He had not thought about their daily activities as being so dull. He wondered if the others also believed they were pointless.

But he did not consider that long. Instead, he felt bursting, unreasonable anger.

Without even a warning, Lard smashed his hand across the other's face. "How dare you talk that way to me!"

Jake hardly reacted. His eyes only narrowed danger-ously; his face deepened in color.

"What's the matter with you, Jake?" Lard snapped, half rising from his chair. "If anybody else had said that, he'd be sorry. Damn! I'd kill anybody else! Don't you like the way things are being run?"

"Fine. Fine. As far as they go, sir," Jake quickly as-sured him in a tightly constricted voice. "Just wondering when we start building a town. We can't keep up like this forever, I guess. Can we?"

"Are you questioning my judgment?" Lard jumped to his feet. "Are you?"

"No, not at all, sir!" Jake looked frightened as he stared up at Lard.

"But you are questioning it, aren't you? You don't like the way I'm taking care of things. Guess you think somebody else might do a better job. You, maybe?"

"No, sir."

"Grant? Is that it? The insane Grant? I'll tell you one thing: I've kept you alive, you ungrateful brat. I've kept all of you alive!" He was suddenly breathing hard. His hands were wet with sweat. He could hear the pounding of his heart, like some giant pump working with frantic speed. "We're going to have children. The colony will grow. We're going to conquer this world without losing a man or woman. And—"

"Grant said something about danger to us all," Jake abruptly blurted out. He sat there like a man expecting to be shot down, body rigid, hands clutching the chair's arms.

Lard felt a sudden sickness. Grant, always Grant. "What do you mean?"

When Jake did not answer, Lard screamed, "Did you hear me? When I speak, you give out! And fast!"

Jake looked as if he felt death choking him. His lips started to move, then froze. His features were drained of all color.

"I asked you a question, man!" Lard fairly yelled.

"He said...we were in...danger!" Jake stammered. Then he quickly added in a more steady voice, "But of course we didn't allow him to continue talking, and—"

"He's mad. That's what he is. You don't believe what he said?"

"No, sir. Just wondering about it. You had a chance to talk to him for some time, and—"

"He's mad, I tell you. You can see that, can't you?" Lard's whole body coiled; the muscles knotted tight. "You do see that, don't you? Come on, Jake. Admit it. The man is whacked out of his skull! Forest fever!"

Jake's face revealed quick shock; his mouth hung open. "Sir, you're tired. No need to get so—"

"Don't tell me I'm tired. Don't tell me anything! I'll tell you! Get out of here. Now! Get out!" He drew his laser and aimed it at Jake, resisting the overpowering urge to press the firing stud.

200

Jake waited only a moment, then quickly slipped from the chair and from the room, leaving Lard alone, shaking, frightened, fighting the violent desire to scream at the top of his lungs.

It was some time before he calmed down. Control surged through him until he could think quite clearly, sanely—even laugh a little at his all-but-hysterical reaction. After all, what was he getting so worked up about?

* * * * * * *

As Jake left the main lounge, his mind was numbed by Lard's sudden outburst. Then he reasoned that the man was exhausted. His own night had been restless. Only exhaustion had made it possible to mention Grant to Lard. That had been a foolish move. Yet his doubts as to the colony's future, his fear that they had not been handling things right, still hurt.

Jake made his way to the room in which Barry was confined. He impulsively knocked on the door, waited until Barry's voice inquired who it was, then opened it.

"How're you feeling?" Jake greeted him softly, closing the door behind him.

Barry was lying on his back on the bunk. Since his arrest and punishment, Barry had been denied the pleasure of any female company, though he was free now to return to the woman with whom he had been sharing quarters.

When the man did not immediately answer him, Jake repeated his words. "How're you feeling?"

"Since when did you care?" Barry snapped back icily. His eyes burned with hatred.

Jake shrugged. "We've been hard on you, haven't we?"

Ever since he had turned Barry and Flip Kord over to Lard, Jake had felt a sense of terrible unrest. Only by attempting to forget the event had it been possible to live with himself. What had brought him here now, he did not quite know. He stared at the small, rather mousy man lying in bed and felt sick.

Barry finally broke the silence. "You've been hard."

201

"Guess you wouldn't understand that I'm sorry and that—"

"Like fun you are! You and Lard and Whets are—"

"I don't need to be told—" Jake broke off. "Grant's returned. I guess you heard."

"I heard." Barry had twisted away. His eyes stared at the ceiling.

"He's confined to quarters until Lard decides what's best to do with him."

"Sure, I can guess what he'll decide." Every word was hard, bitter, filled with hate.

"It's not safe out there alone. That's why Lard didn't want anybody going to the alien village. You can see that, can't you?" Suddenly Jake felt a crushing need to have the man forgive him, understand.

"Lard's crazy. That's all I understand."

"Look what happened to Grant," Jake pointed out.

"I don't know what happened to Grant." Barry slipped out of bed, sat on the edge. "Do you?"

"He didn't sound sane. He claimed that we were all in danger. Said the aliens could kill us off!"

Jake wanted to stop talking, but found the words would not halt. "Lard talked to him for some time, said he's had a nervous breakdown. Claimed the man was raving mad."

Barry's eyes had become alive when Jake had mentioned the aliens and the danger Grant claimed they presented. "What kind of danger did Grant say we're in?"

"I don't know," Jake admitted. "Can't see where the aliens could create much of a threat against laser beams. But—"

"What if he wasn't insane?" Barry fired back. "What if Grant knew what he was talking about?"

Jake shook his head, now frightened by what he had told Barry. "No, no chance. He's shot his rocket. I'm sure of that."

"What if he hasn't?" Barry insisted, now standing. He started to slowly get dressed, as if each move were still painful.

"Lard wouldn't be foolish enough to ignore a real

threat."

"I don't know what Lard would do," Barry countered savagely.

"Look, you might not like the way Lard's running things, but I'll tell you this: the man has personal interests involved. Surely the fact that he'll be a father soon would make him seriously consider all threats to the colony. He's kept us all alive and safe. Maybe he's used a hard hand now and then, but it was for our own good. He's like a father caring for his children: he punishes them when they're bad. Lard could have killed Art Rent that day and been justified. He didn't. Like a father, he merely punished the man, got him out of the way, so that his sick mind wouldn't threaten others. Lard's no fool, believe me."

Barry started to say something, then closed his mouth and sat down on the bunk. "Maybe you're right, Jake. Maybe you're right."

"I am right. Believe me. I am right," Jake announced, almost desperate to convince the man. "After all, it's ridiculous to believe that primitive creatures could stand up against modern weapons. Look how we cut them down in the village."

Barry remained silent.

After a moment, Jake turned and left without another word.

He stopped outside the door to Grant's quarters. A flickering doubt assailed him. Then he shoved it away and started for his own door. He was tired, and his thoughts were distorted. Maybe he should sleep a little before the day's activities. And in any case, he reasoned, there was nothing of real importance to do. He did need to catch up on all the sleep he had lost.

* * * * * * *

Barry waited some time before he left his room. Ever since the beating, he had remained confined to his quarters mainly because he was controlling a seething desire to kill Lard. Now he needed to remain calm, unemotional—at least on the surface. Never before in his life had he wished to commit murder. Life had always seemed so valuable, so important, possibly more so for him because his own life had been filled with intimate knowledge of dead civilizations. He had seen too many great monuments of the ancient past that recorded the pitiful traces of those who had lived ages before. He had become aware of the dusty memories etched into ruined structures. Life seemed much like a dim light passing in the dark. It seemed a sin to snuff such a short flame before its time. All died, but why rush the process?

And then, also, too much death had plagued Barry's personal life. A first wife had died in childbirth, the baby girl not living past her fifth year. A second wife was killed in a rocket liner crash after only fifteen years of marriage and the birth of two children.

Long years of loneliness had followed while he probed into the ancient ruins of past cultures, reliving the glories of Rome, Greece, the Incas, the Aztecs, even colonial America. How many lost dreams had bloomed into reality in these ruins, only to fade with the demise of their civilizations?

Barry was ninety-eight when he remarried. He had outlived his wife and the two children they had. His five grandchildren through the second marriage survived him, but they were now long dead for centuries or held in Deep Freeze.

Death had never frightened him, but it had given him a respect for life and the living. Death had always seemed a mockery of life, the black shadow that was inescapable, the crushing blow that made all personal vanities absurd.

In the last few days Barry had defeated the irrational desire to become the hand of death.

The moment Jake had said that Hal Grant believed the colony to be threatened by aliens, Barry made up his mind what must be done..

He stepped down the empty corridor, not certain where Grant was confined.

He finally made his way into the main lounge to find Lard sitting there alone.

Lard turned, saw him.

Barry moved to the monitor screen that showed the

forest outside the ship. He said, "It's a beautiful world."

"What are you doing up from bed?" Lard demanded.

"The wounds have healed."

"I hope you've learned your lesson."

"Sure. After all, the security of the whole colony is your responsibility," Barry forced himself to say. He turned and faced Lard, fighting down hatred. "I heard Grant returned."

"Yes. But something happened to him out there," Lard stated in a flat voice. His eyes did not meet Barry's.

"Amazing he's alive." Barry shrugged as if it did not matter one way or the other. "And Miss Hitten?"

"Dead, I imagine. We don't know for sure."

Barry didn't dare ask directly where Grant was being held. "But Grant—he's okay? In his quarters?"

"He's here, under lock and key!" Lard's eyes met his. There was mockery in them. "Right under your nose, too!"

"What's that mean?" Barry tried to appear casual.

Lard's laugh was high-pitched, grating, a mocking sound that bounced through the room like a plastic ball. "Not nine doors from you. If that's what you wanna know!"

"You're kidding!"

Lard's voice sounded threatening as he stated: "Yes, five doors. S-A-3, to be exact!"

Those cold eyes grew wide with alarm. Lard's gaze had gone to a monitor screen behind Barry.

"What's that?" He sprang to his feet. "Look!"

Barry turned to see a tiny dark figure emerge from the underbrush at the base of the forest several thousand yards from the ship.

Just then Whets came rushing into the room.

Lard called to the man, "Get Jake, fast!"

Then he added, half to himself, "Whatever it is this time, it isn't human!"

Barry was left there, standing alone. He rushed back down the corridor, towards Room S-A-3.

* * * * * * *

Grant had waited for maybe an hour, pressed against

the side wall just to the left of the door. His fingers felt cramped, his muscles ached, but he kept to his post, waiting, ready. In his hands was the knotted cloth he'd stripped from the bed. He now awaited the first throat to come through the door. If Gattia sent a messenger to the ship and Lard killed it, there would be little hope for human life on Addoria.

Grant had no way of knowing what time it was, because the ship's lights had gone out for the night. All he knew was that morning should be coming soon.

When the lights did finally brighten to announce a new day, Grant was momentarily blinded. His eyes squinted, and for a brief moment his mind clouded. Sleep took over. He swayed, then jerked awake, alert.

Footsteps stopped in front of the door.

His body arched slightly as the muscles tensed. A deep breath sucked into his lungs.

Then a bolt slipped; the door swung open and was quickly pushed shut.

Grant's body went into automatic action. The arms reached out, up, then down; the hands gave one quick jerk; he closed the cloth around a human windpipe.

Maybe size, maybe something about the lack of struggle in his victim gauged the constriction of muscular power. His attack metamorphosed from pure wrist and forearm energy to a quick action of his knee slamming up against the other's spine.. At the same time he released his right hand and jerked the limp body around.

He did not know the man. For a split-second, he looked into the agonized features of the small, harmless looking face before him. Then his right fist slammed brutally into his victim's stomach. A second later, another blow knocked the poor fellow unconscious. He could not risk anybody being able to set an alarm.

Grant wasted only a glance to determine that there were no weapons on the man's body. Then he moved to the door, opened it a crack, and stepped out into the empty corridor beyond.

Weaponless, and theoretically in an enemy camp that could be turned into a deadly weapon against him, Grant boldly made his way down the corridor, as if it were his everyday habit. If anybody saw him, Grant would bluff his way through or attack without mercy. The lives of everybody here depended on his gaining command before Lard could stop him.

He rejected the idea of getting weapons from the armory. His only hope was to find Lard, attack, disarm the man, and call an immediate meeting.

A young woman stepped out of her room, smiled, and then showed sudden recognition.

"Why, Mr. Grant!" she cried.

"Get all personnel into the main lounge!" Grant snapped at her in his most authoritative voice. "Mr. Talor is calling an immediate emergency meeting."

She hesitated, then nodded. He had been lucky on that one.

Grant moved briskly toward the main lounge, expecting to be stopped at any moment.

As he came to the large entrance, his body took on a new level of alertness. It was ready for any action necessary. The next moment might be his last.

As he stepped into the lounge, he came face to face with Whets.

Surprise and the element of the unexpected gave Grant the edge he needed.

One swift forward movement at the throat cut all air from the stockier man. Another chop by his right hand threw the laser gun from Whets' holster and into his own fist.

Several people were already in the lounge, eyes focused on the monitor screens.

Lard was standing with his back to Grant. Next to him stood Jake.

The sound of Whets' body slumping to the floor brought all eyes in Grant's direction.

Both Lard and Jake moved with amazing speed, each capturing his laser. The two men shifted positions, creating distance between one another.

Grant flattened to the floor, took aim at Lard, fired, and missed. Almost at the same time, a laser beam burned the metal flooring inches from his right side.

Somebody screamed.

Lard shouted, "Shoot to kill!" while firing a second time, missing by inches.

The others in the room disappeared behind large lounge chairs, out of the line of fire.

Grant aimed at Lard's right leg, pressed the firing stud, and watched as the man screamed in agony, grabbing at his sheared leg. The man's laser flew some ten feet across the room.

Grant swung toward Jake. "Hold it."

Everything had taken place in no more than ten seconds.

Jake's own gun was focused on Grant. A dead stand-off.

The man who blinked first would die.

At that instant Grant felt a stunning blow at the side of his head. Something hard struck his right hand, and the laser slid away. A heavy body slammed down hard to his, pinning him to the floor.

Lard's voice gasped out, thick with pain: "Kill him. Kill him! For God's sake, Jake, kill him!"

Grant tried to focus his eyes, attempted to regain his mental equilibrium. He saw a fuzzy shape coming towards him. When his vision cleared, Jake was standing like some giant high above.

"Get up, Whets," Jake ordered.

The dead weight lifted and Grant slowly pulled his body to a sitting position.

"Execute him!" Lard's voice screamed over and over again, raging. "Now! Now!"

Grant looked up at Jake and saw confusion and torment on the man's narrow face.

Hope quickly sprang to life.

"Wait a minute, Jake," he commanded softly. "you can kill me any time."

"Don't wait!" Lard was twisted up on the floor half-way across the room. "What are you waiting for? Shoot."

"Let me speak, first," Grant said in a firm but soft voice. "A dying man's last wish?"

Whets' voice sounded cold behind him, "Just kill him like Lard says."

Jake shook his head. "No. I don't think I will...yet."

"You're a dead man, too, then!" Lard promised.

"I don't think so." Jake's voice was strangely firm. He stepped back several yards, swung the laser in a wide arc to take in Lard and Whets. "Move over there, friend. Both of you together."

Whets did as commanded as Jake backed away to a position where it was possible to cover all three men.

"Okay, Grant, have your say."

"I'd like to address everybody. This concerns the whole colony. What I have to say is important to all of us."

"Don't waste time. You don't have much," Jake warned, eyes icy.

"If we want to survive—"

Lard's scream interrupted. "Don't let him speak. That's an order!"

"Shut up or you're a dead man, Lard!" Jake commanded without taking his eyes off Grant. "Continue."

"What I have to say can easily be proven. I told Lard this, but he wouldn't do anything about it, for his own reasons," Grant began, carefully phrasing his sentences so there would be no doubt about his sanity. He glanced at a vid screen and saw the figure making its way to the ship. "There, on the plain, is an alien who can back up my story—at least enough so that you can investigate the rest. There is a means to communicate with them."

"Get to the point," Jake said.

"The aliens, as we call them, are from an advanced cultural civilization that wiped itself out in total war. They still have at their disposal the information to recreate weapons of highly advanced sophistication. They are peace-loving by nature. They have offered either peace or war, a war which under any circumstances we could not win in the long run. Twenty-four humans can't war against a whole planet and win. They threaten that such a war would end in the destruction of this ship and every human. Peace means an exchange of cultures—and punishment for the man responsible for the attack on the alien village!"

As these words were spoken, Whets slowly moved away from Lard. The look of silent fury and disgust in the man's eyes was mirrored in every other face in the room.

Once the rest of the colony had arrived, Grant told his story in detail.

From then on, it was easy.

EPILOGUE

Grant paced nervously outside the spaceship, smoking one of the cigars that Flip Kord, Ltd. manufactured. It was one of the many "personalized" products made to satisfy the individual tastes of the different people of the colony. At Grant's request, cigars without nicotine had been produced, and they caught on with a bang. Most of the people knew nothing about cigars other than what they had learned from history books. Another product was the Luto Liquor Cocktail, made at Jake's request, which served as a very popular before-dinner and after-dinner drink, working both as a stimulant and relaxant. Such products, while of little importance in the overall plans of the colony, were considered necessary to provide creature comforts.

He looked up at the evening sun, which was streaking the low hanging clouds in a splendor of reds and oranges. The sunset was more vivid than it ever could have been on Earth.

He told himself to relax, to take it easy, but the more he attempted to make the mental strain go away, the greater his anxiety grew.

His eyes turned to the small group of buildings scattered along the riverbank. He looked at the tiny shadow box where he and Lena lived. It was a painfully simple four-wall structure, with a combined living room/kitchen, a fireplace, and a partitioned bedroom. The kitchen was highly sophisticated from Grant's point of view, yet primitive compared to the ship and what Lena had been used to on Earth. The furniture was handcrafted by the Jake & Hattie Furniture and Construction Co. In time he would have a mansion, but that would have to wait. There were more important projects to

211

take up their time.

A lot had happened in the last nine months. Proving his announcement about the aliens had been simple enough. Once Gattia was introduced to the members of the colony, arrangements were made to have Art Rents and Barry take a scientific group out by copter to the city. Within a week, the promised peace offer had become a reality. The Ladda willingly set about proving their friendliness by serving as a strong working crew alongside the humans. When the sentence of Deep Freeze for five hundred years was imposed upon Lard Talor, it was reduced to a hundred years at their recommendation, under the condition that total mental deep-brain surgery was successful in making radical changes in the man's thinking. Lena or some other newly trained expert in that field, yet to be born, would be put to the task of restoring the man to an acceptable norm. Lard's greatest punishment was the fact that he would not see his child grow up.

Whets stepped around the ship and grinned. "Well, Hal, I guess this is your day. I just came back from the hunt with Bel Lon and Art Rents. Couldn't miss this. We were a few hundred miles south of here this morning. You should see the game there—fantastic!"

"You're doing a grand job, Whets." Grant managed to smile.

"What's to do? A police force is wasted energy now, don't you think?"

Whets took a new ultra-thin cigar that Grant offered him and stuck it in his mouth. It automatically lit at his first drag. Smoke billowed out on the cooling air.

Grant said, "A police force, guarding troop, hunter corps—all wrapped up in one man. You have an important role in our blossoming community. Good meat is hard to find for those who don't have time for hunting." Grant nervously dropped his half finished cigar on the ground, and pressed it out with sandal.

"How's the ship coming?" Whets inquired, looking off across the plain to the east. "Any progress?"

"Some. But it takes time, even with all the high-tech equipment in the ship. Remember, it took thousands of years for man to conquer space, plus the high cost of dedicated

212

work. Yet here, our lives are hardly more advanced than the primitive nomads who conquered the ancient worlds—while we're trying to build a spaceship! Almost seems impossible. But one must learn to adapt, change with the times."

"The Ladda are anxious. They want to prove their theory about not having originated on this planet," Whets observed, turning his gaze to the town. "And I guess most of us are pretty hopped up on the idea."

Grant nodded. "I never believed much in space travel—not until I woke up here on this planet. Now, in a short time, as time goes, we'll have a chance to explore a whole new solar system. I'll admit Flip had to talk some before I was convinced and excited by the idea. It seemed so much easier simply to settle here and expand quietly. But one can't ignore the pressures of human curiosity. That's where Lard failed most disastrously. If you stand still, you stagnate. We have to expand all of our horizons as quickly as there is a human demand and need. So we have space travel for a bunch of primitives."

"We aren't quite primitives, Hal. We have the combined knowledge of mankind and a viewpoint that takes in a cross-section of cultures that existed over a span of several centuries." Whets chuckled. "In a way, I'm like you, but more simple. I lived a soldier's life—though different from yours—and never was given to deep thoughts. I guess we'll all become sort of a combination of human mentalities— well, maybe you might describe it as—"

"Symbolically, a test-tube humanity?" Grant mused. "And like the Ladda, the inheritors of our species' history, culture and wisdom. All banded together in a unified search of all that's up there."

Whets laughed. "Guess I won't ever learn to express myself the way some of you do."

"We're limited as any unit is limited, Whets. Each person here has his own limitations—also his place, his virtues, his talents. We'll survive because there is so much time before us, so much to live for. And as long as each of us has dreams, as long as we keep asking unanswerable questions, we'll keep our youth."

Grant lit another cigar. "We've managed to make a

lot of progress already. A small town, each man and woman seeking out and finding a place for himself. The beginnings of factories, industries, trades, the forming of a government, organizing an exploration force, the beginnings of a hunting and farming industry, and the making of a spaceship. The forming of laws, the birth of children—and all is peace in the world."

"Barry came in from the city," Whets said, "dusty and with that quiet, distant look in his eyes. Never can figure the guy out. Always off in a dream."

"Dreams of the past." Grant grinned. "A marvelous mind! We can learn a lot from him. He's found his place in our society. He's going to make a good historian, if he ever gets time to write."

"The Ladda are doing everything in their power to help him with his diggings and research. They seem as interested as Barry."

"Nice of the guy to come for the celebration," Grant observed.

Deep shadows were now falling across the evening world as the sun dropped lower. Several couples were beginning to make their way to the ship. After taking another deep pull on the cigar, he looked up at the airlock.

"How much longer?" Whets inquired, following Grant's gaze.

"I don't know, really. Mardi said I had to wait. That's all."

"It's a great day. After all, you are the most important man in the colony. Your name will go down in our history books as the father of our civilization on Ladda. A great man!"

"Hardly. Time creates its heroes. Heroes rise and fall; a star shines for a moment, only to be darkened by another brighter star. In any case, I had enough of the hero thing on Earth. Each man does what is necessary. I happen to be the most qualified person for leadership at this moment, but others will come, and I'll gladly move aside. There will be another place for me then—what, I don't know now. Wouldn't mind looking into Barry's line of work, then expanding it when we search the stars. Who knows? In any case, for the first few hundred years, I would think the Ladda civilization should be interesting to study."

Several people joined them. The whole colony would be there in a short while. Flip Kord and his wife Jeeni stepped up to him. "Well, I see you're making money for my enterprise. How do you like the new crop?"

"Fine mini-cigar, but I can't get used to not lighting it. Seems that was part of the pleasure—at least, part of a lifetime habit," Grant commented dryly.

"We can make them that way, if you really want it," Jeeni offered with a smile.

Grant laughed and shook his head. "We have to learn to accept the new. Besides, it is less work—quicker."

Flip said, "We have the television sets almost perfected, using the raw materials found around us here on the planet. I think we've done a quick job! In another week each house will have television, and we'll beam closed circuit from the ship's library."

"A time waster!" Grant observed, pleased.

A dark shadow moved in the airlock.

"Hal," a woman's voice called from the gloomy darkness.

Dropping the cigar, Grant started for the airlock.

Without a word he made his way through the corridors and up the stairs until arriving at the hospital lab. Mardi took him to an open door, beyond which rested a large bed. She was becoming a good nurse.

Lena smiled up from the pillow, her face tired, but happy as he had ever seen it.

He thought about the immortality which faced him, remembered what the two of them had said about it being a long time to spend with one person.

At this moment, he did not think it would be long enough. Of course it was not logical or reasonable to think that two people could stand each other for eternity, but it was the kind of idea a young man would believe in.

Grant came to Lena's side and took her hand.

"It's a boy," she murmured happily. "Don't you want to see your new son?"

"I'll have a lifetime to see him," Grant said huskily.

"So long?" She laughed.

"Forever, I guess." But he was talking about love, the great, wonderful love he felt for Lena, and knew she understood.

"Yes, maybe that long," she agreed, lifting up as he reached down to gently kiss her.

www.ingramcontent.com/pod-product-compliance
Lightning Source LLC
Chambersburg PA
CBHW020656030726
47498CB00002B/536